FRIGHTMARES

FRIGHTMARES

Eva V. Gibson

UNDERLINED

Text copyright © 2022 by Eva V. Gibson

All rights reserved. Published in the United States by Delacorte Press, an imprint of Random House Children's Books, a division of Penguin Random House LLC, New York.

Underlined is a registered trademark and the colophon is a trademark of Penguin Random House LLC.

GetUnderlined.com

Educators and librarians, for a variety of teaching tools, visit us at RHTeachersLibrarians.com

Library of Congress Cataloging-in-Publication Data
Names: Gibson, Eva V., author.
Title: Frightmares / Eva V. Gibson.
Description: First edition. | New York : Underlined, [2022] | Audience: Ages 14 and up. | Summary: "A summer acting job at a House of Horrors turns into a real-life nightmare when a cast member turns up dead—then disappears"— Provided by publisher.
Identifiers: LCCN 2021042552 (print) | LCCN 2021042553 (ebook) | ISBN 978-0-593-48687-0 (trade paperback) | ISBN 978-0-593-48688-7 (ebook)
Subjects: CYAC: Haunted houses (Amusements)—Fiction. | Murder—Fiction. | Anxiety—Fiction. | Dating (Social customs)—Fiction. | Florida—Fiction. | LCGFT: Novels. | Thrillers (Fiction)
Classification: LCC PZ7.1.G523 Fr 2022 (print) | LCC PZ7.1.G523 (ebook) | DDC [Fic]—dc23

The text of this book is set in 11-point Janson MT Pro.
Interior design by Jen Valero
Cover art used under license from Shutterstock.com

Printed in the United States of America
10 9 8 7 6 5 4 3 2 1
First Edition

For Jill, an eternal reminder
to always Dave everything

chapter 1

This whole night sucks.

The second-to-last working bulb flickered in the cobwebbed chandelier, gave a final flare, and went dark, throwing the room into shadow. I stepped back and peered up at it, sucking air through my teeth as I knocked my hip against the antique dresser.

Josie Manning's eyes blinked open. She squinted into the gloom, peering through the lock of hair caught in her smeared eye makeup. The wrought-iron bed frame creaked as I leaned over her. She shifted, her breath catching in her bloodstained corset.

"Hold still," I hissed, tightening the worn leather restraint around her goth-pale wrist. I'd be lucky if it lasted through Sunday. "This piece-of-shit buckle—"

She opened her mouth to answer, then paused, listening. I heard it too—shrieks and clattering. Hurried footsteps, closer than they should be. Her finger tapped my knuckle: one, two, three. Ready or not.

She started screaming right before the curtain swung open.

It was reflex by now. The ax was in my grip, swinging an arc above her tear-streaked face. I brought it down hard on the clean

1

sheet covering her legs, buried it in the mattress just below her knee. Blood welled and blossomed around the blade; the toes on her severed foot twitched, drawing gasps and laughter.

"SEE? SEE WHAT YOU MADE ME DO? TRY TO RUN AWAY NOW. GO AHEAD, SEE HOW FAR YOU GET *WITH-OUT YOUR LEG*."

"Dude, that's messed up."

The voice—belonging to some douche in a Tapout tank shirt—sent a wave of giggles through the crowd. A bunch of high school kids, most around my age, most of them grinning and taking pictures. We'd be all over the #FRIGHTMARES hashtag by midnight, swimming in well-deserved ridicule and emoji-driven mockery.

Thank God I look nothing like myself.

Josie screamed louder, pleading for help. I left the ax buried in the mattress and reached for the coiled bullwhip hanging on the wall above the bed. Even Tapout flinched at the first downswing. I cracked it again and again against her thighs, striping the sheets bloody. Striping the air with her broken wails.

The whip did most of the work. One more tweaked shoulder would derail my swim training, and I'd have nothing to offer in the fall season but weak form and a shitty backstroke, so a half-assed performance it was. No way was I going to let a terrible summer job mess up my swimming scholarship. It wasn't an option.

The group eventually shuffled into the corridor, heading for the next scene. About a nanosecond after the door closed behind them, I was moving: smearing fresh F/X blood on the whip; coiling it and hanging it back on the wall; yanking the ax out of the mattress; ripping the stained sheet off Josie's "legs" and stuffing it in the basket under the bed next to her actual legs. Her torso sprouted from the cutout in the mattress, ramrod straight and prickly as a pissed-off cactus. I snapped a fresh sheet over her, tucking it around her waist to hide the hole, and repositioned the severed leg so it was even with the other prosthetic. The mechanical toes wriggled beneath the sheet like trapped mice.

"You okay?"

"Well, Dave," she answered, "I'm starving and dehydrated, and my ass has been asleep for the past twenty minutes. Oh, and as I'm sure you've noticed, this corset is a size too small, and it's sapping my will to live. Other than that, I'm great."

"Shift's almost done." I adjusted the pillow behind her back and ran a comb through her bobbed black hair. One thing we'd learned over the past five months on this set was it was way faster for me to do all this bullshit for her, rather than undoing the restraints so she could do it herself. "You still good with the lipstick?"

"It's drying out. Water first, then another coat. Red, this time."

I rummaged through the dresser drawer with one hand, squeezed the sport bottle over her open mouth with the other. By the time she swallowed, I was poised and waiting. A quick pat dry with the towel, a swipe of scarlet over the smeared pink, and she was good to go. I checked my reflection in the mirror: my waistcoat was straight; my cravat was dapper. My cape fell over my shoulders like a swoop of night. I adjusted the wig, smoothed the long blond locks, and dusted another layer of powder over my sweaty makeup. I looked stupid as hell. In other words, ready for the next group.

"Soon as we get out of here, I'm kicking Seth's ass," Josie breathed. "Every run tonight—every single run—he's let them in early. There's no time to reset the scene."

"Better cover up first," I muttered, refreshing the saline tear streaks on her cheeks and smearing them through her eyeliner. Seth Tinetti never stopped checking out our female castmates, Josie included, and made zero attempts to hide it—not in front of his girlfriend, Bethany, or Josie's boyfriend, Ollie, or Loretta, proprietress of Frightmares House of Horrors, our boss, and his actual mother. Not much hope for a guy who has zero chill even when his mom is literally standing there.

"Oh God, you're right," Josie said, groaning. "I swear, I do not get paid enough to deal with this. You kick his ass for me, then, and I'll owe you one."

"I'll kick it for myself. He has us in here with a broken strobe and one working light bulb. I can barely see."

"I doubt the customers can, either. Which is for the best, since half these props are basically garbage. How's the duct tape?"

"It's holding fine, but it looks like shit."

"At least it's holding. If the ax head comes off again, just start beating me with the handle."

"I'm not beating you for real, Jo."

"Dude, I don't mean actually— Know what? You might as well. This bullshit—three years of auditions, two agencies, my freaking SAG card—I should at least be basic Disney cast by now, not stuck in a bed at goddamn Frightmares House of Horrors, being fake-tortured by a very tall child. No offense." The racket started up outside the room. Early. Again. "SETH. WHY."

The broken restraint fell off her wrist as the next crowd shoved through the curtain. We improvised.

The night only got worse. The tours piled up one after the other, until they were practically overlapping. We had no time to reset the scene, and no choice but to go off-script, which meant the entire show was just me cracking the whip, Josie screeching, and the mechanical toes wiggling endlessly beneath the same bloody sheet. Worst of all, right when I'd finally found a rhythm, an actual real wolf spider had dropped from the chandelier onto Josie's bare shoulder, triggering a scream that would've been perfect for the performance had I not echoed it in both volume and pitch.

That spider ended up *jumping*—actually leaping off her shoulder and scurrying down her corset, over the sheet, and off the far edge of the mattress. I then spent the rest of the scene flailing the bullwhip at tiny, spidery shadows as we cleared the room with our ragged howls. We never did find the little bastard, and we never recovered our act—not that it mattered how badly we sucked once the final light bulb blew out.

By the time the crew gathered in the greenroom for postshift notes, Josie was furious beyond speech—which was just as well, since everyone else was at full volume, shouting over each other as Loretta emerged from her office. She'd been into the eighties Elvira look lately, which was a hard bar to clear for anyone, let alone a sixtysomething former B-movie scream queen who wasn't Elvira.

"Enough of this." She fanned herself with a clipboard, gently stirring the ends of her wig. "If your room ran smoothly apart from the tour timing issue, you're free to go. Everyone else, get comfortable."

She waited until the cast members from the rooms who'd held

it together—Dolls Alive!, Murder Circus, Swampland Cannibals, and Demented Doctor—filed out the door before she eyed each of us, one by one: Me and Josie, slouched together on the gross, moth-eaten couch. Ollie West, a few feet to our left, shifting from foot to foot and fidgeting with his headset. Slim, long-haired Chet Perez, holding up the wall with his spine and sneers. Bethany Blake, blond and furious, fighting back tears as she kicked off her stilettos and flexed her left foot against the worn carpet. Seth, slouched on the chintz love seat, pouting like a kid beneath his messy platinum surfer hair. All six-foot-seven of Mickey Styx, broad and solid as the oak wardrobe at his back, his deep brown skin showing through his smeared gold body paint. Josie liked to say that God built Vin Diesel out of Mickey's leftovers.

"Now." Loretta adjusted the rhinestone bifocals on her nose and squinted through them at the clipboard, eyeliner smudged from wings to feathers. "Would anyone care to tell me exactly *what in the world* happened here tonight?"

Turns out, what had happened was your basic amateur-hour haunted house shitshow. In addition to our mess in Captive Countess: Chet had tripped on a severed zombie head in Undead Graveyard, rolled his ankle, and yelled the *f*-word in front of customers. In Vamp City, Bethany had snuck an iced cappuccino into the room and accidentally kicked it over—which had, apparently, been her breaking point. She'd burst out crying in the middle of her act, breaking character and ruining her story arc. The smoke machine in Attack of the Mummy malfunctioned, leaving Mickey blinded and stumbling around until he ran right into the sarcophagus, which had tipped off the platform and swung open, pitching the mummy straight at him. He was able to catch it and shoulder it back into place, then tried to play it like part of the scene, but the mummy's arm flew off, taking half the bandages and the rest of the ambience with it.

It was a pretty apt metaphor for the entire night.

"I don't understand this." Loretta fluttered a sun-wrinkled hand over her face, shifting her focus to her son. "All these problems in one shift? Sethy, I put you on crowd control. You were supposed to be timing the tours."

"Tell her, man," Ollie muttered.

"*You* tell me, Oliver," Loretta pressed when Seth remained silent. "I promoted you to management because I trust you, of all people, to keep me informed. If it's too much responsibility—"

"No, ma'am, it's fine. I found him in the breakroom about an hour into the shift. He was . . . taking a nap."

Every eye in the room went to Seth. He sat there like a tool, arms crossed over his formal butler costume, likely not realizing he might be safer in a real-life horror house than he was with us.

Loretta's fake eyelashes fluttered.

"Taking a *nap?* Timing is everything, Seth—you know that. One group goes too fast, it rushes the actors. Too slow, and you get a pileup. If this keeps happening and word gets around, I'll have to close the doors for good. Do you want Ma to have to close the doors for good? Or spend money we don't have on a trained tour guide?"

"No, Ma. No tour guides. I'm sorry."

"Oh, he's *sorry*," Josie butted in. "That's *nice*, isn't it? That makes everything all better. Murder Circus gets to leave, and I get to explain all the ways in which life sucked tonight, in the lightless spider hole that is my workspace."

"No need to shout, dear, we're all in the room together. Now, then." Loretta swung her gaze from Josie to me. "Davis. *What's* happening with the lights?"

"There *are* no lights. Seth took the strobe for repair two weeks ago, and we haven't seen it since. The last bulb in the chandelier died tonight. There was no time to fix it, so we finished up in the dark."

At that, Chet pushed himself off the wall, shouldered his backpack, and limped across the room. Loretta gave a loud, pointed "Ahem." When he kept right on going, she tottered after him, waving her clipboard.

"Excuse me, Mr. Perez. We're not done here."

"Yeah, well, *I'm* done. Broken sets, no lights, this guy sleeping—godspeed, lady." He gave her a sarcastic salute and opened the door, swiping a smear of leftover zombie makeup off his face. "I'll send you the clinic bill for my foot."

"Chet, man, don't do this to me," Ollie said, groaning. "We already sold out two tours for tomorrow night. We need everyone we've got this weekend, and—"

His words were drowned out by a loud sob. Bethany shoved past Chet and took off down the hall, both hands pressed to her tearstained face. Seth ran after her, ignoring Ollie's raised voice and helpless pleas for order as Chet let the door slam behind him. My mind wandered away from the chaos as I picked absently at the stray glob of F/X blood that had dried to a tacky mess between my fingers. I rubbed it on my shirt, a casual swipe that caught Loretta's eye.

"What happened to your hand, Davis? Is that a cut?"

"Nah, it's the fake stuff."

"Well, your costume is not a cleaning rag, young man." She

leaned in to examine the stain, then recoiled, like she'd bounced off a force field surrounding my pants. "What is that smell?"

"Oh. Probably me." Between prom, graduation, my family leaving town, and assorted work- and now-ex-girlfriend-related drama, my unwashed costume had spent the past two weeks of daylight hours seething in its own funk on the floor of my Honda. "I should maybe throw this in the laundry tonight, huh?"

"Please do, before you kill us all. Go wash up, and you're free to go."

The water in the employee restrooms ran lukewarm, but the soap was industrial-strength, and it didn't take long to scrub away the F/X. I heard them arguing through the thin walls before I even dried my hands.

"I told you it's over, Seth. Leave. Me. Alone."

"Bethany, come on. I know we have our problems, but we can make it work." Seth's voice was low and subdued, soft at the edges like I'd never heard before. "Just talk to me. Please."

"There's no *problem*, don't you get it? This has nothing to do with whatever we had. I don't need to talk to you. I don't need *you*."

"But—"

"Hey there." They both jumped as I burst through the door. Seth had Bethany backed up against the water fountains. Her eyes were wet, her mouth a quivering smear of ghoulish black lipstick. The hall smelled of sweat, and hair spray, and the faint, skunky undertone of weed. "Everything all right, Bethany?"

"Fuck off, Dave," Seth snarled. "She's fine."

"Wow, that's fantastic, Seth. But know what? I asked *her*."

Seth uncoiled all at once, squaring up to me like I wasn't a six-foot-tall swimmer with biceps bigger than his calves. I smiled at the way his face changed when he realized I hadn't flinched.

"I'm okay, Dave," Bethany cut in. "Thanks."

She shoved past Seth and sidestepped me, heading for the greenroom. I stared at Seth until he blinked, then hurried after Bethany. I caught up with her right before the bend in the hallway.

"Um, did you guys just break up?"

"Once again. And unless he gets clean and straightens out his head, I think this time it might actually stick." She pressed her hands to her flushed cheeks and let out a watery sigh. "Sorry you had to see it."

"No problem. Let me know if you need a ride home. My car's messy, but—"

"You're sweet. But I'm fine."

We rounded the corner together, and even through the walls we could hear them: Loretta and Josie, continuing their light bulb argument. It would've been an off night if those two *weren't* clawing each other's faces off. I pushed open the greenroom door, practically slamming into Ollie, who was hovering nearby like a tweaked-out ghost. His pale blue eyes were wide and skittish; his thick, dark hair was a mess beneath the headset, which he still hadn't removed.

"Hey. You sick or something, Beth?" He gave her a once-over, wincing as he met her teary eyes. "If you didn't feel well, you should've said so."

"I," Bethany drawled, "am absolutely *fine*. Super pumped for your busy Frightmares weekend. Happy?"

She stalked off before he could answer. Even if he had, the words would have been lost in the bang of the door against the wall and the reappearance of Seth in the doorframe.

"I quit, Ma!" he yelled. "I'm not taking the fall every time we have a bad night. Yeah, so the tours got screwed. I get it, that's on me. But I didn't break the props, or drop a spider on Josie, or mess with Mickey's fog machine, or drain all the light bulbs. And still, everyone blames me. I'm sick of it."

"Man, seriously," Mickey cut in. "What all *did* you do, besides sleep on the job? Anyone can have a bad day, but when *all* the days are bad? Come on."

"Shut up, Mickey. You're up there in the mummy room, you don't know how people are. They'll scream in your face all day, and even when you give them exactly what they ask for, it's not enough. It's *never* enough. And now, I've *had* enough."

"Yeah, you tell 'em, *Sethy*. You rage against that machine." Mickey walked away midsentence, leaving Seth babbling at empty space.

It would've been sadly hilarious if he'd just kept ranting, feeding the vortex of melodrama that served as crossbeam support for the entire place. Instead, he trailed off. He looked around at Ollie's tense shoulders, Mickey's broad back, Josie's rolling eyes, Loretta's sad, disappointed mouth. My own face, frozen somewhere between neutral and Awkward Monkey Meme. His eyes caught and held on Bethany. She met his gaze, shook her head, and looked away, fresh tears rolling down her cheeks.

It was a first for Seth—giving in. Shutting up. Walking out. He was gone before Loretta could unhinge her jaw to call him back.

Beside me, Josie rubbed her temples, letting out a long, slow sigh. I nudged her with a stinky elbow, offered her a consolation grin as she met my eyes.

"Want to go to Blacklist, Jo? I'll drive."

"God, yes, as soon as I change. You're the only port in my storm, baby son." She turned to Ollie, mirrored his smile as she smoothed a lock of hair off his forehead. "You ready to go, baby? Dave's driving."

"Can't. I still have to count the drawer, clean the coffee out of Vamp, apparently find some light bulbs, and—yeah. You two go on. Relax, have some fun. We can meet up once I'm done. Okay?"

"Really? After everything, with—Ollie." She leaned in, her gaze a sudden, dark threat. I shifted unconsciously backward. "You know how I feel about this. It's *not* 'okay.'"

"And you knew my schedule would change with this promotion, Josie. You said you were fine with it, but—"

"Mostly I *am* fine with it. But sometimes I'm not. Right now, we seem to be sliding together down a slippery slope toward 'not.'"

She swirled away from him, ignoring the way his shoulders slouched in defeat. I took my cue and trailed her to the breakroom, head down, mouth shut. Ollie had landed himself in the doghouse for at least the next hour, but at least I'd get a free latte out of it. On nights this bad, you had to take what you could get.

chapter 2

Much like our workplace, Blacklist Beans & Beats looked smaller from the outside and unremarkable, like any other shitty strip-mall coffeehouse. The owners, however, served their espresso drinks strong and their alcoholic drinks stronger. They also didn't check ID at the door—all details that made it the obvious gathering place for us late-night employees of the off-off-Disney tourist industry. My being seventeen, over the driving age yet under the drinking age, made me Josie's obvious choice for permanent to-and-from transportation.

The front door opened to a steampunk scattering of brass tabletops, exposed pipes, and long, leather couches, all washed in gleams of copper and chrome. The crowd was a lean, listless sigh, weighed by vodka and Friday night relief. People slumped against wherever—a wall here, a chair arm there, faces turned toward the open-mic performance. Some of those faces swiveled as we passed by, following Josie's tiny black dress and knee-high boots and—thankfully—ignoring me. I'd ditched my wig but hadn't bothered to change into street clothes—the only way I could guarantee my costume would make it into the house, let alone the laundry, was to literally keep it on my body until I walked through the front door. If that meant wearing it around greater Orlando for a few hours, so be it. More than half the Blacklist crowd owned waistcoats and capes unironically; if mine had stunk of cigarettes and ennui instead of sunbaked scrotum, I'd have fit right in.

"Not too close. You know I love you, but you reek." Josie hitched the strap of her dress back onto her shoulder, yelling over the acoustic mess on stage as we bellied up to the counter. "You were, however, the only one who had my back tonight, so coffee's on me. I'll get you something nice and sweet."

She caught the barista's eye easily. I leaned against the counter, scanning the room, waiting for that tug. Finding it in the silk lines and silver glints of the girl stepping onto the stage.

Maya Green. My best-kept secret.

She'd been one of those quiet kids who grew up tucked between book pages, then turned tragic in the space of a summer. Her face was a mess of angles and angst, lips frozen in a suspicious frown; her overlong hair and overlarge eyes absent any trace of the bright, sunshine splash that translates to Florida-hot. She wasn't a loser, she was just sort of *there*—a vaguely familiar, vaguely scary slice of background.

Then two months ago, what happens but my goddamn family shows up at my goddamn workplace on a Saturday night, right before the end of my shift. My parents and my fifteen-year-old sister, eager for the Frightmares experience. They took the tour and everything—Roz had howled with laughter and filmed it all for her TikTok, while my dad badly faked polite fear, and my mom took pictures for some godforsaken Dave-themed scrapbook project. They dragged me out to Blacklist after, to watch

Roz tear the heart out of every would-be musician in the room with her piano skills.

It was the longest night. Full bands and solo songwriters. Guitarists forever. A freaking juggler. The entire population of Central Florida, all scheduled to perform ahead of my sister. I hadn't known Maya was even *in* the place before she took the stage. I couldn't miss her, though—not once she opened her mouth and let the words ooze out, washing us in waves of bright and bloody poetry. Dragging me off my feet and out to sea.

I'd been no good to anyone after that—not through Roz's crowd-crushing performance; not through the remainder of that night, or the next, or the day or week or ever after that followed. This girl, who I barely knew—who'd never been more than a blip in the hallway—was suddenly blotting out the sky. What had happened in that moment that I, after years breathing fine on my own, couldn't help inhaling her like air?

"She's cute."

Josie appeared, silent as a cat, each black-clawed paw curled around a steaming glass mug. She passed me the legal one, smirking at my terrible nonchalance.

"Yeah? Who?"

"Don't say 'who' to me like an asshole, Dave. The child on stage. The one you drag me here every goddamn weekend to pretend to ignore, like I'm oblivious to your motives. The one responsible for the big, dreamy look on your big, adorable, forgot-I-had-a-girlfriend face."

"We broke up." I turned my back to the stage, and Maya, and the swell of steady applause that followed her set. The glass burned my fingers as I took a sip—too hot. Too much. I set it on the counter. Josie's elbow appeared next to it, face following as she leaned into view, a pale canvas of skeptical eyebrows and smeared, bright lipstick.

"Stop lying."

"Swear to God, Jo. Last week, at graduation. She dumped me in the auditorium parking lot, right after we walked."

Her brow furrowed slowly, as if a sudden move might transform me into a puddle of tears. But my ex, Cate, and I had been clawing toward our Happily Never After since junior year. When she'd euthanized the skin-shredding facade of us, in the Cate-est of Cate-like ways, I'd been the only one not surprised. As far as the world was concerned, we'd been nice and solid—but a nice, solid turd is still a turd.

"Wow," Josie drawled, cutting her eyes back to Maya. "And you're already getting back out there—getting out on the town. Doing your thing. You go, Dave."

"Oh, I am definitely not 'doing my thing' right now. We're basically from different planets. She's a wild card by definition."

"Sweet Jesus, have I taught you nothing? You don't live your life in fear of the wild card—you *become* the wild card." Her eyes darted over my shoulder, lips twisting into a wicked smirk. "Heads-up, baby son."

And she shoved me—just put her hand on my arm, sent all six feet of me flying sideways—and disappeared into the crowd. I stumbled over my own feet, felt my heel come down hard on someone's toes.

"Ow. Watch it, dude. Just trying to get a coffee."

I turned to apologize, the blood already draining from my face. I knew whose toes those were without having to look. We'd never spoken, but I'd know that voice anywhere.

And yep, that definitely was Maya Green, glaring up at me through narrowed, unblinking eyes. Her gauzy dress was the same red as her lipstick; a tiny, silky braid snaked from her temple, losing itself in her tangled curls.

"Whoa, sorry," I stammered. "I'm sorry. I didn't—"

"It's fine. Could you move, please?"

"Oh, shit. Sorry." I grinned down at her, wishing I didn't suck in so many, many ways. "Actually, I wanted to say. I liked you. Your poetry, it was . . . I'd love to see more. Hear it, I mean. I mean, your stuff—"

"Next Saturday," she deadpanned, cutting me off. She turned to the counter to place her order, tossing the rest of her sentence back over her shoulder like a scarf. "Spoken word, after the scheduled acoustic set."

"Nice. I'm Dave, by the way. Dave Gardiner."

"I know who you are, dingus. We went to the same schools for, like, a decade."

"Yeah, I know. I just wasn't sure you'd—"

"Recognize you? Everyone recognizes *you*, Dave Gardiner."

"I don't know about that," I muttered, wincing at the way my name left her mouth, each syllable steeped in disdain and douchewater. She hated me. She *pre*-hated me.

"Yes, you do. I almost *don't* recognize you, though, with all that"—she turned back to me and gestured to her face— "stuff on? Oh God, did you really go goth on Cate Tanner? Oh, tell me she literally imploded. Please."

"Goth?" I brushed a finger carefully over my cheek. My makeup. My terrible, half-melted stage makeup I hadn't bothered to scrape off. Awesome. "Oh. No, that's for work."

"Um, wow. What . . . do you do?"

"I'm an actor—sort of. I work a room at Frightmares House of Horrors. The haunted house off I-Drive."

"Oh, yeah—I went there a couple years ago. The one with the creepy doll room, and the cursed mummy, right?"

"That's the one." I grinned at her like a dumbass, through layers of cracked, caked powder. "We added some new stuff since then—you should check it out. I'll be the one beating and dismembering my tied-up coworker."

The words leaped from my mouth like methed-out greyhounds, sailing around a track to nowhere. This had to be a nightmare.

"Okay." Maya picked up her coffee and backed up a step, putting a depressing amount of distance between us. "Well, have a good summer. Enjoy dismembering people for money, I guess."

She turned away, ready to slide through the crowd and into the future. It was too weird, all at once—she'd be gone in the next minute, maybe forever. I'd never catch her storming through the halls or catch myself scanning classrooms and assemblies for a glimpse of her eyes. I'd never hate myself for checking the bleachers at a swim meet, on the nonexistent chance she'd even consider showing up to watch. I'd never do any of those things again. And now I stood there watching her leave, and as usual I was that tongue-tied jerk in every movie with an angel on one shoulder and a devil on the other. In my case, both Shoulder Daves wore the same dumb costume and said the same dumb shit.

Don't you tell her you're single, Left-Shoulder Anxiety Dave hissed in my ear. *Don't you goddamn dare.*

Let her walk, dude, Chill Dave on the Right whispered. *Let her go.*

"Cate broke up with me!" I yelled, loud as hell. "After graduation."

Maya glanced backward, eyebrow arching, chin tilted quizzically. A reluctant smile licked across her lips like flame.

"Oh. I'm sorry to . . . *Should* I be sorry to hear that? You seem fine with it."

"I *am* fine with it. I'm *great* with it, actually."

"Well. That's *great,* then. And, like I said, I'm here every weekend. So." Her sigh was halfway to a chuckle, like she'd be mad at herself later for reminding me. But not mad in the moment. Not mad right then, at all. "Maybe I'll see you around, Dave Gardiner."

She ducked away from me, balancing her drink, shoulders braced against the crowd's stray elbows and careless, drunken stumbles.

"Oh, she's an absolute peach." Josie eeled her way into the vacancy beside me. "She's skittish, and petty, and absolutely belligerent. I fully approve. You're welcome, *Dave Gardiner.*"

"My God. You were lurking for all that?"

"I was definitely lurking for all that. It was unmissable." She upended her drink over her open mouth to catch the last drops and slammed the empty mug back on the bar. "Ollie should be done closing by now. I'll text him to meet us at Denny's. It's too loud in here, and I'm starving."

We were halfway across the room when I felt eyes on my back—the slick, crushed-ice slide of an unseen, unblinking gaze. Someone was watching me.

I about gave myself whiplash looking back, hoping it was

Maya. Craning for a last look at that face before it vanished into the distant stretch of maybes.

I was too late. I didn't see her anywhere.

The eyes still followed me, though. They drilled into my skull, trickled through my hair. Seeped deep beneath my skin, until the door swung shut behind me.

chapter 3

The thing about my job is that someone is always screaming.
When I pushed open the greenroom door for Saturday's preshift
notes, it was to a full-on face blast of Loretta's howls, blaring
through her closed office door. The cast was scattered around
the room in unusually quiet clusters. I made my way to the couch
and plopped down, sinking way too deep into the worn cushion.
Josie, who was perched as usual on the arm next to me, gave a
sullen nod, barely taking her eyes off Ollie. He darted back and
forth between groups, barking instructions and making notes.
Checking his phone every two seconds, which, judging by his
wild eyes and grinding teeth, did nothing to make whatever re-
plies he waited for appear.

"Everything okay?"

"This is already bad," she muttered. "Chet's a no-show, and
Seth's in there getting his ass chewed."

"How is that different from any other night?"

"Because Loretta was losing her mind before any of us got
here," Mickey said, sidling up to lean against the wall at Josie's
side. "She was yelling when I clocked in an hour ago, and she's
still going. So, unless you want—"

He swallowed the rest of his words as the office door banged open. Loretta swanned through it as if on wheels. Her eyes were wide, and her cheeks were red. Her mouth was an overdone smile, ringed in hot pink lipstick.

"Oh good, everyone's here. Let's get started now. . . ." Her eyes roamed the room, landing firmly on my dumb grin. "Davis? Are you a little cleaner, and a lot less fragrant?"

"Yes, ma'am."

"Excellent, dear. I hope you thanked your poor mother for taking the hit for us all."

"Oh, I did it myself. She's out of town."

"What, you mean gone? You're home alone, sweetie?"

"It's fine." I shifted in my seat, ignoring the muffled chuckles-turned-coughs bubbling up around the room. "It's only for a couple weeks."

"And you did your own laundry? Well, what a nice young man you are. I'm impressed."

"The low bar of basic hygiene," Josie scoffed as Loretta moved on to the Swampland Cannibals group. "Very impressive, indeed."

"Maybe he'll save you a load next time, Jojo," Mickey stage-whispered. Josie threw an elbow into his side, cackling along with him as my face caught fire at the innuendo. There was literally no limit when the two of them got started.

"He should be so lucky." Her voice went low and creaky, like a witch reeling me toward her house of sweets. "Better watch out, Dave—all alone in that big, empty house. Anything could happen. If you slip and fall—if someone steals you away or cuts your throat in the dark of night—no one would know until it was too late to save you."

"Whatever." I yawned. "If I go missing, you assholes can just assume I quit. Like everyone smarter than us already has."

"Yeah, about that." Ollie appeared behind Josie, Loretta's clipboard jutting from his white-knuckled grip. "Jo, we need you in Vamp tonight. Bethany's a no-show."

"Are you kidding me? She quit too?"

"Bethany Blake has left the building? WHAT. A. TRAGEDY."

Our heads turned in the direction of the chintz love seat, already well aware who was at the other end of those words: Maggie, from Murder Circus, prepping the set of stilts lying across her knees. Her and Bethany's mutual hatred predated their time as coworkers; it was less a secret and more a workplace fixture.

"That's enough, Mags," Ollie said.

"Oh, but I'm being *absolutely serious,* Ollie," she drawled, adjusting the hardware on a stilt and smirking at us from beneath her harlequin face paint. "How will *any* of us, let alone the show, go on without our resident diva? Frightmares as an institution will simply fall to *pieces.*"

"*Enough.* Second and last warning." He turned his back on her too quickly to catch her raised middle finger. Maggie's set partner, Dara, bit back a smile, nudging an elbow into Maggie's ribs. "As I was saying," Ollie continued, "Bethany's not here. And, unless she shows in the next five minutes, we're pretty much screwed."

"Two down in two days," Mickey mused. "A new record. I never saw her at the coffeehouse last night, did you?"

"Last I saw her she was dumping Seth again," I said, racking my memory for any sign of Mickey at Blacklist, let alone Bethany. "Maybe he knows where she is."

"Seth barely knows where *he* is most days." Ollie sighed,

running a hand over his face. "But yeah, we have no vampire. Unless you're volunteering?"

"If you want to see me in those heels, we can work something out. But as far as me taking that room goes, I don't know the routine. Like, at all."

"And if I'm in Vamp, who's strapped into my bed?" Josie said. "Is Dave supposed to stand there whipping himself?"

"Josie, I need you to work with me here." Ollie turned to her, jaw set, voice hard. "Do me a favor and don't argue. For once."

"She's got a point, though," Mickey said, cutting Josie off before she snapped back. "Someone needs to be in that bed for the scene to work. With the options we have, Dave would be a sorrier sight than Jo."

"He's right," I confirmed. "I really would."

"And at the same time," Mickey continued, "Vamp is hard even when you know the drill. We can't afford any big fails after last night."

"Speaking of big fails," Josie muttered as Seth exited Loretta's office and sat down heavily on the love seat's matching ottoman. "If he's on tour duty, Ollie, you can go ahead and start looking for my replacement, too."

"I think even Loretta knows better than that. She's taking on tours tonight herself. So, okay, here's the lineup: Jo, you stay in the bed and play helpless prisoner. Act like your captor could return any minute, or whatever. Mickey, you know Vamp. Dig up the guy costume and tweak the script."

"Just like old times. Got it."

"Good. Dave, you take Mickey's room. I'll be coordinating with Loretta on the headset and working ticket booth and front of house. Seth can fill in for Chet. It's not ideal, but we don't have a choice, and he won't have to remember lines. It's pretty hard to screw up zombies. Even for him."

"Did he at least fix the tomb?" Mickey asked. "Or is Dave about to have a one-armed mummy climb up on his back in front of God and everyone?"

"Shit. I don't know. Loretta said she'd have someone deal with it this morning, but I never got a chance to follow up, so—I don't know, okay? Test it out, Mickey, you'd know better than I would if it still needs work. And if Seth got his hands on it, I'm guessing it does."

I stole a sideways glance at Seth. He sat slumped forward, elbows resting on his knees, head buried in his hands. His fingers dug through his thick, pale hair to find his scalp, and his shoulders weren't exactly heaving—even if he were crying, he wouldn't do it in front of us—but they were trembling. It had to be rough, being that big a mess *and* being just self-aware enough to realize everyone around you knew it. He was a douche and a slacker, but he wasn't clueless.

Or maybe it was simpler than that. No one had to tell *me* how much it sucked to get dumped in public with zero warning. I didn't miss Cate, but I still couldn't think of that moment without wincing.

Loretta flicked the lights on and off to get our attention, clapped her hands, and waited until the room fell silent.

"All right, everyone. We have a few things to tweak for tonight's performance. If Oliver hasn't already confirmed your role this shift, please see him. Otherwise, break a leg. Let's all do our best, have a great time, and a great show." Her usual bright smile was feral around the edges. "Places!"

"That was the saddest motivational speech I ever heard."

Mickey's enormous hand fell on my shoulder as I peeled myself off the saggy couch. He guided me away from the swarm of cast members surging toward poor Ollie and steered me into the hallway. "Okay, kid, come on. Time to get you shiny."

Mickey wasn't kidding about the shiny part. He raced to Attack of the Mummy while Josie rushed me into the breakroom, where she wiped off my usual makeup and stripped me down to boxers, tossing my costume and wig to the side. Once Mickey appeared, they double-teamed me. I smeared my face, arms, and shirtless torso in shimmery gold body paint, which Josie also spread over my shoulders and back before basically safety-pinning Mickey's giant costume into submission until it fit my significantly smaller hips. Meanwhile, Mickey lined my eyes in black and brushed contour shadow beneath my cheeks and along my abs, defining muscles no one had seen up close since my last swim meet.

"Man, this sucks," I griped. "You really paint yourself up every day? Front and back, and abs, and everything?"

Mickey smirked at me over the contour brush.

"Not by myself. Dara usually gives me a . . . hand."

"Dude. Nice."

"Pigs." Josie smacked the back of my head. "Are we done here? I need someone to strap me into that stupid bed."

"Can't," Mickey said. "I have to wash this gold off my own face, dig up the old Vamp suit, and hope it's not too musty. Or soaked in rat piss."

"Ugh, do we have rats *again*?"

"We have something. Egypt stunk like hell when I grabbed the costume. Probably something nasty in the vents. Or Seth left another Publix sub out overnight."

"I swear to God, if this place burned to the ground, it would only increase the property value."

Josie dragged me down the hall to Captive Countess, leaving Mickey to rummage through Wardrobe on his own.

"Dave, is your mom really gone this week?"

"My whole family is. This week and next." After dropping Roz off at an intensive music sleepaway camp, my parents had veered east to Port Canaveral, and practically dove onto a Caribbean-bound cruise ship. They'd invited me along, but no thanks—I'd spend the whole summer laced into Josie's corset before third-wheeling their second honeymoon.

"So, no curfew. Nice. You should come out with us tonight. Assuming we all survive."

Our room was in mild disarray, which was less surprising than the fact that it now contained working lights. Ollie had replaced the chandelier bulbs and removed the broken wrist bindings from the headboard. A coil of black nylon rope lay on the mattress, beside the evening's stack of clean, folded sheets.

"Wait." I glanced between the bed frame and Josie, who was eyeing the rope, lips pulled into an apprehensive red pucker as she scrubbed the gold makeup from her hands with a baby wipe. "I'm supposed to tie you up and leave you alone? With actual rope?"

"Yeah, I'm not super comfortable with that, either." She picked up the end of the rope, inspecting the texture and flexibility. "Huh. At least he got the silky kind."

"Who cares if it's silky—what if there's an emergency? Like a fire? Or some dude tries to grope you? You'd be stuck in the bed, with no way out."

"God, you're right. Maybe we could leave my hands free but

set up the fake leg like it's already been amputated, and I could act like you're coming back to take off another piece? And obviously with no foot I can't run away. . . ." She tapped her chin, tilting her head to the side as she studied the bed. "Or did I just go too dark?"

"Yeah, I think you might've. Hold on a sec, I have an idea."

I spooled the rope out and went to work. By the time she'd touched up her makeup and situated herself in the mattress, I'd solved our problem. After making sure the fake leg was in place and the sheet was tucked around her waist, I presented her with the finished product: the entire length of rope, each end tied into a miniature noose and only slightly smudged with gold glitter.

"The nooses are for your wrists," I explained. "They look real and, like, cliché-sinister, right? And they're tight enough that they won't slip off, but you can adjust them without getting them knotted up. So, what I'll do is wrap the ends around the bedposts and thread the rope through the headboard spindle, but leave it hanging down the back of the bed frame. The crowd can't see it, but it's enough that you still can cross your arms in front of you. If worst comes to worst, you can get to your own wrists, slip out of the loops, and free yourself. Simple as that."

"This is genius. And these knots are great. You were a Boy Scout, weren't you?"

"Way back when. Long enough to learn knot-tying, at least."

"My hero. Okay, then, Scout, strap Mama in and get your ass over to Egypt." Her finger tapped mine as I bent over her, securing her safely in place: one, two, three. Ready or not. "It's almost showtime."

The Frightmares building was a long, rectangular blight of black-painted stucco that absorbed heat like a bitch and was divided into nesting-box compartments inside. The employee spaces—Wardrobe and the greenroom, Loretta's office, the breakroom, supply closet, storage room, and restrooms—those were clustered in the center of the building, connected by the shiny, dark and light green checkerboard linoleum of the interior hallway. The exterior hallway ran the circuit of the outer wall, leading from the pretour showroom, directly through the eight fright rooms, and back around to the lobby and exit doors. The rooms themselves were separated by closed-off vestibules about fifteen feet long, with a heavy curtain at each end. The vestibules were quiet and eerie, and nearly pitch-dark, allowing the customers a transitional space between spectacles while ensuring that the lights, screams, and sound effects didn't bleed from one scene into the next. Which was really all for the best, considering the stranglehold of utter chaos that gripped the place at any given moment.

I'd thought my usual work routine was bad, but that was only because I'd never worked Mickey's room.

It absolutely reeked in there, but the fog machine was working, releasing puffs of mist on cue. The lights flickered (on purpose, at least) and thunder crashed as I leered at the first tour group, waving a curved dagger over the half-bandaged "corpse" on the stone slab. Mummification herbs, bandages, and tools lay scattered around it, decorating every unoccupied inch of surface. A bowl of F/X blood sat near the head, a bowl of water at the foot. Whether my character was supposed to be Ra the Sun God, a pharaoh, or King Tut's actual sarcophagus was unclear—what *was* clear was that the costume consisted of no more than

29

a loincloth, a bulky headdress, and the body paint, which might as well have been made of liquid poison ivy. None of it made any sense from the perspective of science, history, or decency, but that was Loretta's problem. She went for visual impact over authenticity every single time.

Quality control had been ditched back at the starting line, of course. Mickey had crashed through the employee door at the very last minute and given me the briefest of briefings before rushing off to Vamp. Basically, I was to perform vague spellcasting rites, wait for the light cue, then trigger the mechanics via a button on the control pad at my feet. The tomb would open at my back, and the mummy within would rattle out on its apparatus, allegedly functional arms extended. Once I felt it touch my shoulders, my job was to play it from there and struggle with it until the crowd was gone. Then I had to flip another switch on the control pad, which would retract the mummy back to its starting point. Simple enough, but there'd been no time for Mickey to demonstrate, or even test the mechanics, before the tours began. All I could hope for was to get through the shift without having the whole thing fall on my head.

The lights flickered again, then went to strobe, signaling the scene's climax—the literal attack of the mummy. I fumbled my foot around beneath the slab, searching for the control pad, found a button, and pressed it. Nothing. My other foot slid through a smear of F/X—I barely caught myself on the slab, managed to turn the gaffe into a spin, and gave a deranged bleat of triumph as I stomped the pad again, finally toeing the correct button. I heard the mechanics whir behind me, heard the sarcophagus door creak open, and then—

Nothing. Again.

I waited for the bandaged hands to land on my shoulders, my cue to drop my herbs and dagger, and give myself over to wailing and terror as the featured creature dragged me backward to join it in eternal entombment. What actually happened was me blinking at the silent crowd, hands frozen in midair, mouth frozen in a goofy, gaping gasp.

It was night-terror awful. Frightmares House of Horrors was a disorganized shitstorm on a good day—I'd spent more shifts scrambling to cover someone's ass than I'd spent adhering to any script—but I'd never full-on choked before. Josie and I always had a backup plan: if we couldn't wing it, we'd fake it. We made up lines and played off each other, threw props, kicked and screamed, or acted out any number of improvised scenarios from the grab bag of options that didn't include standing there like a dumbass. Attack of the Mummy wasn't a hard gig, but it also wasn't *my* gig. What was I supposed to do with a mummy that didn't attack?

I stomped on the button again, then a fourth time. It didn't help. A few of the more polite customers grimaced in sympathy and looked away as they shuffled through the room toward the exit. Most of them dissolved into scoffs and sighs, punctuated here and there with mocking giggles. I snapped out of my fugue state, waved the dagger at the crowd, and belted out a couple more maniacal cackles, fighting the urge to raze my itchy skin until I was nothing but a gold-painted skeleton. The last customer disappeared through the exit door, shaking his head.

Immediately, I dropped the dagger and turned to deal with the mummy, cursing my terrible, bullshit dump of a job. Not that I had a hope in hell of fixing anything mechanical at all, let alone before the next group arrived, but maybe I could rig up a temporary solution—yank it out of there and grapple with it on my own, or at least try to figure out the problem.

And the problem, as I discovered when I finally got a peek at the broken mummy, was quite simple. It wasn't a mummy at all.

Instead of the usual bandage-wrapped automaton, some dumbass had stuffed a mannequin into the sarcophagus.

It was propped diagonally inside the space, head skewed to the side, black dress torn at the hem, blond wig knotted over its face. Not that mannequins were an odd sight at Frightmares; we had a ton of them, both whole and unassembled. Bins of limbs and baskets of detached heads in the greenroom; more than one closet packed wall to wall with torsos. Sometimes they even ended up where they belonged: in the storage room, stacked inside labeled Rubbermaid totes.

But this one—what the hell?

Was it a placeholder gone wrong? A joke, or a prank, as if Loretta wasn't already poised to flay us all alive at the slightest hint of a second consecutive bad night? And where the hell was the mummy?

I cast a wild glance around the room, like it was going to crawl itself out of hiding, watch me soil myself in fear, and have a good laugh at my expense. It didn't appear, of course, and I had to act fast. I had to make a choice, and my choice was to close the sarcophagus and play off the idea of an imminent mummy for the rest of the night. And if I hadn't acted so fast—if I hadn't instinctively reached out to shove the door into place instead of activating the mechanics via control pad as intended—I wouldn't have knocked the whole thing off-balance, just like Mickey had the night before.

It was hardly a shock to realize no one had double-checked

it after that whole mess. Dysfunctional props were a feature, not a bug—it was part of the general suck of the place, and we all knew it.

Really, though, it just sucked a whole lot more when said prop was bigger than you and tilting off its platform in your general direction. It sucked big-time when you were nowhere near strong enough to catch it, much less wrestle it back into place. Instead, you had to take it head-on, let it take you to the floor, stepping back just far enough so it missed crushing your skull, but not fast enough that you didn't end up pinned beneath it from the sternum down, wind gone, the rogue mannequin sandwiched between the tomb and your sweating, sparkling, itching skin.

And it really, really sucked when you realized the mannequin was soft, and pliable, and, suddenly, horribly familiar. When you realized it was far too heavy and dead-sweet fragrant to be nothing but plaster and paint.

When you knew, beyond a doubt, that it wasn't a mannequin at all.

chapter 4

Feeling and thought returned to me in sparks: A blare of pain beneath my headdress. My stinging arm, skinned shoulder to wrist. A body, curved into mine like a hug gone wrong. Devastating as a fallen tree. A heavy, crooked head lay on my shoulder, its long, thick hair covering my face, filling my mouth as I sucked in a gasp of air—the strands stuck to the back of my throat, which already tasted of stomach acid and bitten-tongue blood, and oh dear sweet God, her hair was in my mouth. A dead girl's hair was in my *mouth*.

The thought surged through me with a jolt of adrenaline. I scrabbled beneath her, flailing and jerking, frantically spitting until my arm popped free, and I swept the rest of the hair off my lips and face. My wind came back then, whooshed into my swimmer's lungs on a fog-machine gust of decay and dried sweat. All those things smashed together inside me, reversed course, and blasted back into the world.

I was already screaming when the curtain swung open.

"HELP ME. SOMEBODY HELP. THIS ISN'T PART OF THE SHOW, I SWEAR TO GOD."

The fourth wall was nonexistent. I reached as hard as I could, clawing at people who refused to reach back. My veins popped. My neck muscles howled. I strained and struggled, barely rattling the seventeen tons of sarcophagus. It shifted maybe a hair to the left, then settled back down, cutting off the blood flow to my leg. It was ridiculous—the scenery, in shambles; the stupid gold paint; my very vocal, very real terror that left zero room for scripts or character nuance, or anything that wasn't an unhinged shriek.

"I NEED HELP! PLEASE, THIS IS REAL. SHE'S DEAD. *OH MY GOD, SOMEONE GET HER OFF OF ME, SHE'S REALLY, REALLY DEAD!*"

The audience loved it.

They looked me over, took in the set and the fog, remarked on the realism. Passed me by, chatting with each other like I wasn't lying on the floor at their feet screaming, trapped beneath an actual corpse.

"This isn't so bad, huh? Cheesy as hell, but the actors really go for it, don't they?"

"Yeah, this kid's decent. Better than the guy in that shitty zombie room."

"SOMEONE, PLEASE, GO GET HELP!" I howled. *"I'M SERIOUS, I'M NOT ACTING—YOU HAVE TO HELP ME. SIR. SOMEBODY HELP ME, PLEEEEEEEEEASE."*

A nervous chuckle skittered through the crowd, crackling like an electric current from person to person until it dropped off the end of the line and sought the ground. I watched their heels disappear dutifully, pair by pair, through the vestibule curtain separating Attack of the Mummy from Murder Circus.

The last guy left in the room, however, was a straggler. He trailed behind the rest, tapping his phone, probably shitposting the tour in real time. He was distracted and chuckling, drifting off the curve of the path and into my reach. That was how I got my fingers around his ankle. That was how I managed to dig my nails into his sock and yank until he stumbled.

"Whoa, what the—get off me, man."

"Please," I whispered, voice ripped to rags, all but literally dying for someone to save me. "Help."

He leaned back, ducked to peer under the rail, and looked right at me, eyes jumping between the sarcophagus and the bandage pile, the splayed, dead girl, and my wild, contorted face, glistening with glitter, smeared with sweat. Then his mouth cracked open his expression somewhere between a leer and a sneer. He stepped on my wrist with his free foot, grinding it into the carpet.

"Eat it, bruh."

The air left my lungs in a final, nearly silent whimper as the guy disappeared into the vestibule. My head dropped backward, bouncing painfully off the floor. The dead girl's head flopped way too far to the left. The kind of far you can only flop when your vertebrae are no longer stacked end-to-end like they should be.

I had maybe three minutes at most before the next tour group appeared—assuming Loretta wasn't ruining the timing, in tribute to her son. I had to get it together.

Not that I cared about the job in any sense. I was fine coming off as a giant crybaby to anyone who happened by, as long as it meant getting out of this waking nightmare. But I couldn't count on any of that. I had to free myself. And before I did that, I had to take another breath—I had to refill my lungs with the sickly scent of her shampoo and face powder; the industrial plastic reek of vinyl; her faded perfume, wrapped in rot and edged in rust. Tinged with the faintest whiff of salt, dried stiff on a low-cut costume. Before I did anything else at all, I had to take it in.

I didn't want to see her. I didn't want to know.

And isn't that just too damn bad, Dave.

Yeah. It was.

So, I choked back a moan, and I set it all aside. I cut my brain loose from my body, wound my fist through a clump of hair. Tugged it up and out, angling her face toward my own, and oh Jesus holy mother, human heads weren't meant to tilt like that. But what the hell did it matter anyway—she'd have said it, too. She'd have laughed at the absurdity.

There's one perk of a broken neck—am I right, Dave? Twist your head any which way you like, and good for headbanging too, right? You know? DO YOU KNOW WHAT I'M SAYING, DAVE???

Right. Yeah.

Bethany would have found it funny as hell if the neck in question hadn't been hers.

chapter 5

I gave up yelling for help. I lay there, struggling uselessly beneath the sarcophagus, Bethany's cheek pressed against my shoulder. I'd taken one look at that face—her blank, wide-open eyes; the broken, blood-crusted nose; the slack mouth; that chilly, blue-and-gray-tinged skin, stiff with stage makeup—and loosened my grip, letting her head drop. The crunch of her nose hitting my collarbone ripped me up from the inside out.

The room tilted; the walls breathed. My skin screamed with sweat and pain, and burning, unrelenting panic. It wouldn't end. None of this would ever end.

You're right, it won't—unless YOU end it. Dave. Get. Up.

Her voice—Bethany's voice—clattered through my mind, sending a jolt from my skull to the base of my spine. I shifted my head to the right, braced my shoulder against the floor. Gathered every nerve left in my pathetic guts and kicked my leg as hard as I could—not upward, but outward, an emulation of the world's worst half-assed snow angel.

It worked. My leg slid free, and the sarcophagus tilted to fill the space. Its lower edge struck the floor where my leg had been; the upper edge rocked against my thigh. It barely missed my nuts, but I was no longer pinned by its full weight. I managed to reach around poor Bethany and lift the edge off my leg, press the rest upward, and finally shove my way out in a surge of desperate adrenaline.

There were only three ways into the set rooms at Frightmares House of Horrors: the two vestibule curtains at each end of the tour path, one leading in and the other out; and an employee entrance on the other side of the path. Those doors were hidden by floor-to-ceiling black curtains, and opened onto the interior hallway, which was halfheartedly nicknamed "backstage." Backstage consisted of the greenroom, the breakroom, and other employees-only areas. The employee exits gave us quick and easy access to each individual set so we cast members wouldn't cross through the lobby during business hours, and so we didn't have to take the entire goddamn tour ourselves every time Loretta called places.

In two of the rooms, however, were fourth doors—emergency exits leading straight outside to the employee parking lot. Captive Countess, my and Josie's usual room, had one. The other was only steps away, tucked behind the painted pyramid backdrop.

I lunged for it, leaving rationale beneath the curling layer of fog. The stiff curtain buckled in my clawing fists as I hauled it aside, my triumphant yell cracking into a shriek. I skittered backward and fell over the sarcophagus, landing right on my ass, inches from Bethany's outstretched arm.

The mummy stared at me from the space between the set and the wall. It sat propped sideways against the doorframe, arms raised halfway, like it had fallen asleep in the middle of its planned attack. Someone had tended to the whole missing limb issue, but what the fuck was it doing *there*? Who had taken it off its mechanism and stashed it behind the scenery to make room for Bethany?

And that's when it hit me, for real—that's what it took to shake the most basic realization from my baffled, broken brain.

Someone had done this.

Someone had walked into this room, dismantled the sarcophagus, and hidden the mummy. Then they'd filled the space with the dead, broken body of my friend.

What was *happening*?

DAVE. GET OUT OF HERE. NOW.

The words were a kick in the ass, driving me upright, sending me toward the exit in a full-tilt rush. I all but leaped over the mummy, hitting the door's push bar with both hands. It slammed open onto a napalm blast of heat and sunshine that nearly scorched the eyes from my skull.

The employee parking lot re-formed in spots and flashes of scattered vehicles: Mickey's motorcycle, squeezed casually into the too-small space between the company van and Ollie's Jeep. Loretta's Subaru cozied up next to Seth's douche-ass F-350. My own crappy Honda parked too close to the chain-link security fence. I stumbled toward it, shredding my bare feet on the alternating landscape of sandspurs and molten gravel, got halfway there before I realized it was no good. My keys, my wallet, my clothes and shoes—everything was stuffed in my locker. If I wanted out, I'd have to go back in.

Oh, HELL no.

I hit the fence already climbing. Somehow I made it up and over in a weird, cartwheeling scramble of bruised knees and bloody palms. I didn't stop. I just ran.

Two city blocks later, I was done whether I wanted to be

or not. I was a mess of sweat and glitter, face paint melting and dripping down my burning shoulders. My feet were hamburger meat. My head was a muddle of color and sound; of bruises and pain and relentless itch; of wild, gasping breath, and her voice, again—Bethany's voice—cutting through it all like steel, clear and bright as the daytime sky.

So you're just going to leave me there? Throw me aside and take off? You asshole.

"I didn't." An SUV of college-age girls blew past me in a swell of horn blasts and catcalls. I swallowed the rest of my words, redirecting them, as I always did, to the mind pocket where I kept my Shoulder Daves. *I didn't mean it like that.*

Well, how you meant it sure doesn't get me off the floor and out of the fake fog cloud, does it, Dave?

She was right. Bethany and I hadn't been super close—she wasn't my partner, not the way Josie was—but we'd worked together for months. We'd inventoried props and gone on food runs. We'd bitched to each other while applying eyeliner. She'd always laughed at my dumb jokes. She was my *friend,* and I'd left her there on the floor of our awful workplace, facedown, half stuck under a broken set prop, and I *knew* how much of a punk move that was. I knew it so completely, I'd conjured her voice in my head, specifically to berate me for being such a colossal turd.

God. I'm sorry. I—oh, Christ, Bethany—I have to help you. I have to DO something.

You'd better.

My body spun without me, ignoring my screaming lungs, the sandspur in my instep, and the molten concrete. I threw myself back into gear, grateful for the hundreds of hours I'd spent in the pool and the gym, for the squats and presses that kept my legs strong, for the endurance training that forced my blazing, mangled feet forward.

Considering how I'd left things in the mummy room, a little pain was no more than I deserved.

If I didn't get back and handle the situation, things would only get worse. Someone had committed *murder* and hadn't even tried to hide it—and I'd spent an entire tour cycle trapped under a goddamn dead body, which was not something I could ignore until closing time for the sake of ambience.

Frightmares House of Horrors loomed just ahead, a long, dark beast poised to catch the dipping sun. I pushed past the line of customers and crashed into the ticket booth window, pounding on the glass separating me from Ollie's stunned face. He blinked at me through a stray lock of shiny, dark hair. Sweat shone at his temples, and his bow tie was askew.

"Dave? What the—oh my god, *why are you outside?*"

"Dude," I wheezed as he opened the door and yanked me into sweet, air-conditioned relief. "You have to—"

"Man, we've been slammed since we opened—this line hasn't let up even once. I just let, like, a twenty-person group into the intro room, and you're on break? Loretta's going to kill you. She ripped me a new one for taking a piss, and I was barely gone five minutes."

Tell him, Dave. Bring him back there and let him see me.

"Come on," I panted. "I have to show you. She's—"

"I'm not playing with you, Dave. Move your ass now, or I'll—"

Make him SEE.

I was at least four years younger than Ollie, comparatively green as grass. I was also three inches taller, powered by pain, shock, and unchecked adrenal fear. It wasn't difficult to drag him

42

through the lobby, then the backstage hallway, by the fabric of his uniform jacket.

"It's bad, man," I managed, hacking up the last of the outdoors as I butted in front of him, slammed through the employee entrance, and shoved through the concealment curtain. "You need to see this, and I'm not even joking, because—"

He ran face-first into my back. That's how suddenly I froze.

The pyramid-set curtain was drawn smooth and flat, pulled neatly back over the exit door. The tools lay in order on the slab beside the perfectly arranged mummy-in-progress. The sarcophagus stood on its pedestal, closed and still, presiding over a floor space empty of all but mist.

Bethany was gone.

"Dude, *what*?" Ollie pushed past me and scanned the room, cocked his head as a scream drifted through the vestibule from Undead Graveyard. "Oh shit, here they come. If you need something fixed, you need to tell me *now*."

"But—she was right—" I sucked in a lungful of air, choked instead on a puff of artificial fog. "Listen, you have to believe me. When I left this room—"

"Look, Dave, I don't know what your deal is, but I gotta get back. Will you be okay in here?"

"I—" Nothing else came out, because what else did I have to say? *Never mind, seems someone took care of that whole dead body issue? Things were pretty wild a minute ago, but the corpse is all cleaned up now, so we're solid?* Where would I even start?

"Yeah," I finally croaked. "I'm good."

He clapped me on the shoulder and booked it back through the employee entrance, drawing the curtain and closing the door behind him. On autopilot, I stepped around to my assigned place and swiped a finger under each eye, like that would do the trick. I took my place at the slab, hefted the dagger, turned it over in my hand as the vestibule drape swung open.

Ready or not.

The customers streamed into the room, still giggling at Seth's zombie antics. The giggles died off damn quick, though, as my show wore on—less than a minute in, and even the rowdiest were staring, silent, and boy, did they look unsettled as hell. Maybe it was my empty, bloodshot eyes. Could've very well been how the dagger shook in my hands, or the way the small, feral moan leaked from my mouth as the strobe activated and I toed the hidden button. It could be the water leaking from my eyes at the creak of the sarcophagus, or the whir of the gears as the mummy rattled out, reaching for me with its working arms, exactly as it should.

Everything perfect. Everything in its place.

My scream, when its fingers brushed my shoulders, was as real as it'd ever been.

chapter 6

I finished the shift.

Instead of calling the cops, instead of howling through the building, telling everyone with a pulse what happened, instead of shredding the sets like Wolverine until I found some answers, I pulled the ultimate Dave move and finished my goddamn shift.

I stayed in that room, hit those buttons, reset the scene, and played it out over and over, because what else *could* I do? Bust into every room, one by one, hurling accusations at my coworkers? Describe in detail how our friend and castmate had fallen onto me from inside one of the set pieces and performed her final act postmortem? Scream about the dead body that had randomly appeared in Attack of the Mummy's sarcophagus, then somehow disappeared in the space of—what?—however long I'd been outside?

No way. They'd Baker Act me before the last customer left the lobby, no matter what I said. There were no witnesses—unless you count the dozens of people who'd traipsed past, all failing to acknowledge us as anything but the show they'd paid for. There was no proof.

I couldn't even tell anyone about the body—because there *was* no body.

Only one other person knew Bethany was dead. And that person knew because they'd made it happen.

By the time the last tour passed through, I was a husk of a human, focused on a single goal: getting out of Frightmares alive. I skipped the postshow meeting, went straight to the breakroom for my stuff, then left without a word to anyone. The employee parking lot was a balmy, seventy-six-degree stretch of gravel and sandspur-scattered dirt, washed in floodlight-white. I squinted into the headlights of passing cars, thumb fumbling over my key fob. The Honda honked and flashed in my startled face as I accidentally hit the panic button. The blare drowned out my frustrated yell as I smashed all the buttons at once, desperate to do anything right.

"Dude, what are you doing? Since when do you skip notes?"

I blinked at Josie, who'd appeared at my side in a blur of fourteen-eye steel-toed Docs and short shorts. Sweat shone along her collarbone, dampening the edge of her crimson cami top. Her wide, dark eyes held mine, concern softening their usual stony glint. She took the fob gently from my hand, silencing the Honda with a single, logical click. I swiped it back, clenching it too hard in my clammy, shaking hand.

"Bathroom emergency," I lied. "Code brown."

"That's *it*? Loretta's already at the brink—not that she can afford to fire anyone right now, but you really couldn't hold it?" She glanced sideways at Loretta's Subaru and lowered her voice, as if Loretta herself were crouched in the shadowy space behind the wheel, ear pressed to the window to catch our words. "Ollie said you were *outside* during tours. What happened?"

I almost told her. My mouth fell open, ready to exhale. Ready to unleash.

It closed at the snarl of Mickey's motorcycle, revving to life at the far end of the lot. It leaped from its parking space and growled past us. By the time it faded, I'd lost my nerve.

"No big deal," I croaked. "Felt like I had to puke. I went out the fire exit, forgot to prop the door open, and got locked out."

"Oh God, is it norovirus? Please tell me it was something you ate, and if you can't do that, you need to take a big step back from me."

"I'm okay."

"Okay, but unless you're actively contagious, don't you dare call out next shift. I'll get you, like, a decorative urn or something. Blend the puke bucket right into the mummy set. But we can*not* handle another missing player."

"Jo. I'll be fine." I swallowed a glut of contradictory words, thick with panic, acid-hot. "I should head out, though. Get some rest."

"Dave? You're still here?" Ollie appeared at Josie's side, sliding an arm around her hip. She nuzzled his cheek with her nose. "You okay, man?"

"Dave feels pukey," Josie answered for me, "so he's blowing us off. Which means you get to be the driver."

"Is that why you tweaked out earlier?" He shook his head sympathetically at Josie's nod while I stood there, dazed as shit, my brain three steps behind. "Man, that sucks. You should get home, get some rest. All I ask is that you don't pull a Bethany two-point-oh."

"WHAT THE HELL IS THAT SUPPOSED TO MEAN?"

They both jumped at that, and who could blame them? *They* hadn't been trapped beneath a slab of dead Bethany flesh. They didn't know she was dead, and now missing, decomposing in an undisclosed corner of the world. Jesus. Jesus God.

"Hey, settle down," Ollie said. He took a small step back, disengaging from my spiral. "I only meant, she was a no-show, remember? If you need to take off tomorrow, at least give me a heads-up."

"Yeah, I think you *should* go home and crash, baby son," Josie said, "before you crash for real, facedown in the dirt." Her eyes darted to the ground and moseyed back up, drawing a clinical line from my toes to my face. "You *are* getting dressed first, right?"

I squinted at her, then down at myself—my aching bare feet and shiny legs, the drooping folds of a costume too heavy for its safety pins. The bare torso, caked with paint and dirt.

My teeth caught on my lower lip; my brain ticked backward to the employee locker room, the pile of street clothes I'd dropped on a folding chair. I'd totally meant to put those on.

I wiped my hand across my face, rubbing fresh sweat through streaks of grit, fighting down a wild, ragged sob. I was so close to losing it.

Fuck, who was I kidding? "It" had slipped through the cracks long ago.

"I—yeah. Yes, I'm getting dressed. I—I mean—I was thinking that I should maybe—"

"Dave, I'm not your confessional camera. You can drive home naked for all I care, as long as you make it back in time for tomorrow's shift."

She stood on tiptoes to muss my hair, wrinkling her nose at the handful of grime rewarding that little show of affection. Ollie gave me a tight, apologetic smile as he followed her to the Jeep, leaving me standing like an idiot in the middle of the lot. Any other night, I'd have chased him down and apologized, made sure beyond a doubt that I hadn't crossed a line or rocked the boat.

Hey, man, are we okay? Don't be mad. I know I'm a tool, and I'm sorry. First round at Blacklist is on me. Instead, I stalked toward the building, striding right across the path of another moving vehicle—the company van, Seth behind the wheel, pulling out far too fast. His brakes squealed, his horn blared at my retreating back.

I didn't stop. I didn't even turn my head.

chapter 7

I slammed back through the building on pure adrenaline, forcing myself to pass each doorway and turn each corner. All I needed was my clothes, and—

Do you really NEED them need them, Dave? Are you, like, soul-bonded to your Naruto T-shirt?

"No," I answered Bethany's voice as I barreled down the hall toward the breakroom, "but—"

Are those cargo shorts so irreplaceable that you're actually walking BACK INTO THIS LITERAL CRIME SCENE TO PUT THEM ON YOUR MIRACULOUSLY STILL-BREATHING BODY, DAVE? MY GOD.

I nearly skidded to a stop as her words sank in. Any sane person would torch the whole property before setting foot in it ever again, and there I was, heading right on in to grab my street clothes. What the hell was I doing?

But I was already at the breakroom; my hand was already turning the knob, autopiloting my dumb ass through the door-way, like I hadn't whiled away an evening under the same roof as both a corpse and her murderer. I grabbed my stuff off the folding chair, shoved my poor, sore feet into my Vans, and practically teleported back to the car.

My hands glittered gold in the dash lights, clenched at ten and two like the steering wheel was the detonation trigger of a bomb. A shiver scuttled over my shoulders, stirring a cyclone in my gut. Forget logic—I had no clue how to *process* the shit I'd seen, much less stumble through the end of the day without crumbling. As for the "what's next," and whether that involved calling the cops, or quitting my job, or leaving the state . . . well, all that was a problem for Future Dave. Present Dave was moment to moment—and at that moment, all I could do was drive.

I had to keep going. I had to make it home.

I blew out all my breath and held it, forcing myself to take small, controlled sips of air until my heartbeat slowed to normal. I drove ten over the limit, wove the car in and out of traffic, swerved off the main road onto a residential shortcut. Frightmares House of Horrors slid from the rearview, making room for a soothing swatch of night.

The Honda seemed to sigh along with me as I eased off the gas. Mist accumulated on the windshield until my squinting-through-the-fog dumb ass finally realized both the headlights and A/C were off. I flipped the lights on and opened the vent, let the muggy night invade and gather on my dirty skin. The full, thick whoosh doubled onto itself like cloud cover, broken only by the tiny, crackling crunch from the back seat.

What. The. Fuck.

My brain scrambled into reverse, ticking off all the routine parts of functional vehicular operation I'd neglected during my hasty departure: I'd skipped throwing my clothes in the trunk; those were wadded on the passenger floorboard. I'd forgotten my headlights. I'd forgotten to open Spotify and pick a playlist. I'd completely blanked on the AC. I'd managed to yank the seat belt across my bare torso as I'd fishtailed out of the nearly empty lot, but that was one hundred percent force of habit. Hell, I was lucky I'd made it into the car in the first place—I'd fumbled the key fob so spectacularly, Josie had actively intervened.

And then—what? Had she fully reset the alarm, or merely silenced the panic button, leaving it unlocked? Had I automatically hit the fob to relock when I'd walked away, or had I left it open, an invitation to anyone who wanted to climb right on in, and oh my holy god, what if someone *had*? What if that had actually happened, in the time it took me to storm to the breakroom and back?

I wouldn't know. I hadn't checked the back seat.

Keep driving, Dave, Bethany whispered. *Don't slow down.*

My vision tunneled to the road ahead. My throat closed to a pinhole. The streetlights shone dim on quiet sidewalks, each one swooping its way through the car in swells of dull, broken yellow. I flicked my eyes halfway to the rearview, then punked out, then steeled myself and—

DON'T DO THAT. DO NOT LOOK BACK.

A drop of sweat cut an ice trail down my neck. I stared at the empty lane, suddenly certain—suddenly *sure,* with every nerve and fiber—that mine wasn't the only heartbeat in this tiny space. If I acknowledged that back seat in any way, I was dead.

Once my eyes met his—once they caught and held the gleam from the silhouette rising into view in that mirror—it was over.

Ostrich time, Dave. If you don't see him, it's like he's not there. That's how this goes, right? Keep your foot on the gas, your eyes on the road, and you'll be fine. You'll be safe.

Bethany made perfect sense. That urban legend—the one with the back seat, supposedly empty but actually occupied by a serial killer—the girl in that car was inches from death, but she'd kept driving. She'd persevered. She'd never seen the silhouette, never acknowledged her attacker, and she'd lived. Bethany was right. All I needed to do was keep going.

But what if she was wrong? What if it didn't matter what I did? Every house on this street was dark. Orlando's nightlife was miles behind me. There wasn't another car in sight. What if, while I was busy driving and not looking back, the killer was rising behind me anyway? I'd have a knife in my neck before I could even tap the brakes.

Should've checked the back seat, Bethany hissed. *There's that male privilege Josie's always howling about. In case you need it spelled out for you.*

Don't yell at me, I thought at her, blinking back the burn of tears. *I can't breathe.*

Must be nice to live your life in such a way that you can just climb on into any car on earth without checking the goddamn back seat, DAVE.

I'm sorry, okay? I'm sorry. Just help me, Bethany. Oh God, is there really someone back there?

How the hell should I know? Do I have eyes in the back of your head? Stop talking to me and drive us out of here. Foot to the floor, and don't look back. Her tone smoothed to soothing, sending a warm rush of comfort across my cheeks. *Look, stay calm. Steer back toward town. Find a safe, crowded place to pull over. If you don't look back, you'll be okay. Everything's going to be fine.*

I let my foot rest heavy on the gas, blowing through cross

streets and stop signs until I saw it: a beacon in the night. A silver gleam on the horizon.

The 24-hour RaceTrac gas station, pulsing with people, teeming with life. Lit with banks upon banks of bright, fluorescent lights.

I practically ran over the median. The Honda swung across the turn lane, nearly clipping two parked cars and a trash can as I slid up next to an unoccupied gas pump, slamming on the brake just in time to avoid running the whole car into the Hummer in front of me.

My controlled swimmer's breathing had turned to gasps— the suck and blow of small, thin screams. My fingers fumbled at my seat belt, clawed and caught at the door handle until it gave. I landed on my knees, scrambled up, then fell again, skinning them bloody on the concrete. I slammed the door shut with my shoulder and collapsed, shaking, in a puddle of motor oil and melted Icee.

"The hell? Kid, you okay?"

I blinked up at the guy standing beside the Hummer—a mid-twenties dude built like his vehicle, in flip-flops, camo shorts, and a worn USMC T-shirt. He balanced a pack of Pampers under one arm, hands occupied by a travel mug twice the size of any cupholder.

"There's somebody. In. My car," I stammered. "Back seat. Hiding."

"Someone's in there?" He set the mug and diapers on his roof, opened the driver's-side door, and pulled a hard-shell firearm case from beneath the seat. A baby rattle fell out the open door and rolled under the vehicle. "Is he armed?"

"Don't know. He's been—and I was driving—and—"

"Okay, settle down. Let's check this out."

He approached the Honda carefully, pistol pointed downward, motioning me back with his free hand. I sort of rolled out of the way, cowered next to the front tire as the guy sidled up to the window, peering up and over the back of the driver's seat, then inching forward. I cringed against the hubcap as he squared with the back window, bent down, and pressed his cupped palm to the glass.

"Hey, kid? There's no one in there."

"What?" The blood drained from my face, then recirculated, burning hot across my cheekbones and neck. "You're sure?"

"Not many places to hide—car looks empty to me. Unless you got yourself a ghost." His brow furrowed at my involuntary moan. "You sure you're okay? Need me to call someone?"

"No. Thanks anyway."

"Sure thing. Get yourself on home and take care of . . . that." He gestured to my filthy, sparkling skin, and what remained of the ruined costume. "You'll feel better once you clean up. Rest up. Get whatever's in your system out."

I nodded through the fog of weary humiliation, too stunned to protest. Too relieved to feel much shame, even though I was shivering in a parking lot, hiding from nothing like a little kid. I wasn't even mad he thought I was high. It was as safe an assumption as any, considering I looked like piss-drenched roadkill shot from a confetti cannon.

The guy was kind enough not to offer me a hand up, leaving me at least that little bit of dignity. He drove away with a careful wave. I dragged my sorry ass up little by little, ignoring the sideways glances and flat-out stares of other, saner, customers. The forgotten baby rattle rolled toward the pump in a slow arc as I made my way along the car and pressed my face against the window, staring as hard as I could at the empty back seat.

chapter 8

Man, you are so right. Bethany sighed. *Sno Balls are best when completely dismantled.*

"It's a flawed snack to begin with," I boomed. No need to whisper in my empty bedroom. My sister's mini-pinscher, Trent Roznor, was the only one around to hear me, and he was too busy licking the leftover cheese from my empty nacho container to care. I leaned over the semicircle of snacks, plucking an unopened pack of Sno Balls from the selection. A drop of shower water plopped from my wet hair onto the cellophane. "The cake part is garbage, but there's no way around it. The marshmallow, though? Peel that off and it's perfect, just as is."

Unarguably. We should eat this one, and then the other one.

"We should. We will."

Funny how writhing all over a gas station parking lot erases whatever you thought your low point was and replaces that with itself. There was no way to come back from it, so instead of slinking into the car and driving straight home, I'd fished my T-shirt off the passenger floorboards, pulled it on over my messy torso, and descended upon the convenience store.

I'd emerged ten minutes later, a shamefully heavy bag of

gas station junk food in hand. After ensuring the back seat was murderer-free, I'd climbed into the driver's seat, cranked the engine, and very nearly shat my loincloth at the sound of that same dry crackle. I'd about snapped my neck twisting around, immediately finding the source: a stray Taco Bell wrapper, Roz's garbage from the week before, shimmying in the blast of the back seat vent.

Bethany had been quiet during the ride home. Not that I blamed her.

The Shoulder Daves did their part to fill the silence, at least—Chill Dave on the Right, mostly. He talked me through the stop signs and darker streets, checked the curbside shadows for leering faces and hidden blades. Guided me through my subdivision, then my neighborhood, until my house loomed ahead in all its safe, palmetto-framed, Mediterranean Revival glory.

The first turn of the doorknob was as bad as it got. I'd stood there with my key in the lock, tense from hairline to toe knuckles, fresh sweat gathering on my upper lip.

We have an alarm system, right? Chill Dave prodded. *That we armed before leaving the house?*

"Yeah. It's habit—we always set it, even just to take the dog around the block."

And do any non-Gardiners know the code?

"No." That thought alone helped more than anything. Our alarm code was an ever-in-flux parade of seemingly random numbers, significant only to the family, yet arranged out of order and pretty much unguessable. I'd changed it myself the morning my parents left, actually—I was literally the only person on earth who knew its current configuration. If the house was silent, it was safe.

Go on, then, dude. Let's get inside.

The untripped alarm, while reassuring, didn't stop me from double-locking the doors and resetting the thing before I even kicked off my shoes. It also didn't stop me from checking every room in the house, and every single space in each room—under beds, in closets, behind doors and drapes and shower curtains. All the window locks, even on the second floor. Under the table in the breakfast nook, thanking every god I could think of that we didn't have an attic or basement to tack on to the worst scavenger hunt ever.

Both Daves eventually fell silent, which was about the time when I realized Trent Roznor, for all our mutual dislike, was better company than none. He'd followed me around the house during my search, then butted his way into the bathroom, where he'd spent the duration of my necessary but harrowing shower running in circles, scratching at the vanity, and barking at the doorknob. Once he'd figured out Roz was not, in fact, on her way to tend to his every whim, he'd shredded the toilet paper and gnawed a hole in the bath mat before settling into a corner to glare at me between intermittent licks of his own crotch.

Bethany hadn't reappeared until I was dry and settled on my bedroom floor, pajamas on and snacks arranged, the bedroom door locked tight. I'd just begun to savor the second Sno Ball when my phone vibrated way too close to my bare foot. I bit down reflexively on my own lip, choking back a scream behind my bloody, sugared tongue.

> Checking in on your alleged norovirus.
> Are you awake or asleep?

Josie. I blinked at the screen, mind scurrying between possible answers. How could I tell her? How could I not?

> Awake. Not sleeping any time soon.

> You okay?

"No." My voice startled Trent Roznor out of his cheese coma. He heaved himself up with a grunt and sniffed around the empty snack wrappers as I fumbled over the keypad, trying like hell to form a coherent reply.

> Not really. I'm actually really fucked up, Jo. Bethany's dead. I need your help.

Her call came through before I could send the text. I answered, unleashing a blast of voices, laughter, and the rhythmic wail of badly played instruments.

"Hey, Dave, how's everything? You holding up okay?"

"I guess," I croaked. "I mean—no, I'm not. I'm really not."

"What? I can't—hold on. *What*, Mickey? I don't know, that's what I'm asking. Well, if you'd LET ME TALK TO HIM, I'll find out. GOD." Her voice redirected back into my ear. "Dave? Are you there?"

"Yes."

"I won't keep you, just making sure you're still alive. You looked like hell earlier, so I won't hold a grudge, but be aware that right now I fully hate you for ditching me with these two. Yes, Mickey. OKAY. YES. Dave, tell Mickey you're okay, before he dislocates his conscience."

"Jo, wait. I need to talk to you. Something happened today, and—"

"DAVEY. TELL ME YOU'RE OKAY."

"I'm okay, Mick," I lied. "Just unwinding."

"Good. Good boy. I'll swing by and check on you, no problem. It's right on my way. Tuck you in good night. Keep our little guy safe."

"Time's up." Josie reclaimed the phone, sending Mickey into the background garble. "Sorry, he's relentless."

"Jesus. He's not actually swinging by, is he?"

"He's had four drinks since I got here, and I don't know how many before. He's not 'swinging by' a damn place. Ollie's wasted too. I'll have to leave Mickey's bike here and stuff both these assholes into the Jeep by myself."

"Yeah. Hey, I—it sounds like you can't really talk right now, but do you think we could meet up some time tomorrow? I need to tell you something."

"Sure, hon. I have stuff to do before work, but we can go out after, while Ollie closes up. Would that help?"

"Yes." I wobbled. A shudder of relief traveled up my spine, threading through and knotting around the fear. "Thank you."

"Um, you're welcome, Dave." She paused. "Look, are you sure you're okay? Do you *want* us to come check on you? Pick you up a Frosty, or some Tums?"

"Nah, it's late." Not that the Frosty didn't sound like the most wonderful, horrible idea ever, but still. "Go deal with those two, I'll be fine once I get some sleep."

"I'm a text away if you need me. I—dammit, Mickey, give me the phone. Give it—MOTHERFU—" There was a sharp crack, then the call dropped. I was alone.

Well, alone except for Bethany, my trusty Shoulder Daves, and Trent Roznor, who'd seized the opportunity during Josie's call to drag a half empty Fritos bag under the bed and crawl halfway inside it. I tossed my phone aside and reached for him, earning a nip on the thumb. Despite his hostility—which, to be fair, he extended to everyone on earth except Roz—Trent Roznor was something solid, at least. A living creature. A tiny, black-and-brown tremble of muscle, with fifteen feet of bark in his minuscule bite.

Something more than a medley of invented, synaptic whispers.

Much more than that in a literal sense, actually; namely, the shrill whine that suddenly drifted from the confines of the bag. The very specific, very familiar warning that signaled an impending mess. Trent Roznor knew exactly where his doggie door was; he trotted through it just fine when he was home alone. However, he'd decided not to bother when we were around—not when we could hand-carry him through the house like the little prince Roz had raised him to be.

I grabbed the Fritos bag, dog and all, picked the whole thing up, and headed for the stairs. I bypassed his doggie door— when the whine reached a certain pitch, he'd go the second he touched the ground, whether he'd made it outside or not—and slid open the glass door off the living room, disarming the alarm. The motion-sensor floodlights switched on, illuminating our pool, patio, and a semicircle of manicured lawn. Beyond that semicircle was nothing but darkness, stretching out to our six-foot privacy fence—which, of course, was where Mom insisted we take the dog at times like this, so he'd do his business as far from the house as possible.

Nope. Not tonight.

I carried the bag across the patio, setting it down where the flagstones met the grass. Trent Roznor scrambled out and trotted right up to the edge of the darkness. I cringed instinctively, waiting for leather-gloved hands to reach into the light and grab him up. Instead, he squared up his haunches and took a massive dump that, as far as I was concerned, could remain there until morning. Leaving it violated yet another of my mother's rules, but she wasn't here. I wasn't about to risk death over a literal turd.

It was a chickenshit thought, and unrealistic. Trent Roznor wasn't good for much, but he was better than any home security system when it came to sounding an alarm. I'd once watched him bark for a solid five minutes at his own tail—I had no doubt he'd let me know if an unwelcome third party set foot near the property line.

The *ifs*, though.

If I went out there—if I stepped into the shadows and someone *was* waiting, what then? My family was away. My next-door neighbors were elderly, and likely asleep. On a scale of aggressive sidekicks, the dog was a nonentity, more likely to hinder than help. If the worst happened and I disappeared, no one would even notice I was gone.

Employee turnover at Frightmares was a running joke, one appreciated most ironically by the small handful of employees who'd been there longer than six months. I hardly knew half the cast in more than passing. Chet wasn't the first person to rage-quit, and he wouldn't be the last. No one ever called in sick—we didn't get paid time off, and we were so chronically short-staffed that Loretta wasn't about to fire anyone over something as minor as not showing up. It was far easier to ghost on a shift than it was to get permission to skip it. It would've been weirder if Bethany actually *had* given us a heads-up.

And what had I done? I'd skipped postshow notes, set off my own car alarm, and lost my shit at Ollie—who was my friend, but also my manager. Plus, I'd lied about being sick, which meant if I didn't show up—if I got sick for real, or hurt, or, say, murdered in my bed—they'd naturally assume I'd caught a bug and stayed home. They probably wouldn't even bother to worry. Great job, Dave.

I thumbed open my phone screen and stared at the text I'd been composing when Josie called. *Bethany's dead. I need your help.* The cursor blinked at me, waiting for my next move.

One tap. That was all it would take to turn the idea into a con-crete statement, timestamped and unretractable. An admission, not just of knowledge, but of guilt—sure, why not send that one out into the world at two a.m., casual as can be? And if I *did* send it, what then? I'd only sat on the information all goddamn night, long past the rational window of action. How would I explain the delay? How would I even start?

I'd known Bethany was dead, and I'd done *nothing*.

I'd been scared, yeah. I'd damn near been paralyzed with fear. But Bethany's body had disappeared, and the sarcophagus had been repaired—which meant whoever stored her in there in the first place knew I'd found her. There was no getting past that fact—they *had* to know I knew. Which made me a liability.

If I told Josie, she'd become one too.

I couldn't risk it. The second that text hit her phone, it would transform from a secret warning into a paper trail, both on our phones and in the records of our cell carriers. It would become a black-and-white fact that someone else might see. If I told her—and I would; if someone at our job had developed a sudden taste for coworker blood, I would damn sure put my partner on high alert—it would have to be in person. And we would have to be alone.

My breath leaked out in a long, weary shudder as I undid the text letter by letter. Then I followed the dog back inside, reset the alarm, and locked us both in my bedroom, not bothering to turn off the lamp. The last thing I needed was another cluster of shadows.

I was almost asleep when the memory hit—the grit of the floor beneath my back, the ends of her hair tickling my throat, the gummy press of her lips slack against my neck. The weight of her body, cold and heavy, clothed in an air of early rot. My stomach rocked; I was up and lunging toward the bathroom, barely making it before unleashing a Sno Ball–pink slurry of sugar and salt. I puked until the world went hazy, then slumped to the floor, throat scraped raw by sharp-edged bits of unchewed chips.

You okay, man? Left-Shoulder Anxiety Dave, the conscientious one. Always checking in.

"I don't think so, man," I croaked at the ceiling. "Feels like I'm about to freaking die."

DUDE.

Dude. Really?

"Oh God, I'm sorry," I babbled at the overlapping Daves. "I didn't mean it. I—I'm sorry."

The words welled quietly into being, from a place that went further down than sorrow. It wasn't shock or confusion that choked me. It wasn't terror, or even self-preservation. It was sorrow for my friend, raw and real. Unmuddied by fear.

Bethany was gone.

I curled onto my side and let the knots in my back and neck and jaw go soft. I let my heart unclench, drain, and finally feel. Tears ran steady from my swollen eyes, disappearing into the mat beneath my cheek.

chapter 9

I stood on the sidewalk outside the empty ticket booth, hands fisted around yards of wrinkled fabric. Frightmares House of Horrors loomed silent against a backdrop of billboards, palm trees, and blistering blue sky. I tamped down the acid rising from my gut and forced myself to reach out and yank open the entrance door.

What was I doing here? What the hell was I *thinking?*

You don't have to do this, Dave. Going back in there—back to that room—

"Oh, trust me," I reassured Bethany's voice. "I'm returning this costume, and that's it. I'm extra super officially done with this bullshit job, and I don't care what they—"

"Oh, thank god. You're here." The sudden grip on my arm would've sent me into a flurry of high-pitched shrieks had Josie's familiar voice not been on the other end of it. She was in full makeup and a headset, already sweating into the seams of her corset. She pressed a button on the headset and spoke into the mic as she took off across the lobby, dragging me along. "Ollie, he's here. Yeah, we're on our way."

"Josie, I'm not staying. I just came back to drop these off, and to warn you."

"Did you bring Mickey's costume?" We slammed through the door to the employee corridor, not even slowing down on the turn. "You're back on whip duty. Me alone in our room didn't go over."

"Yeah, it's right here, but—"

"Good, because he's down to undies and gold paint, and neither is mixing with his hangover. What, Ollie?" She cocked her head, attention focused on the headset. "Which costume? No idea—I guess Bethany still has it. Almost to the room. He's changing there."

"Josie," I cut in, low and urgent. "About Bethany—"

"Yeah, she fully bailed on us. Dara's taking over Vamp tonight, so Ollie's moving Brennan over to Murder Circus from the Swamp, but he doesn't know how to walk in stilts. So Maggie got pissed and yelled at Ollie, and now he's writing her up. Yay for another fun-filled, drama-free shift at Frightmares."

"Why doesn't Ollie just move Brennan to Vamp?"

"Not my call and not my problem, baby son. Now, you need to get your happy ass in gear and into costume. Here, give me that." She yanked Mickey's costume from my weak grip and sprinted down the corridor, leaving me standing like an asshole in front of our set door, pulse racing, throat stuck around a whimper, as she yanked open the door to Attack of the Mummy.

I braced myself for the death blow, waited for the downswing of an ax, or a crowbar, or the quiet snick of a switchblade. Waited for hands to reach and claw and drag Josie, screaming, into the room. Instead, she threw the loincloth and headdress through the doorway, spun on her heel, and flew back to me, Mickey's whoop of relief trailing at her heels. She was at my side, shoving me into Captive Countess before my feet remembered how to function.

I couldn't speak. I couldn't breathe. The world was a flashback pulse of laughter and fog, and the memory of Bethany's chilly, lifeless skin. I vaguely registered Josie's hands on my T-shirt, tugging, pulling it over my head and replacing it with the blousy costume shirt like I was one of Roz's old Ken dolls. My shorts followed, and I complied automatically, stepping into the pants, then the boots, shrugging into the waistcoat as I pieced the room back together in snippets of color and sound—most of which were provided by Josie, who was doing a damn fine auctioneer impression into her mic. Finally, she switched off the headset and threw it in a drawer, touched up her lipstick, and turned to me, taking in my sloppy, partially costumed form from the floor up. She eyed my shaking fingers as I tried and failed to close my waistcoat buttons.

"Look, if you're still sick or whatever, we can switch," she offered. "This bed sucks, but at least you'll be sitting down. I can grab a crinoline and skirt from Wardrobe."

"I'm not sick." I fisted my hands at my sides, zeroed my eyes straight in on hers. "Josie, you have to listen to me. We have to get out of here. *Now.*"

"On second thought, if you think you might puke, you probably shouldn't be stuck in the bed. This isn't *The Exorcist.* Here, I'll help. We don't have time for this."

She flew through the buttons, tied the cravat, and yanked the wig onto my head. I stared past her into the mirror, blinking at the bloodshot eyes and specter-white skin, plenty harrowing even without the usual makeup. Josie had already slid into the bed's seating contraption, triggered the mechanical leg, and fixed the noose cuffs over her wrists. My mouth wobbled around a glut of sticky, sour thoughts, unable to form my lips and tongue into the right ones.

She was so *vulnerable*, stuck in there like that. Hands tied. Legs trapped. *We* were vulnerable. Anything could happen.

It hadn't truly sunk in before that moment; now it hit me like a club to the back of the head. Bethany had died in one of these very rooms, at some point between Friday and Saturday's showtimes. We had locks, an alarm system, and only three doors leading in from outside—two of which were key-only emergency exits. No one could sneak into Frightmares and bypass all those things undetected—which meant Bethany was killed by someone we worked with. Someone we knew.

Someone who was, at this very moment, somewhere in the building with us.

They could be anywhere. They could bust in right in the middle of a tour, and the crowd would probably file on past in a cloud of chuckles and sighs, chalking up our ongoing murder to a planned performance. I couldn't guarantee anyone's safety, not even my own. Even if I fought the good fight, it would still be one on one. If they had a weapon, we were even more screwed—all I had was the whip and a perpetually broken foam ax.

And if they overpowered me, Josie was toast.

Go with it, man, Chill Dave whispered. *You won't get her out of here unless you drag her, so you gotta stick around. Make sure she makes it through the shift and talk to her after.*

Nope City, folks. Anxiety Dave. The voice of reason. *Forget professionalism, and tact, and fuck this job as a whole while you're at it. Drag her if you have to, but get. Her. Out.*

He was right. It was too much to ask that I continue the act, pretend like everything was cool when it definitely wasn't. No way was I leaving my friend to fend for herself when she was literally one of the only reasons I was still working at this garbage place. I had to warn her. I had to get us both out.

"Jo," I hissed, reaching to undo her left wrist. She frowned, eyes closed, tilting her head toward the sound of the approaching crowd. "Let's go. We need to go."

"Hush." Her finger tapped mine: one, two, three. Ready or not. "Trying to get into character here, dude."

"Look, we can't stay here, okay? Bethany's—"

"Bethany owes me a strong drink and a groveling apology for many things, including ditching us last night. Lucky for her, she caught me in a forgiving mood."

"She—what? A forgiving—"

Her eyes blinked open and fixed on me, a tiny crease forming between her brows.

"I said I was in a forgiving mood, Dave. This afternoon." She shifted against her restraints, fingers curling carefully around the length of safety rope. "When I talked to Bethany."

The world seemed to fall away from beneath my feet.

"You—*talked* to her? Face to face?"

"Over text. Mickey broke my phone at the coffeehouse, so I was checking my Instagram on Ollie's phone. I was literally holding it when the message came through."

"What . . . what did it say?"

"That she wasn't coming in today, tomorrow, or ever, because this place is a literal portal to hell. Not that I don't agree, but way to screw us over endless nights in a row, right?"

"It wasn't her, Jo. It *wasn't* her—it couldn't have been."

"It was her name on the caller ID—who else would it be? We even chatted for a second."

"About what?"

"I don't know, something generic. Like, okay, no hard feelings. Best of luck. That kind of thing. And she said same to me, and to take care, and we should hang out sometime, so—"

Her words ripped into a scream as the tour group appeared. I went through the motions automatically, chopping and whipping, head spinning. What was going on?

"What happened next?" I demanded the second the curtain rustled shut behind them. "Did you tell Ollie she quit?"

"Yeah, but he already knew. Bethany sent a formal email resignation before she sent the text. Ollie was with Loretta in the office when it hit her inbox—apparently, it was *not* well received. And you'd know all this if you'd bothered to show up to preshow." She glanced at the door, listening for the sound of footsteps. "Dude, did Seth, like, finally get you into shrooms? Why do you look like you've seen a ghost?"

"I—" The words skidded to a stop just past my lips, barely louder than a breath. I cleared my throat and forced them out again. "I mean, I—did I?"

I don't know, Dave. Did you?

"Dave." My name from a real live mouth brought me back to Josie, who stared at me with wide, apprehensive eyes. "What's going on?"

"I don't know. Oh God. I don't know."

Josie's lips closed over whatever she'd been about to say. I felt her worried gaze on me, but the room was a blur, shards of reality sloughing off in layers. Like the world was chipping away at itself, changing shape beneath the pressure of its own hands.

What the hell was happening to me?

"What, are you stalking me now? That's creepy as hell, Dave Gardiner."

My coffee leaped up the wrong tube, scalding the inside of my nose. She appeared against the crowded backdrop of Blacklist in a swirl of incense and espresso steam, eyes heavy, lips a wrecking-ball smirk. I stared up at her from the couch for a hideously silent beat, too rattled to conjure a coherent answer but way, way too knee-jerk-infatuated to blow her off. Not that words mattered. I was eternally destined to present as a dumbass in the vicinity of Maya Green.

"Oh. Hey."

"Yeah. 'Hey.'" She slid onto the arm of the couch, tucking her feet into the space between the frame and cushion, and rested her elbows on her knees, drink cupped in her hands. Her hair zigzagged over her shoulders, winning the battle against what must have started as a low bun. A drop of coffee fell from the rim of her cup, landing on my T-shirt sleeve. "So. You're here alone? On a Sunday night?"

It was a good question—a normal question. One that would've been easy to answer if the truth hadn't been such a trash mosaic of the unknown, but what can you do.

"No. Sort of. I'm waiting for my friends."

"The Varsity Douche Squad?"

"What?"

"Nothing. Your friends from school?"

"From work," I muttered, gaze dropping back to my coffee. Charming *and* articulate. Get it, Dave. "Haven't really hung out with the school friends since graduation."

"Oh. Sorry." She sipped her drink, squinting against a curl of steam. "Why aren't your work friends here yet? Did you have the night off?"

"I quit."

"Wow. Really?"

"Maybe. I think. I walked out, and I'm not going back, so I'm probably fired, anyway." My eyes skittered to the door and back again, restless as my shredded nerves. "They should be here soon."

That last bit was half expectation, half wishful thinking. I'd completely ditched Josie after our shift. I'd helped her out of the bed, walked her down the hall, waited until she was crossing the threshold of the crowded greenroom, then turned and flat-out booked it back down the hall. Six minutes later, I'd peeled out of the parking lot in my thoroughly inspected car. I'd left my costume and wig in my unlocked locker; I'd send my resignation in the morning. Since supposedly living Bethany had gotten her closure via email, Loretta could damn well accept the same from me.

In the meantime, no way was I spending another second in that building. I also wasn't aching to sit alone in my empty house all night. We'd already planned to end up at Blacklist—if Josie still wanted to talk, or hang out, or even chew my ass out for leaving, she knew where to find me. As for Trent Roznor, he had his toys, his bed, his doggie door, and plenty of self-dispensing food and water. He'd be fine on his own for a couple extra hours.

You, probably not so much.

Bethany's voice slapped the back of my head, dislodging a shaky gasp—shock, washed in relief. Rising terror, at her abrupt return.

"Dude. Hey. Are you okay?"

I blinked up at Maya's narrowed eyes, and the dark brows drawing together above them.

"Are you crying?"

"No." The word sailed past my teeth and into the room. I plonked my cup onto the low table in front of me. Coffee sloshed over the rim, scalding my already shaking hands. "I'm not crying, I just—"

My eyes were burning, though. I was as close to breaking as I could be, right in front of her. My ego was in full cringe. The rest of me, though—far beyond giving a shit.

"Right," Maya said softly, scanning the room, understandably searching for an out.

I wasn't even mad. I pressed my palms to my face, like I could somehow rub some self-control back into my nerves. Maybe salvage a scrap of dignity if I really dug in deep. Her hand on my shoulder almost sent me out of my skin.

"Come on," she said. "Let's get out of here."

chapter 10

It was a fever dream. The room swam in swoops of noise and spots of bright, nauseating colors. Maya cut through the crowd, reaching back to take my hand when I lagged. She pulled me free of the ennui logjam that was Sunday night at Blacklist, tugging me toward the door. Her slim fingers threaded through mine, an all-business grip that sent sparks along my palm.

She let go as we stepped out into the soupy air, gathering her hair back into its original bun, then turned to me, eyebrow arched over a wary, watchful gaze.

"Which one's yours?"

Her phone blew up as we settled side by side on the hood of the Honda, my legs dangling, hers crossed beneath her long, flowy skirt. She began texting, not bothering to hide the screen; I eyed her reply, and the resulting explosion in the group chat:

We're in the parking lot. Nothing to worry about.

MAYA. Wtf are you doing???

Dave Gardiner? Really??

I mean, I would

We know you would, Amber

Climb that boy like a tree

Wow, TMI. Maya, you okay?

I'M. FINE. Just talking. Going dark now,
be back soon.

Be safe, hon

"Um," I hedged, "do you need to go, or . . . ?"

"They saw us leave together. Safety 101."

"Jesus. Do they think you're, like, in danger?" I scanned the
parking lot for accusatory glares. "If this is too sketchy we can go
back inside, or—"

"Nah, it's not personal. We check in with each other no matter who's involved. And if I thought you were sketchy, I wouldn't be out here." She smashed a mosquito into a bloody smear across her shoulder, wiped the mess on her skirt, then turned the phone facedown in her lap. "Now. Dave. What the hell is going on?"

I know why I told her. It was a terrible idea, but it was no mystery—I'd spent the past twenty-four hours forming my head-whispers into my friend, who may or may not be dead; then, my definitely living friend, Josie, had added another facet of doubt to the hypotheticals. My family was away, and my old friends might as well be smoke. I needed to talk to someone who wasn't in my skull.

Plus—well, it was *her*. Maya Green, washed in streetlights and neon, skin a sweat-sheen shimmer in the hazy night. I'm a mess around that girl even when I'm *not* freshly traumatized.

She watched me silently, eyes wide, lips pressed to her steepled fingers as I told her every goddamn thing, from Seth's assorted pooch screws to the employee drama, through my horrifying stint in Mickey's room, and the subsequent hellscape of fear that had taken on the shape of my life.

"And I'm hearing her voice now," I babbled, my gaze roaming over every shadow of the parking lot. Wishing like hell I could begin to grasp what had happened. "She's in my head, like the Shoulder Daves. I don't know if I should call the cops, or if I'm losing it, or which of those is the better option, or—"

"Wait. Stop." She pressed her palms into her eyes, took a deep breath, then shook her hands out, as if waking up the blood flow to her fingers. "You're laying down some pretty wild stuff here, so I may have missed this detail, but . . . *what* is a Shoulder Dave?"

Shit.

"It's this thing I do," I muttered. "A Dave on each shoulder.

They help me keep an open mind and look at things from all angles. When I'm dealing with a tough situation, I fire up the Daves and get myself through. It's—it's my only way of coping sometimes, you know? With—everything." I swallowed back the ache in my throat, cheeks blazing, heart cringing. "It started forever ago. Way before yesterday ever happened."

"Well, are you sure you're doing the Bethany voice yourself?" she hedged. "Did she, like, join forces with the, um, Daves, or is it—I mean—"

"A ghost?" Man, this talk had jumped all the way off whatever track it had been on. Really hadn't planned on bringing the Daves into the mix.

"I was going to say a mental break." Maya's voice was wary, but sympathetic. "You said she might not even *be* dead, Dave. She's emailing and texting left and right, according to your friend. So what if she *is* alive?"

"If she's not dead, then what did I see yesterday? Because either that was real, or my brain is playing tricks and I hallucinated the whole thing. And right now, I honestly couldn't say which."

That was it, really—the core of the problem. When you don't know what's real in your head, what does that mean for the rest of the world? If I couldn't separate fact from hallucination, how was I supposed to do anything at all?

"Okay, then," Maya said. "For now, let's assume she really is dead. The Daves are, like, your little sidekicks, right? They're always there for you, even when no one else is. And you're sure this is more of the same?"

"Yes. The Daves are weird, I know, but they're *conscious*. I invented them *knowing* they weren't real. I didn't mean to start a Bethany voice, but it feels the same."

"I get that. Since that's your safe way of dealing, your sub-conscious probably conjured up her voice in response to what happened. I mean—you were trapped on the floor under the body of your dead friend. That's *horrific*."

"I know it sounds fake," I insisted, "but—wait. What? You actually—"

"Look, I'm not a fan of bullshit, okay? I've spent a lot of time around people who make it their personalities, and I'm pretty good at sniffing it out. And even though this is, like, the literal definition of bizarre, I'm not getting that vibe off you right now."

I let myself stare, for once—took in her face, the curve of her jaw, the stubborn set of her mouth. Her gaze, sure and tranquil, the stable singularity in a field of madness. An oasis.

I was pathetic. Totally sad and obvious, with my dumb, grate-ful smile and my dopey gaze—I could *feel* the puppy eyes forming in my own head. Dave Gardiner, Sackless Wonder. No dignity whatsoever. Nothing to salvage.

I wasn't even ashamed. She believed me.

"You're serious?"

"I am." She returned my smile, damn near stopping my heart. "I don't think you're lying to me, Dave. And I want to help."

chapter 11

If anyone had told me Friday night that, come Monday morning, I'd be standing on Maya Green's welcome mat, four streets over from my own house, I'd have demanded their dealer's contact info. I'd trash seventeen years of solid, straight-edge discipline and body-as-temple self-denial for a hit *that* good.

There I was, though, poised to knock on the bright scarlet version of my own olive-green front door. My knuckles had barely dusted the wood when she appeared in an air-conditioned whirl of incense and unbound hair. Her feet were bare, her shorts tiny, her T-shirt an enormous homage to Baby Yoda. A silver anklet, restless with tiny bells, jangled as she absently flexed her toes against the floor. Her eyes roamed the six-foot distance from my head to my flip-flops and back up again, ending with a raised eyebrow.

"Good morning, Dave Gardiner. Long night?"

I couldn't even bring myself to cringe. You couldn't stay up into the wee hours, staring into the darkness and listening to Trent Roznor relentlessly tongue-bathe his own ass, and still come out presentable on the other end. I'd pulled it together this morning long enough to stumble into the shower and burrow my way into a clean shirt, but honestly, to say I looked like hell was generous. I didn't need the worry lines forming around her eyes to clue me in on that fact.

"You could say that." I glanced past her into the silent house. "Are you sure it's okay with your parents? Me being here? If you'd be more comfortable in a public place—"

"It's fine. I'm almost eighteen—house rules are minimal, as long as we don't literally burn it down." She stepped aside to let me in, motioning to an assortment of neatly paired shoes just inside the doorway. "Come on."

I added my flip-flops to the shoe row and followed her down the hallway, the textured tiles cool beneath my bare feet. The floor plan of Maya's house was nearly identical to my house, but flipped—the kitchen on the left, living room on the right. A huge, busy aquarium and floor-to-ceiling bookshelves in the sitting room, instead of curio cabinets and a piano. A home office in place of our dining room, messy with scattered paperwork and clusters of potted succulents. Framed family pictures stared at us from all sides: Maya and a younger sister, both aging in staggered rectangles across the soft blue walls.

We were halfway to the stairs when my phone buzzed in my pocket. I fished it out, welcoming the distraction, but Ollie's message stopped me dead in my tracks.

Dave, you know I love you. With every last shred of my heart

"What the hell?"

"What?" Maya doubled back to where I stood, peering over my arm. "Who's Ollie?"

"My manager. But this can't be—"

> But so help me JESUS if you ditch your shift tonight and leave me alone in that bed, I'll make a midnight snack of your soul

"Josie." Recognition and relief double-punched my sternum. "It's Josie, not Ollie. She's still got his phone."

> Ollie said if you don't show, SETH will have to stand in for you, and that scenario WILL end in blood—HIS. So I shall SEE YOU TONIGHT IN OUR VERY OWN LABYRINTHINE HELL, MY BEAUTIFUL BABY SON. BE THERE –j

"Josie your partner?" Maya frowned. "Why is she on this Ollie guy's phone?"

"He's her boyfriend. Her phone broke the other night, and—"

"Wait. Isn't she the one who talked to Bethany?"

"Yeah, that's how it happened. Bethany texted her resignation to Ollie's phone, and it came through while Josie was using it."

"Right. That's not convoluted at all." She squinted at the message, chewing thoughtfully on her lower lip. "When do you go into work?"

"Usually around four, but not anymore. I told you, I quit."

"Does Ollie know that yet?"

"I—" He didn't, actually. Emailing a resignation to Loretta, let alone sending Ollie a friendly heads-up, had completely slipped my mind. Maya watched that information creep across my face and nodded to herself.

"Good. So we have until around three-thirty to put our plan into motion."

"If 'our plan' involves me going in to work like everything is cool and getting sucked back into that mess like I did yesterday, forget it."

"Yeah, whatever." She swooped in and grabbed my phone, firing off a text before my dumb ass realized what was happening.

> Worry not, my lady, your baby son will be there

"I will not 'be there,' Maya. And I would never, ever talk like that. And she knows it."

I made a grab for the phone, but she danced out of reach. It buzzed again, flooding us in a wave of confusion emojis:

> My lady??? Christ, Dave, don't make it weirder than it has to be

I glared at Maya's smirk, managing to swipe my phone back and shove it in my pocket before she could make things worse.

"See?" I told her.

"And yet, it's still less weird than her allegedly texting a dead person, right?" She stared into the middle distance, brows drawing slowly together until she was flat-out frowning at it. "If things work out, maybe she'll—"

"Nope, she's not involved. Moving on to option B."

"There's no option B yet, Dave—the plan hasn't evolved to that stage. The events of the afternoon won't exist until the events of the morning play out in real time."

"What events? What are you talking about?"

"It's easier to show you." She turned on her heel, crooking her finger over her shoulder as she headed for the stairs. "Follow me."

I don't know exactly what I expected to see when Maya opened her bedroom door. Whatever was in my head, though, I do know that the reality of lavender wallpaper, hanging spider plants, and blue-patterned crazy quilts were not on the list. Neither were the two lace-trimmed throw pillows, arranged facing each other on the white carpet, or the well-worn Ouija board poised for action in between them.

Yeah. Really hadn't expected that one.

Well, this is just insulting, Bethany drawled from out of nowhere. *How about a big old bowl of Nope to start the day?*

"Hey, so," I began, watching Maya move around the room,

draw the window shades, and grab a lighter and a giant Yankee Candle from her nightstand. "About this setup. A Ouija board? Really?"

"Process of elimination. You don't think it's a ghost, but you can't be *sure*-sure unless we fail to establish contact, right? Hence, Ouija."

"Maya, I'm here in the first place because Bethany's spent the past couple days yelling inside my skull. Contact has one hundred percent been established."

"But not," she insisted, "in a way that's been confirmed by anyone *outside* your skull. We need solid proof one way or the other."

She cupped her hands around the lighter and leaned over the candle. I heard the flick, smelled the burnt metallic whiff give way to the scent of vanilla cupcakes. She settled herself on one of the cushions and raised her eyes to mine. I didn't even argue. Whatever I came up with, she'd have six rebuttals waiting to dismantle it. Maya's words, and the way she said them, were the catalyst for my entire crush—and what that meant, apparently, was that I was about to get comfortable and watch this girl, who I'd drooled over for months, talk to the possible ghost in my head while we sat in her cake-scented bedroom. This life.

"Okay, then." I took my place on the cushion opposite her, careful not to jostle the Ouija board. "Have at it."

Maya let her eyes drift shut and leaned over the board, placing a fingertip on the center of the planchette.

"We open ourselves to the world beyond the veil today, imploring those who hear to lend us their voices. We call upon the spirit of Bethany . . ." Her forehead scrunched, and she opened her eyes. "What's Bethany's last name?"

"Blake. I think."

"You think? This girl is in your literal head, and you don't know for sure?"

"That's what's on her headshot, but it might be a stage name. Josie goes by one, and Mickey—most of the cast. Loretta likes us to use stage names in the workplace if we have them. Says it's more professional. Less confusing on industry résumés."

"Yeah, I get it." She sucked in a long, slow breath, letting her eyes slide closed on the exhale. "Bethany Blake, we call to you. We beseech you, show yourself to us."

She did not just say beseech. Bethany was there, all right, and she was talking—but only to me. *This is ridiculous.*

"Bethany, we seek answers," Maya continued. "We need your guidance. Help us bring the truth to light."

"Wait," I cut in.

Maya's eyes cracked open, aiming all the questions my way.

"What exactly are you asking?"

"I'm trying to find out what happened to her. Obviously."

"I thought you wanted to negate a haunting. You never said anything about—"

"She's dead, Dave. We don't know how, or why, or who did it—or if anyone even *did*. What if she slipped, or something fell on her? What if it was an accident? Or even natural causes?"

"Natural causes? She didn't put herself in that sarcophagus, Maya."

"Well, obviously. But whoever did—do we know for certain that they *killed* her? What if there's more to it? Are we looking for someone who found her dead, and panicked—or are we looking for a murderer?"

"How the fuck am I supposed to know any of that?"

"You aren't. It's why I'm asking Bethany, not you. I did go into this with an objective, you know—to figure out what we're dealing with."

This is bullshit. All of it.

"She has a point, though."

I spoke the words. I can't believe I did it, but I answered Bethany aloud. Like Maya needed a backstage pass to this mess in my head when she already had front-row seats.

"What? Is she here?" Maya's hands went slack on the board, fingertip nudging the planchette to the left of center. "What's happening?"

How badly do you need to get laid, Dave, for real? The board game, the beseeching, the fucking candle—it's condescending. And after everything we've been through, you're just going along with it. Pitiful.

"Tell us," I pressed, wondering, for a moment, if maybe this would work after all. Maybe I'd seen or heard something vital and blocked it out. Maybe my subconscious had guessed at and buried a truth I couldn't bear to face. Or maybe I really was haunted. I leaned forward, catching Maya's wide, dark eyes. "Tell me how you died."

The air stilled. The candle flickered. We sat there, barely breathing. Maya's finger trembled on the planchette; my hands clenched into fists, like I was gearing up to take on the whole room, never mind that there was nothing in there to fight. The silence pooled and thickened, filling our ears and throats and hearts.

Because that was really all there was: nothing.

"Okay, then," Maya finally said, way past a reasonable wait time. "I don't know what to tell you, Dave. But I wasn't lying." She sat up and crawled across the Ouija board, taking hold of my hunched shoulders. Making me look her in the eye. "I believe your trauma is real. I set up the Ouija to take the question of a 'ghost' out of the equation. Now we need to figure out our next steps."

I almost left. The idea of laying it out there—of blowing it open and officially declaring Frightmares a crime scene—was too much.

"I don't know. Maybe you're right." I rubbed my eyes, pressing back the burn. "Christ. I think we need to call it in."

"Call the cops, you mean? And tell them what? That your friend is dead, even though no one's reported her missing? That your other friends say they've talked to her since you found her body—which *is* now missing?"

"Okay, I see your point, but—"

"But say she *is* dead," she continued, talking over me. "Say someone *did* kill Bethany and hid her in your workplace, then covered it up once you found her—and that other someone already knows you know. You've kept your mouth shut so far, but—"

"—if an OPD car rolls up to work," I continued, a sick, hot flush creeping across my skin, "and that person thinks I'm planning to talk—"

"They could try to shut your mouth for good. This is— I don't—" She got to her feet and crossed to the window, lifted the corner of the shade to peer up and down the block. "Did you tell *anyone* else about this, besides me?"

"No. I tried to show Ollie when I found her, but by the time I got him back there, she was gone. I didn't—" I stared at the candle flame, backtracking my thoughts to that moment. I'd manhandled his ass across the building, but I'd been out of breath and largely incoherent. I hadn't said a word. "I didn't tell him anything. Or anyone else."

"Not even your parents?"

"They're in Aruba. I'm sort of on my own right now."

Maya's eyes drooped shut, as if trying to unhear that particular detail. She ran a weary hand over her face, leaving eyeliner smears across her temple.

"Wow. Okay. So, I'll brainstorm on my end, and meanwhile, I'm thinking you *should* call in to work after all. Officially tender your resignation."

"I can't."

I didn't know I was saying it until it came out. Once it did, though, I knew it was true.

This was bigger than me. Bigger than my sanity or my confusion, or my paralyzing fear. Bethany deserved justice. To do right by her, I had to keep it together, keep my mouth shut, and start digging. And maybe I *was* having a mental break, or would soon enough.

But it didn't matter. Sticking my head in the sand was a hard no.

I had to know what happened to her.

I had to go back.

chapter 12

The sun shone warm on my back and neck as I doubled my pace, arms pulling, legs propelling me across the pool. Lungs and limbs and muscles slipping into a rhythm they'd perfected long ago. I needed the calm that went hand in hand with submersion, where my mind was clear, and sharp, and thankfully, wonderfully, empty.

My body was a vessel I trusted. *That* was a reliable place to live—a strong, healthy place that looked good in even the dumbest Frightmares costumes. That cut through the water exactly how I told it to, without slowing or tiring, fed off the sun and exertion and repetition until it was everything the world loved about me.

Dave swimming was Dave at his best. My times didn't lie—neither did my school, district, and county records, my state championship medals, or my full-ride scholarship. Nor did the top-tier social standing that accompanied all those things, or the way all of it fell away to nothing as soon as I hit the water. None of that mattered. None of that was why I swam.

In the pool, I didn't have to talk. I didn't have to smile, or listen, or worry about the excruciating things that might fall from my mouth if I relaxed enough to let my guard down. I'd gotten a *ton* of passes on that stuff just by being Dave Gardiner—Dave, whose smile charmed and flustered in equal measure. Whose tongue-tied silence came off as cool and mysterious. Whose bashful laugh turned awkward into cute.

Still, it never got easier to live in my own head. It was a mess in there. It always had been.

The water was where I went to find peace.

I'd brought Trent Roznor out in the yard for company, hoping he'd chill in the shade of the covered patio while I swam. He'd cooperated for about seventeen seconds, then brought his stuffed possum squeaky toy over to the edge of the pool, where he dropped it in the water and proceeded to bark at me every time I swam past. After the fourth time I stopped to fish it out, I'd pretty much given up on relaxation. A solid half hour later, and I was no closer to calm than when I'd started.

Instead of churning out more laps, I pulled off my goggles, settled on the steps, and threw the possum across the yard. Trent Roznor bounded after it and brought it back over and over, barking at nothing, as always. Maybe he'd exhaust himself and pass out, and I could get some thinking done.

Now you're just stalling, Dave, Bethany said. *Put doggo inside and get your head straight. Figure out how you're going to deal with everything tonight.*

It was all well and good for her to say, but *how* was the query of the day, was it not? Frightmares was nothing if not a giant question mark. The séance had been useless, but the morning at Maya's house hadn't been a total waste. I'd helped her pack up the Ouija set, then stood there like a tool while she tidied the room, fluttering between her bed and desk like a nervous moth.

"I don't like it, Dave," she'd said as we made our way downstairs. "It's not safe for you, going in there on your own. Who else can you trust with something like this?"

"I trust Josie, but I don't think she'd believe me. Mickey would think I'm pranking him. Ollie would probably call the cops—which puts us back at square one, with no body and no evidence. And Loretta—"

"No, you're right. It's a bad idea to bring anyone into it. For now, if you're really going back, you have to act normal and see what you can scrounge up on Bethany—her address, her contact info. Her actual name, not that 'is-it-her-last-name-or-her-stage-name' crap."

"What for?"

"We need to go out to her place, check if anyone's seen her around." She'd rolled her eyes at my huff. "Look, I believe you. I know she's dead. But we need to establish a last sighting. If someone saw her come home on Friday, that means she wasn't killed until Saturday. That makes all the difference in the world."

"Okay. I can try to get her number off Josie. She might know Bethany's real name, also."

"Right on. If that doesn't work, your boss should have everything on file."

"Yeah, well, I may not exactly be on her good side." I'd cringed as we stepped onto the porch, another detail worming its way into the mix. "I sort of skipped the last couple postshow cast meetings."

"So, you kiss her ass. You go in there, give a full Anne Shirley apology, and you ask her how you can help solve her staffing problems. Tell her you want to talk to Bethany on her behalf."

93

"Got it. What's an 'Anne Shirley'?"

"You—ugh. Of course you don't know. Just do your charming Dave Gardiner thing. And be careful."

I'd left her house more confident than when I'd arrived, but that had waned fast enough. If even one thing went sideways, I might as well call the cops on myself now. How the hell was I supposed to launch a covert investigation when I'd never even had detention? I was Golden Boy Dave—an eager, dedicated employee who did his job and nodded his head.

But I sure had been a hot mess since Saturday, hadn't I? Leaving work; skipping notes; showing up late. Acting unhinged in the parking lot and blowing off my friends. And the really fucked-up part was that now, in my safe, familiar surroundings, I was almost able to forget it had even happened. In the light of day, it was easy to believe this was nothing but a nightmare.

Must be nice.

Bethany's mutter made me wince. None of this was okay.

I wanted to tell someone—I wanted to scream it from the bottom of my swimmer's lungs. Of all the times for my usually involved parents to go full world-traveler. Their presence wouldn't change much about the Frightmares situation, but at least they'd *be* here. The cops wouldn't believe me without proof, and I couldn't trust any of my other castmates. I had nothing but a vague, shitty plan, and Maya Green on the fringes, awaiting further instruction.

I had to get her out of this. I had to clear my head.

Trent Roznor nudged me, snapping me out of my thoughts and trampling over my last nerve. I climbed out of the pool and led him back toward the house, chucked the possum overhand through the sliding door. He scrabbled after it. I shut the door behind both of them, chills breaking out over my arms. Stomach knotting up as I realized those chills had nothing to do with the waft of air-conditioning from the living room.

Something was wrong.

A sound had registered in my distracted senses—a metallic, distinctive clunk I'd heard countless times before. A clunk that absolutely should not have rung out across my yard at this particular moment.

The rattle of the gate latch. Someone was here.

Who would drop by unannounced on a random Monday? We weren't expecting any packages. My neighbors knew my family was gone, as did Roz's grand total of two friends, neither of whom would try to come in the back way even if they did drop by. I used to leave the gate unlocked for Cate, but the chances of her showing up here at all, let alone unpreceded by a string of dramatic texts, were at dead zero. The only person who'd texted me in days was Josie—and that was from Ollie's phone. Maya and I had exchanged contact info, but her number had yet to appear on my screen.

I didn't even have my phone *on* me, I realized—it was in the kitchen, sitting on the charging station, and had been since I'd gone outside. Maybe Maya *had* texted me, or tried to call, then got worried when I didn't answer. Maybe she'd come over to check on me. You couldn't hear the doorbell from the backyard. Maybe she'd rung it first, then circled around to try the gate.

Maybe, Bethany whispered. *Or maybe it's not Maya. At all.*

I stared at the gate, fear prickling over my shoulders. Waiting for the latch to—what? Explode into shrapnel? Rattle again, as some unknown person tried a second time to gain access to my yard because—why? No one had a reason to ring my doorbell, much less break in through the locked back gate.

Unless.

Josie's words from Saturday's preshow tickled the edge of my memory: *If you slip and fall—if someone steals you away or cuts your throat in the dark of night—no one would know until it was too late to save you.*

She was right. And thanks to Loretta's fixation on my laundry during that little exchange, everyone—*everyone*—at Frightmares knew I was home alone. Whoever killed Bethany might have decided I was a risk after all—and why attack me in the workplace when they could sneak up on me while I swam, blindside and gut me, and leave me to lie undiscovered in my Speedo at my unmonitored, very empty house?

But if I got to them before they got to me, I might be able to catch them off guard. Take them down before they had a chance to strike.

This was my chance. I had to know who was watching me.

Nope, Anxiety Dave said. *Big old bag of rock-solid nope, my dude. Get your ass in the house. Get your phone and call for help.*

No time, Chill Dave on the Right answered. *Anyway, fuck that. If they think they can take* this *on, let 'em come and try.*

I crossed the lawn before I could change my mind and sidled up to the gate, back pressed to the fence like I was on a SWAT team raid, hating the Dave who had led me here. Every hair on my scalp prickled, my arms tensed, my jaw locked around a whimper I absolutely refused to let loose. I pressed my eye to a crack in the fence but couldn't see shit; then I steeled myself, grasped the gatepost, braced my toes against the backer rail, and swung myself upward all at once. My head popped up over the pickets, prepared, for better or worse, to come eye-to-eye with a killer.

Nothing. The side yard was empty.

Feeling like the world's biggest dumbass, I dropped back to the ground, grabbed my towel, and slunk back to the house, a wave of relief soothing the adrenaline burn in my veins. Even if there had been someone out there, I should be safe inside. The gate was one thing, but if they were brave enough to mess with the front door, they'd be greeted by the wail of our alarm system.

Dave. Bethany's hiss stopped me in my tracks, halfway through the living room. *You disabled the alarm when you went outside. It hasn't been on for the last hour.*

The world rocked; spots popped across my vision, blurred the furniture, edged the walls in gray. The floor tiles seemed to double; they stretched from my feet down an impossibly long hallway, to a front door that might as well have been miles away. Someone was here. The alarm was off.

Whoever it was had all the time in the world to sneak in through that door while I was casing the fence.

My towel fell to the floor as I took off down the hall, skidded across those millions of tiles on slippery feet, clawed open the deadbolt, and burst into the yard. I pulled up short on the molten driveway, eyes scanning the street, muscles strung, my voice stuck in my throat.

The neighborhood radiated its usual calm, weekday morning suburban vibe. No one was around, except for a loose cluster of moms in the yard two doors down, standing over three toddlers covered in fingerpaint and sidewalk chalk. My subdivision had been designed with plenty of winding roads, sharp turns, and stop signs to discourage speeding. My house, of course, sat right in the middle of a curve; I could look all I wanted, but the view didn't extend farther past a few houses in either direction.

I checked up and down the street anyway, ears straining for anything unusual—suspiciously hurried footfalls, shouts or car alarms, the deep, throaty barks of dogs bigger and more useful than Trent Roznor. What I heard was the whine of a mower; the honk of a horn; the squeal of brakes on a too-fast sports car; the distant revving of a motorcycle. The music from the ice cream truck two streets over. The screams and splashes of the kids across the street, enjoying their own pool. As far as I could tell, nothing was out of place.

I retreated into the house before anyone saw my dumb ass standing there, dripping all over the driveway in a Speedo. The sight of my normal, tranquil neighborhood reengaged my brain, let logic drift back in to fill the space my fear had siphoned dry. The door had been locked. There were people outside. I was paranoid—my head was a wreck. *That* was nothing new, but there was no reason to wet myself. Everything was normal.

Everything was fine.

chapter 13

The office was lit by three dim, recessed ceiling fixtures, four decorative black wall sconces, and five plastic LED candles, crammed into a wobbly, black-painted candelabrum that looked straight out of a Spencer's. The desk was an ornate, repurposed dining table; the high-backed chairs an ergonomic nightmare of crimson velvet and chrome-studded black leather. Even the walls were weird—they were papered in a Victorian print, burgundy with a darker pattern that looked like either floral arrangements or really jacked-up peacocks, depending on which way you turned your head. Loretta, perched in the middle of it all like a friendly gargoyle, gestured for me to sit.

I flung myself into the chair opposite hers and proceeded to vomit up what dignity I had left all over her cluttered desk. After so many months spent surrounded by actors, the melodrama thing was getting a little too easy.

"Of course I forgive you, Davis," she finally said, stopping me with a wave of her hand. "I wish you'd told us not to expect you, but all things considered, I'm glad you bothered showing up for work at all. I'm not having much luck holding on to my cast."

"Let me make it up to you," I insisted, diving straight into that opening. "I know you've been having a hard time, with people leaving. Maybe I can reach out, talk to them, whatever—I really just want to help."

"You're sweet, hon. Thank you. But for now, all I need from you is punctuality, responsibility, and a good, positive attitude. Everything else will come out in the wash." She squinted at her screen, then at the clock. "As for the staffing issue, Oliver posted an ad on the Craig List—he's interviewing a replacement for Vamp right now, actually, and has three more lined up for Undead Graveyard. We haven't heard a thing from Chet either, I'm sorry to say."

"You're already replacing Bethany? But—"

"The last I heard from her was her resignation. If she changes her mind I'll happily take her back, but the show must go on. Not to mention the building rent is going up, and there're so many repairs—" She squinted at the computer again, finger clicking compulsively on the mouse. "And now *this*. I told them when they installed the cameras. 'Give me a VCR,' I said. Insert tape, press Record. A good, sturdy system I know how to run. But no—no one uses those anymore, they said. Obsolete, they said."

"Cameras?" The words clicked in my head, rolling over each other, picking up speed like the gears on a bike. "We're wired in every room?"

"God save us, I can't afford that. We have four, but it might as well be zero if this keeps up. It all goes into the online, and *poof*." Her hands fluttered around the literal poof of her beehive, like she was fanning away a swarm of lovebugs. "What good is a fancy security system if it never works when you need it?"

"What happened?"

"I found marks on the lobby door this morning. Scratches

around the keyhole, like someone tried to break in. I checked the cameras, but all of them were dark. Must have had a glitch at some point—there's no footage at all from the weekend, not that I can find. Nothing." She wilted in the chair, one hand drifting up to her earpiece. "Yes, Oliver? Yes, thank you, dear. I'll be right there."

I stood as she locked her screen, trying like hell to keep a straight face over the faraway roar building in my ears.

We had cameras.

That this was breaking news was peak dumbass, even for me—of course we had cameras. Everything and everyone had cameras. But I'd spent the majority of my employ at Frightmares actively failing to give a damn about my surroundings; those cameras were background. Unnoticeable and unimportant, and probably broken long before last weekend, like everything else in the place.

But what if they were the missing piece? If the security system had in fact been up and running Friday night, there was a chance it'd caught something. Four cameras didn't promise much coverage of the enormous, twisty catastrophe of the place, but if I could get a look at Friday's or Saturday's footage, I might be able to pin down a timeline—make note of who'd left, and when; see who was in the building and where they'd been when Bethany disappeared.

Or maybe I'd see, onscreen, the final moments of her life.

It would be horrible. It would be hideous beyond words. But it would be proof—and all I had to do to get it was click around for a few minutes on the company computer. Luckily, Loretta openly sucked at anything Internet—or, as she called it, *the online*. Home of the Craig List. Getting access would be the easy part.

"My parents have a similar setup on our property," I lied, before she made it to the door. "I could take a look at it for you, if you like."

"Oh, could you, dear? I can't do a thing with any of it."

"Sure, Loretta." I stretched my smile until I felt my dimples, clocked her with that easy, good-boy grin everyone seemed to love so much. "Anything to help."

"This boy. This boy, I tell you. I need to run down to the interview, but you're more than welcome to have at it while I'm gone." She leaned back over her keyboard and pecked out her password, not bothering to block my view. Her desktop bloomed to life, a garbage dump of folders and icons scattered over Vampira wallpaper. She clicked into the folder marked *Security Camera,* then swooped around, descending upon my cheeks with her pinching fingers. "You're saving all our lives, Davis."

She sailed out of the office. I settled into her chair, rubbing the sting of her talons out of my face.

The greater good, man, Chill Dave reassured me. *Stay focused. Get what you need.*

There was no reason to argue. I cleaned up the files, to start—Loretta's subfolders were about as organized as her desktop. It was nothing a quick sort command couldn't fix, but after I'd arranged it all by date, the most recent archives still showed nothing after last Thursday. The Trash folder was empty too. I refreshed the feed, replacing the empty black frames with live footage from what appeared to be perfectly functional cameras, and was about to do a hard drive search for the missing files when the door swung open. Ollie's head appeared around the doorjamb.

"Hey, man, Loretta said to pull you outta here. She's got the new hire all signed up, and—" He broke off at the sight of me at the boss's desk, very obviously clicking around on the computer. "Dude . . . what are you doing?"

"Nothing." I leaned back in the chair, giving him a clear view of the screen. "Loretta's having issues with the cameras. She asked me to troubleshoot."

"Oh, right on. Any luck?"

"Seems fine to me. Check it out."

He peered over my shoulder as I clicked back through to the feed, pulling up the four-panel livestream view: The breakroom, empty except for the table and chairs, kitchenette, and row of lockers. The deserted lobby. The interior of the ticket booth as seen from its back wall, and the view of the sidewalk and street beyond the glass. The employee hallway, through which Loretta and the new hire walked side by side.

The chair jerked backward, slamming into Ollie's knee and damn near tipping over as I shot to my feet.

"WHAT. THE. HELL."

"'What the hell' is right, Dave!" Ollie howled. "You almost broke my—"

I heard the greenroom door open and Loretta swan through. I definitely heard the shrill trumpet of her voice, and the answering chorus of cheers and applause, as the Frightmares House of Horrors cast greeted the newest member of the family.

I shoved past Ollie and burst out of the office, just in time to see Maya Green step through the doorway and smile right at me through a set of perfect, gleaming fangs.

chapter 14

She managed to dodge me all through preshow. After the formal cast introductions, Loretta sent Maya off with Mickey for a vampiric crash course, which meant I couldn't corner her for the "What in the almighty hell are you doing here, Maya?" conversation. Not that I'd have had the chance anyway, what with Josie basically adhering herself to my person, leering and giggling all the way to our set.

"Dude, I'm taking *full* credit for this." She wound her arm through mine as we walked, lowered her voice as Maggie rushed past us, carrying her stilts. "I saw you last night, you know—ditching me for our newest victim. Those are some top-shelf recruitment skills you've got there, baby son."

"Josie, I really don't think she's here because of me, so maybe don't—"

"Sweetie. Please. She spent her night out sitting on the hood of your car, then literally got herself hired at your job the next day. That qualifies as 'interested' from where I sit. And to think: none of this would have happened if I hadn't given you that literal push on Friday. You at least owe me Chipotle for getting that ball rolling."

"I will buy you all the Chipotle you want if you stop," I moaned. "Don't say anything to her. Or Ollie. Or—dear sweet God—please don't tell Mickey I know her. He'll never let up."

"Since when do you care what Mickey says?" She squinted up at me, brows arching over a tiny frown. "What's with the nerves, Dave? I thought you two were, like, acquaintances? From school?"

"Not really. We never talked before you literally shoved me into her. She doesn't know I—" I sighed and ducked my head, faking and not faking, blanketing the truth with a safer, spontaneous alternate reality. "I'm barely back out there after what happened with Cate. If it gets back to Maya that I'm into her, and she blows me off—"

"Oh, honey. Bless your sweet soul." Josie squeezed my arm and spun away from me as we reached our room, bumping the door open with her hip. "My silence will know no bounds."

"Thanks, Jo."

It was enough to smile at her in the moment and appreciate the teasing grin I got in return. The Frightmares cast had never been squeamish about dating in the workplace. I could think of at least fourteen cast-member entanglements I'd seen begin and end since I started working here, not even counting the on-again, off-again saga of Seth and Bethany. But Ollie's promotion had gotten him all worked up about boundaries and professionalism, and Mickey loved nothing better than to stir some shit. If he caught wind of anything that might liven up a shift or two, he'd leak like a relaxed baby just to watch the fallout.

Josie, though, would stick to her promise. Not around me, of course—it'd be open season on my ass when we were alone. But I trusted her to keep my secret, or what she thought was my secret, to herself. And really, that was all that mattered.

Because in the grand scheme of things, I gave a little less than half a rat's ass if Maya knew about my feelings. She'd watched me stumble over her feet and stammer over myself through a face full of stage makeup; she'd watched me shudder and babble in a parking lot; she'd watched me talk to the empty air. I'd either already blown it, or I wasn't going to. As for our coworkers, they could talk all they wanted—I hadn't spent high school at the top of the social food chain just to collapse on a fainting couch over some dumb work rumor.

The reason behind my silence was simple: I was a target now, for whoever'd killed Bethany. If they caught so much as a hint of my alliance with Maya, she'd appear in the crosshairs at my side. I had to treat her like I'd treat any other new employee who didn't already have my senses knotted around her every word. To keep her safe, I had to keep my distance.

This was going to be a nightmare.

The longest shift ever finally ended, only to segue into a post-show notes marathon that lasted the approximate life span of a dwarf star. Josie spent the whole meeting staring at Loretta, pretending to listen intently, all the while digging her nails into my arm every time Maya so much as blinked.

Bethany's whisper had been conspicuously absent during the performance, as had both Daves. In fact, I'd been so preoccupied with the idea of Maya alone and unguarded in Vamp that I hadn't even had time for a routine panic attack, much less a sweat-soaked, crippling flashback.

After Loretta finally wrapped things up, I hovered near the door and swooped in on Maya, bundling her off to the side as she teetered past.

"Maya, what the hell?"

"You weren't kidding about this place, Dave," she said, grinning, knuckling a smear of lipstick from the corner of her mouth. "What an absolute garbage fire."

"Why would you do this? This morning you were all worried about me being here with no one to watch my back, and now—"

"And now I'm here to watch that back for you, good sir. And, since we can't exactly advertise our agenda, we'll go full *Hamlet*. Play within a play." She ran her tongue over her fangs, smirking up at me. "I told you option B would reveal itself in time."

"No," I hissed, gut doing a free-fall dive into nothing at the thought of her standing between me and even a whiff of danger. "I don't want you anywhere near this place."

"Look, you *need* me here—you're too enmeshed. You have friends, and biases, and your head is all messed up. I'm neutral. And you're probably already being watched."

"Which is exactly why you shouldn't be involved."

"Well, I wasn't involved at all until you went and brought your fake ghost and your little mini Daves or whatever over to my house. And now my feet are killing me, and—so"—her voice grew louder and more vacuous, lifting at the ends of her words— "I don't really know? What to do about my stuff? The only empty locker has a broken latch."

"What?" I blinked at her wide-eyed gaze, at least ten steps behind wherever she was headed. "I don't—"

"Loretta said two people quit, so is the other locker maybe free? Like, if you know of a way we could cut the lock off, I'd be happy to clean out whatever's left in there. I just really need a safe place? For my bag. It's literally just sitting in a corner right now."

Her meaning snuck up on me and whacked me in the back of my dense head. Chet had spite-emptied his locker Friday night, taking the lock and all his stuff, leaving the latch jacked up and the door hanging wide open. Bethany's locker, however, was untouched—her street clothes and keys and purse possibly still inside. Concrete proof that she hadn't just walked out like a normal, living person.

I leaned casually against the wall, grinning down at Maya, trying like hell to ignore Josie sliding not-so-subtly past, wiggling her hips and winking at me over her shoulder.

"Oh. Yeah, sure, I'll totally take care of that for you, um . . . was it Mia?"

"Maya," said a voice at my back. "Maya, meet Dave."

"Oh, hi, Ollie." Maya turned a fanged smile toward his helpful face. "I was just asking, uh, Dave, I guess, about—"

"Yeah, the locker situation. I heard. I'm on my way out right now, but grab me before shift starts tomorrow and I'll free up that space for you. You'll need to bring your own lock. That cool?" He nodded at her affirmative reply. "Great. Hey, Dave." He turned to me. "We missed you the last couple nights. You're feeling better, I hope?"

Ollie's cheerful, offhanded oblivion made my ass clench. I so, so did not need his input in this totally fake conversation.

"Oh," I answered. "Yeah, I'm okay. Sorry about all that. I have a lot going on, and—"

"Dude, don't we all. Keep your head up and you'll get through. We're heading over to Blacklist if you want to hang out. You too, Maya."

"Oh. Thanks," she said. "I'll text my mom about my curfew."

"No problem either way. Hope to see you guys there." He thumped me on the back, gave Maya a thumbs-up. "Good job tonight, by the way. Welcome to the team."

He caught up to Josie and they left hand in hand. Maya swiveled back to me, eyes darting over the remaining stragglers in the greenroom.

"Ugh," she muttered. "There goes that plan. Might as well go take these teeth out and start brainstorming."

I stopped her with a subtle hand on her arm, kept her in pause as the room emptied out person by person.

"I think we can make it work on our own. Hang back—we'll cut the lock ourselves once they're gone."

"You keep bolt cutters in that fancy waistcoat, huh?"

"We keep them in the supply closet. All the shit that breaks in this place, you better believe we have a loaded toolbox. I'll replace Bethany's old lock with mine and bring a new one in tomorrow. Ollie won't know the difference." I glanced over my shoulder at Loretta's open office door. She hovered over the desk, trying to log out of the computer with one hand while the other gathered the straps of her giant purse. "Follow me, act like we're leaving."

I cleared my throat and raised my hand in a wave. Maya was already halfway into the hallway by the time Loretta blinked up at me.

"Good night, Loretta."

"Same to you, dear. See you kids tomorrow."

We left the greenroom, waited around the corner until she burst out the door in a flurry of clacking heels, loaded down with file folders and various set decor. A severed-arm prop hung over her shoulder, waving to us as she tottered away toward the lobby.

"You really should've taken me on a behind-the-scenes tour before telling me your story," Maya muttered. "There's nothing I wouldn't believe about this place right now."

She giggled at my glare but didn't hesitate to follow me to the supply closet. She also didn't hesitate to let that giggle turn to a cackle when a bundle of net fabric and about eighty bags of that stretchy fake spiderweb cotton leaped out at me the second I opened the door.

"Goddamn it," I hissed as she clapped her hands over her grin. The closet was crammed corner to corner with storage bins and prop boxes. A quick survey of the shelves revealed an empty space where the toolbox should've been. "Thanks a lot, Seth."

"You're, like, the third person I've heard say that exact thing," Maya mused as I shoved all the webs and crap back into the closet. "I don't know who Seth is, but—"

"Zombie room. Loretta's son. Which is pretty much the only reason he's still allowed to work here."

"Oh God, *that* guy? He was creeping me out *all* night."

"Seth?" I'd been so freaked out by her showing up like she had, I hadn't even thought to note anyone else's reaction. "Was he messing with you?"

"Not really, but he was staring. I ran into him, like, twice around random corners before and after the shift. And I thought I saw him in the doorway near the end of the night, as the last tour was leaving my room. Have you ever felt like someone was watching you, and then looked up and it's a zombie? Not recommended. It was just—" She shuddered. "I don't know. Does he usually lurk?"

"He's usually high," I muttered, trying to remember when I'd last seen Seth at all before today. Friday night? Saturday night, when he'd nearly run me down with the company van? I'd missed every other employee meeting since I found Bethany, so that had to be it. I vaguely remembered seeing him at tonight's postshow, but he'd left as soon as he got his notes. "He was pretty messed up when Bethany dumped him, and—"

"When *what?*" she hissed. "Are you serious, Dave?"

"Yeah. She broke up with him Friday night. She was really upset, and . . ." I grimaced, wondering what other pertinent details hadn't made the cut in my rehash of the weekend. "Did I not mention that before?"

"You absolutely did not." She looked past me down the empty hallway. "Do you think—could *he* have been the one who—"

"Jesus. I—no. No way. Seth can be sketchy, but I can't see him *killing* anyone—especially Bethany."

"Okay, but *someone* did, right? When a woman goes missing or turns up dead, the cops look at the boyfriend first for a reason. Who else *could* it have been?"

Her words made my head spin—because she was right. Someone *had* killed Bethany, and it *could* have been Seth. It could have been *anyone* at Frightmares, which meant we'd been shoulder to shoulder with a murderer for the past several hours. Several days, in my case. It wasn't a new thought, but it also wasn't the sort of thought that lost its edge.

"Maya, I have no idea. These are my friends. I can't see *any* of them doing this."

"Okay, well, who else had a problem with her?"

"Plenty of people, but it's all small stuff. Like, the other day she went off on Brennan because he got onto Seth about parking his truck across two spaces. She and Maggie have some weird grudge that goes back to high school. Hank had a thing for her about a year ago when she and Seth were on a break, but she ghosted him to date Ronnie, which ended up being a disaster. Lena used to hook up with Seth, so that's always been awkward. Last Wednesday, Bethany got pissed at Jillian for eating the last bagel in the breakroom, but it was Cori who actually ate the bagel, and it turned into this whole screaming thing. And a month ago—"

"Yeah, I get the point," Maya broke in. "Bethany was a drama magnet, and Frightmares employees are the pettiest creatures on the face of the earth. So that's awesome. And now I'm her replacement, working in her room, wearing her—oh *no*. Is this *her costume?*"

"No, that's a spare. She's much taller than you, and—" I stopped, gulping down the sick swoosh triggered by the realization. "She's still wearing hers. Or, was."

"I'll take the silver lining." She ran a hand through her hair and leaned against the door, shifting her weight in the stilettos. "Does this mean we don't have bolt cutters?"

"Someone didn't put the bolt cutters we definitely do have back in the right place, is what this means."

"I'm somehow less than shocked. What's the last thing that broke around here?"

"There are, like, ten possible answers to that question, Maya. This whole place could fall in on our heads any—the mummy." My eyes fell shut, the memory of the suddenly working sarcophagus drumming a low, painful thud in my temples. "That goddamn mummy. And if someone fixed it so fast—"

"—that means they probably left the toolbox in that room. Which, in turn, means—"

"Yeah. We need to check it out."

She was right. As much as I could've happily climbed into my own grave without ever setting foot in Attack of the Mummy again, we had to at least look. We had to get the lock off that goddamn locker, one way or another.

We made it down the hallway and pushed open the door to the dark, still Egypt room. Mickey had reset the scene for tomorrow's shift—the mummification slab was tidied up and ready, herbs and blood bowls organized artfully around the half-bound corpse. The sarcophagus stood behind it, tightly closed; the mummy, I assumed, nestled safely within, not that I was about to check. Everything was dark and quiet, bathed in the neon red glow of the *EXIT* sign peeking out above the set backdrop.

"Okay, so where is it?" Maya said.

"Probably behind the backdrop. It's the only place in here big enough to stash it without making it part of the set."

I ducked under the barricade and hurried past the props, way too fast on skittish feet. My skin was ice, my gut a volcano, too close to eruption. Whether the night was more likely to end in fear vomit or pee-soaked pants was a question I'd rather not have answered.

I heard her clicking along behind me, slow in the stilettos, muttering *f*-words as she made her way behind the set curtain. I was already rooting blind back there, and nearly jumped out of my skin when her groping hands landed on me.

"Is that you, Dave?"

"Um, yeah. It's my ass, actually."

"Oh God, I'm sorry." The hands vanished, leaving my pulse hammering and my face blazing. "Is the toolbox here, or not? I can see just about half an inch in front of me, and that's the end."

"I don't know. I think—" The words turned to profanity as

I found the ragged metal corner of the toolbox with my ankle. "Yeah. It's here."

"Good. Grab it and let's get the hell back to the light before I break my neck."

"Whoa. Could you maybe rephrase that?"

"What? *Oh.* God, I'm sorry. I—"

She went quiet all at once. I turned and saw the outline of her raised hand in the shadows, gesturing me to keep still.

"What?"

"I thought I heard something. It's—"

Maya's hiss ended in the palm of my hand as the Egypt room employee door banged open. She wobbled, stumbling in her ridiculous shoes. I caught her as she pitched forward, and took a heel spike squarely in the center of my big toe. One of her hands gripped my sleeve; the other slammed over my mouth, just in time to muffle my grunt of pain.

Her fear-wide eyes locked on my face as light flooded the room. My eyes bugged to match and we both went still, the exact instant the door swung shut behind whoever'd just stepped inside.

chapter 15

I couldn't breathe. Not just because Maya's hand was covering all the necessary air holes. One single word screamed through my body, from the core of my soul to the tips of my nerves:

Run.

It was a pointless impulse. Even if I hadn't been made of stone, legs weak, arms occupied with an off-balance Maya Green, where would I go? Our only shot at escape was the emergency exit, steps away, but she'd break both her feet in those shoes before she made it over the threshold. Leaving her behind wasn't an option.

Maya's eyes grew impossibly wide as the footsteps left the carpeted pathway, meandered around the rail, and crossed the room, drawing closer. We listened as they stopped, then started, then heard the scrape of something heavy, a jangle of metal. The footsteps again, slow and deliberate. The person they belonged to was *big*—tall enough for long strides and heavy footfalls.

I forced myself to draw a slow, careful breath from the cup of Maya's palm. It smelled like sweat and makeup, dirt and metal, and it cleared my head just enough to let the panic really set in. Fortunately, it kicked my brain back into gear as well, sending me a single Hail Mary of an idea: lift Maya off the ground and flat-out book it, slam us both through the emergency exit door into the parking lot, which I could only pray hadn't emptied out. If my only choices were fight or flight, I was more than happy to fly the hell out of the situation and deal with my bruised ego at a later date.

We were as good as caught anyway—I had no choice but to make my move.

Slowly, I removed her hand from my mouth, bent down, slid my arms around her waist. Tightened my grip and lifted her off her feet, inch by careful inch. I trained my gaze on her bewildered eyes as they rose level with mine, begging her without words to trust me.

She *had* to trust me, or we were both dead.

Then, the footsteps stopped.

"What the hell?"

The mutter was low and confused, soft enough that I wouldn't have heard it at all if it hadn't been the only break in the ringing silence of the room. It froze the blood in my veins. Maya gasped at the clatter and thud of something hitting the floor. Her fingers gripped my shirt, dug into my shoulders as the footsteps reanimated into a run, heading our way, and then her hand disappeared from my mouth, slammed into the back of my head, and yanked me forward, turning the space between us into nothing.

My brain melted. Her mouth landed hard on mine, then opened, her fangs pressed into my lower lip. I didn't think. I didn't have a chance. What I did do was lean into it, fight or flight a vague idea for another time. It was finally happening. The circumstances sucked ass, and the Shoulder Daves were going wild, but for a single, brief, suspended second, I didn't give one sweet damn if we were about to die, and ah shit, we really *were* about to die, weren't we?

I broke away from Maya with a gasp as the curtain screeched open on squeaky runners, blinked into the glare of the overhead lights—which were very quickly blotted out by a gigantic shadow. My vision doubled, then realigned as I shook off the haze of Maya, squinting away the spots swimming between me and our attacker. Then the shadow shifted, and my eyes started working, and suddenly everything was fine.

Mickey stood there clutching the curtain in one hand, the other fisted and cocked back, ready to swing. He gaped at us like he'd seen a ghost, eyes leaping back and forth between me and Maya. He'd washed the gold makeup off his face, arms, and head, and was in jeans, a T-shirt, and riding chaps. His leather jacket, backpack, and motorcycle helmet lay on the floor behind him, where he'd apparently dropped them before rushing in to beat the crap out of us.

"Dave?"

"Hey, Mickey," I said, setting Maya back on her feet. "Was there something?"

"You tell me, man. My keys fell out of my jacket. I had to retrace my steps." He unclenched his fist and shook it out, gestured at his scattered stuff. "The room had a weird vibe, though, like I wasn't alone. And then I started hearing things—you're lucky I recognized you before I started swinging."

"Sorry," Maya giggled. "Dave was showing me around earlier, and we lost track of time, and . . . you know. Oops."

Mickey blinked at her, then at me. His face disappeared behind his giant hand, and for a second, I thought he was pissed. Then the hand fell away, releasing a whoop of laughter loud enough to make me wince.

"Oops!" he howled. "You damn near gave me a heart attack, and she's saying *oops*. Go do your thing with the new kid, Dave. I promise I won't tell your girlfriend."

"*Girl*friend?" Maya asked, hands on her hips. She was definitely leaning into the act.

"We broke up," I stammered, letting my voice rise an octave, hoping like hell I sounded authentic. Trying to appear nervous about one very specific thing you don't care about at all, when you're actually losing it for unrelated reasons, isn't as easy as you'd think. "I swear, it happened after graduation, and I haven't—"

"Man, that's between you and high school," Mickey cackled. "I gotta run, though. Ollie's holding the door for me, waiting to lock up." He paused, forehead creasing around a leftover smear of gold paint. "You should maybe wait until he's gone to come out of there. He's been all the way up his own ass with the manager thing. He'll be pissed if he catches you in here—and right now, none of us need that."

"Thanks for the heads-up, dude."

"Why cause trouble when there's no harm done, right? Once the alarm gets set, this door arms itself when it closes. Keep it cracked until you hear my motorcycle. I'll stall till he leaves, then the coast should be clear for you to go." He squinted at Maya's wide grin, then cracked up all over again. "The fangs too, man? Goddamn, I miss being young."

"Yeah, yeah," I chuckled, taking the bro punch he glanced off my shoulder. "You know how it is."

"Do I ever. Oh, and Davey?" He tapped his lower lip, then gestured to my face. "Might want to scrub up before you go. Walk into Blacklist looking like that, and what I do or don't say won't be the problem."

He chuckled his way out the door. I swiped a hand over my mouth. It came back smeared with a blend of my foundation and Maya's dark red lipstick. Could I look like any more of a dumbass, even if I tried.

I wiped my hand on my pants leg, head still spinning at the unreal memory of her fangs against my lips, and how absolutely hot that had been, even on the brink of hypothetical death. I gave up trying to be subtle and let my eyes roam over Maya's stilettos, the curve of her calves in the fishnets, the flare of her hips beneath the stretch of vinyl as she paced back and forth, absently swiping her fingers over her own mouth.

"God, this is bad," she fretted, snapping me out of my trance. "Can we trust him?"

"Mickey's cool." I forced myself to speak and move normally. I brushed past her, opening the exit door just enough to disengage the latch, then dragged the toolbox past the curtain and into the light. "He's a pain in the ass, but the most he'll do is say he saw us hooking up, not that we were in here late."

"I don't need *that* getting around, either."

"It wasn't *my* idea," I muttered. I mean, *I* knew it had been for show—it had never been *real*. Obviously. "I was about to run us both out the door. You're the one who leveled up."

"Ugh, sorry about that. I recognized Mickey's voice. We were caught anyway—we needed a reason to be back here. Something unrelated to the toolbox, and our shady little mission."

"Yeah, I get it. But hey"—I cocked my head at her, flashed the Dave Gardiner grin—"if we have to go full *Hamlet*, that was a pretty sweet improv."

Shut up, knob, Chill Dave growled as Maya rolled her eyes. *Looks like* someone *left his dignity in his street clothes.*

Seriously, man, echoed Anxiety Dave. *Just try to be cool, for a single microsecond in time and space.*

"Anyway, I don't think it *will* get around," I said, mentally shushing the Daves and turning away to hide my burning face while I rummaged through the toolbox. "He fixed it so we can sneak out of here—now he's part of the lie. The most he'll do is tell Josie so they can bust on me in their spare time."

"Awesome. Nice friends."

We both jumped at the rev of Mickey's motorcycle, just outside the door. We waited until it had grumbled its way out of the presumably empty parking lot and disappeared into the night; then I grabbed the bolt cutters and headed for the employee door, motioning for her to follow. I hadn't just almost soiled myself in fear in front of Maya Green only to blow what was left of our original mission.

"Jo and Mickey are good people," I reassured her. "We mess around a lot, but they have my back when it matters."

"I hope you're right," Maya muttered, giving the sarcophagus a wide berth. "And what the hell *was* your plan, anyway—were you just going to bust out the side door, carrying me caveman-style? Like that would have looked *less* suspicious?"

"It seemed like a better idea than standing there frozen until it was too late. I *could* just kiss *you* next time if you give me advance consent. Otherwise, you have to make the first move."

"'Next time.'" She ducked under the barrier and fell into step at my side, rubbing a hand wearily over her face. "What the hell have I gotten myself into?"

"I tried to warn you," I said, sighing. "Welcome to Frightmares."

chapter 16

The hallway was empty. Maya's head appeared beneath mine around the doorframe, looking left and right. She squeezed past me, made it about three steps before removing her stilettos, then crept in stockinged feet toward the breakroom, beckoning to me right before she turned the corner. I flicked off the lights in the mummy room and scrambled after her, balancing the bolt cutters on my shoulder like a lumberjack's ax.

The breakroom was a mess of haphazardly arranged furniture and flickering fluorescent lights, which was nothing new. The kitchenette counters were cluttered with stray plasticware and scattered sugar packets. The small, round lunch table had been wiped down, but the chairs were askew, and the napkin holder sat off-center, as if the attempted cleanup had been interrupted—or, more likely, abandoned halfway through. We ignored all that and headed straight for the bank of lockers on the opposite wall.

"Oh no." Maya's moan was soft, but sudden enough in the hushed room to make me jump. She stood there helplessly, shoes dangling from one hand. "Dave, none of these are even labeled. Please tell me you know which one is hers. Or that she's available to let us know."

I sighed at that, knowing it sounded insane. Still, Maya was here, risking her own safety and backing me up. Helping me cope, with nothing to gain. And even though Bethany's voice had gone into hiding hours ago, I knew the answer to Maya's question without having to ask.

"Second from the left."

"Are you sure? If we cut the wrong one—"

"Positive. Josie's is the one on the end, and Bethany's has been next to hers since before I started here."

"Unless she switched."

"Well, yeah, but if that's the case, we're wasting our time anyway. We can't cut off every lock until we guess right—all we can do is go by what we know."

"Okay, then. Let's get it done."

She dropped the stilettos in the corner next to her backpack, padded over to Bethany's locker, and grasped the lock, holding it at an angle. I positioned the bolt cutters and paused, meeting her eyes. In less than a minute, we'd know for sure if Bethany had left on her own or was really, truly, gone.

Maya offered me a shaky smile, eyes wide with fear, and sympathy, and a tiny kernel of optimism. It wasn't much, but it gave me the push I needed to bear down until blades bit through metal.

The lock swung free in Maya's hand. She stared at it for a second, then let it fall to the floor, wrapping her fingers around mine. I dropped the cutters and faced the locker, then ripped off the Band-Aid all at once.

Bethany's locker was tidy compared to mine—not that *that* was an insurmountable feat—and she'd managed to make the small space look somewhat presentable. A magnetic mirror hung on the inside of the door, next to a stick-on air freshener.

A yellow sundress hung by its straps from the interior hook, hem brushing the toes of the matching wedge sandals that sat on the locker floor. Maya reached in with her free hand, gently pushed the dress aside, like a curtain. Bethany's purse sat squarely on top of the sandals, undisturbed. Undeniable.

I heard Maya's breath catch, shudder out, then catch again, as if her thoughts were trying to manifest as words but kept falling short. I could definitely relate.

It was a strange sort of relief, knowing I'd been right. I hadn't made it up, or hallucinated, or blown anything out of proportion, and here was *proof*—irrefutable proof that Bethany hadn't pulled a Chet-style spite walkout, or taken a leave of absence, or even just ghosted Frightmares, like everyone else who didn't want to spend an hour arguing with Loretta while attempting to give a formal two-week's notice.

Told you. Bethany's voice drifted up from the hollow in my middle. I didn't bother answering, silently or otherwise.

"God," Maya whispered. "This is—I mean, I know this is literally why we're—but I didn't expect it to actually—"

"I get it. You were thinking I'd had a mental break. Or was pranking you. Or maybe just talking out my ass." I met her scared, sad eyes, hating the brusque edge to my voice. Hating that I had to sound unbreakable, to stop myself from breaking. "Sorry to disappoint."

"Dave. I don't think any of that. I—"

"Don't worry about it. I wouldn't believe me, either. The whole thing sounds like bullshit from any angle."

I dropped her hand and made my way to my own locker. My legs were heavy, half-functional, like the air had turned to water. Maya sighed behind me, probably realizing there are no pre-existing, socially approved guidelines for acknowledging someone wasn't lying to you about a murder.

We'd confirmed two things, though: Bethany was gone, and her belongings were here, meaning it was very likely that she was, in fact, dead. The whole Bethany's Voice issue was its own thing, but I didn't have the energy, much less the time, to hammer that one out on the spot. First things first.

I swallowed a ball of misery and steeled my nerves, spun the combination on my own lock until it released. My stuff lay in its usual heap: shoes, clothes, keys, wallet. Phone. I grabbed that off the stack, detached my lock, and turned to Maya, who still stood frozen, staring into Bethany's locker. I took a couple pictures of the contents, committing it to official, time-stamped permanence. Maya carefully, respectfully held the dress aside so I could get shots of the purse, then she reached inside it, coming up with an ID holder attached to a set of keys. We didn't find a phone.

"We can't leave all this here," she said. "If Ollie cuts the lock off and finds her stuff all left behind, that blows everything wide open."

"No," I said, an idea dawning in my scattered mind. "We *should* leave it. They'll realize something's off, that she left without any of her stuff and hasn't been back, and then Ollie or Loretta will call the cops. They'll start searching and filing reports and all that without us ever lifting a finger. We'll be completely out of the situation."

"But what if Ollie notices your lock is missing? What if he brings it up in front of the wrong person?"

"What if he does? I'll say mine was broken, so I threw it out and brought in a new one."

"I don't know—that's a big coincidence, don't you think? With the sudden focus on locks and lockers, it could look suspicious."

"I think 'sudden focus' is stretching it." I took a picture of Bethany's driver's license, making sure the address was in focus. Her last name actually was Blake, surprisingly enough. "No one else knows or cares about this lock issue except Ollie, and that's only because it's his job to make sure you have a place to put your stuff. There's nothing suspicious about broken things around here."

"Someone still knows you found her, though. That doesn't go away just because you're not the one reporting it."

"Yeah, I know." My voice was surprisingly monotone, considering I hadn't actually considered that detail before she mentioned it. "But there's nothing I can do except keep my mouth shut, and hope they get caught before they come after me."

"I don't like this," she muttered, stepping aside as I replaced the keys, closed her locker, and fastened my padlock in the latch, using my billowy shirtsleeve to rub away any fingerprints we might have left. The lock clicked into place with a *thunk*, final and binding. "I have a really bad feeling right now, about every single thing related to this place."

"Join the club."

I turned away from the locker and stalked over to mine, gathered my stuff, and slammed the stupid door. From the corner of my eye, I saw Maya shove the stilettos into her backpack and slip into a pair of clogs. I didn't bother to swap out my own shoes, much less my clothes. Ever since I'd rolled around the RaceTrac parking lot in Mickey's loincloth, my wardrobe shame threshold was damn near nonexistent.

We made our way back down the hallway to the mummy room

in silence. Maya trailed a few feet behind me, head down. I could feel my own weariness setting in, mingled with sorrow and defeat. We'd done what we'd set out to do—we'd made our discovery and gathered our evidence. We were safely on our way back to the real world, ready to breathe and rest and hopefully plan our next move.

All of it made me want to puke.

Aside from my Honda, the parking lot was empty, just as Mickey promised. Maya stepped out the door ahead of me, pulling out her phone.

"I know we said we'd be at Blacklist," she said, "but I just want to go home. I'm not really up for the coffeehouse scene right now."

"I'm skipping it too." After the night's events, I couldn't fathom strolling into Blacklist like everything was normal. Josie would be pissed I'd ditched her for the second night in a row, but I had bigger issues. "You need a ride?"

"My mom can come get me. I can text her and wait over at the 7-Eleven, if you need to go."

"I can drive you, it's no problem." I kicked the doorstop out of the way, glancing back into the shadows of the empty room. The door hissed slowly closed as I stepped into the lot beside her. "Looks like we're clear. We can—no. *No.* THE CAMERAS."

chapter 17

I dropped my stuff and threw myself back at the door, shoving my hand into the crack just before it closed. My poor fingers took the brunt, sending a streak of pain up my arm.

"Dude, what the hell?" Maya hissed, right at my ear. "What cameras?"

"We only have four," I gasped, sweat breaking out all over my face and neck. I looked around wildly, slipped back inside, frantically motioning for her to follow. Once she was safely over the threshold, I jammed the doorstop back into place and made my way around the backdrop. "In the lobby, the box office, the hallway, and—" I gulped. "The breakroom."

"*Dave.*"

"I know, okay? I literally just remembered."

"What do we do?" She was starting to panic, wringing her hands and bouncing up and down on her toes. "If there's an investigation, they'll confiscate the footage. We can't talk our way out of this—they could arrest us. We broke into her locker, we know she's dead, we could go to jail—"

"No. We won't," I said, ducking under the barrier. Heading for

128

Loretta's office before the thinking part of my brain could scream at me to stop the madness and get the hell out of that place while I had life left in my body. I was too pumped, though—too jacked-up on fear and nerves. Way too psyched to finally be faced with a problem I could actually solve. "Come on."

"I am *not* going back in there."

"Okay, stay here and watch the door—make sure it doesn't close on us. I'll be right back."

"Like hell I'm staying here on my own—where are you going?" She followed me in spite of herself, grasping my stupid billowy sleeve as we hurried through the employee hall. "Dave, please, we need to get out of here."

"Stick close to me and stay calm. We're fixing this right now."

"How are we fixing this? Smashing the cameras? It won't change what they've already picked up. We're busted. We're screwed."

"We're not. Trust me—in five minutes, it'll be like we were never here."

Maya took the whole "stick close to me" instruction literally— her hand clutched my sleeve all the way down the hall, her shoulder grazing my arm with every step. She followed me to Loretta's office, blinked through bloodshot eyes at the weird decor and creepy fixtures, face weary, bravado drained dry. I knew the feeling. My own eyes burned with exhaustion. My neck and shoulders were tense and aching. My heart lay low in my chest, heavy with loss and grief and fear. An hour at most had passed since we'd snuck off to find the bolt cutters, but it felt like a goddamn day and a half.

I settled at Loretta's desk, determined to tough it out. If I fell apart now, all this bullshit would have been for nothing.

"This should only take a minute," I said. "I'll disable the cameras and delete today's files. Then we'll get the hell out of here before something really goes wrong."

"Seriously? Dave Gardiner is a hacker too?"

"Not quite." I woke the monitor and entered the password—*Sethy*, which I probably could have guessed soon enough on my own, even if I hadn't watched Loretta type it in that afternoon with my own eyes. "Dave Gardiner *is* pretty awesome, though, now that you mention it."

Nice one, Chill Dave cackled. *Atta boy, Dave Gardiner.*

"Right," Maya deadpanned. "Do whatever awesome Dave thing you have planned already and get us out of here before Loretta doubles back for more fake hands or whatever."

"No one's coming back. It's almost—" My eyes flitted to the monitor clock, then bugged at what I saw. We'd wasted way too much time hunting down that toolbox. "Wow. It's after one a.m."

"Amazing." She rubbed her face, leaving ghoulish smears of makeup across her temple. "Is it still cool to take you up on that ride home?"

"Anytime."

Four days ago, the idea of Maya Green riding shotgun in my car would've triggered a mudslide of anxiety, anticipation, and panic sweats. Now, all I wanted was to get her out of this building in one piece and ferry her home to the safety of her pre-Dave life. So much for any chance I'd ever hoped to have. If she didn't regret giving me the time of day by now, she'd get there soon enough.

I accessed the security system and turned off the cameras.

Then I pulled up the stored footage and relived our little escapade in black and white.

"Jesus," Maya breathed. She leaned over my shoulder and stared at the screen, wide-eyed. "We're just *on* there. Like, this is clear-cut, incriminating footage, and we didn't even *think* about it."

"I never saw a single camera in this whole building before today," I said, equally rattled at the sight of myself striding down the halls in my dumb costume, wielding the bolt cutters, like I had a single clue what I was doing with my life. "If I hadn't been in here earlier sweet-talking Loretta, I wouldn't even know about these."

"Wow. God." She stepped away from the desk and turned her back on the monitor. "This is—"

"Yeah."

We'd been too confident. I'd figured we could trust Mickey to keep quiet about catching us in the mummy room because he'd made himself part of the lie. But we'd strung ourselves up in the same conundrum—we'd trespassed in our workplace, we'd broken into Bethany's locker, and now I was sitting at my boss's desk, fingers poised to delete security footage I wasn't authorized to access, much less destroy. All that to cover up a murder I hadn't even committed. What the hell had I been thinking?

That was the problem, though—I *hadn't* been thinking. I'd panicked. I'd acted on impulse. I'd dived into the raw-sewage retention pond of this situation without considering how deep it might go. And we'd crossed too many lines to quit now.

I went through the motions, deleted the past few hours of footage, left enough to make it look like the camera crapped out again midshift, and it was done. This was more than some weird mystery now—this was felony territory. The sewage was way over our heads. There was no sign of shore or safety.

All we could do was try to keep swimming.

By the time we made it back to the mummy room and into the parking lot, Maya was wilting on her feet. She stood by silently while I pulled the door closed, gathered my clothes from the parking lot, and led her to the car. We'd driven most of the way back to our neighborhood in silence before I started to worry.

She's basically the reason you're still holding it together, Bethany said. *You know that, don't you, Dave?*

Yeah, I know, I answered silently. *And if I don't hold it together, she might die. I can't let it happen.*

You "let" her get into this in the first place. You owe this girl.

She was right. Maya had found me at Blacklist on the edge of a breakdown, and instead of backing slowly away, she'd roped herself into a shitty job and jumped feetfirst into a goddamn crime scene, all for some dude she barely knew. I owed her way more than a silent ride home in my messy car.

"You all right?" I finally asked as I turned onto her street, glancing over at her pale, tired face.

"Oh, definitely. I mean, I'll need years of therapy for sure, but we're alive, right? So. Better off than Bethany."

She's not wrong. Bethany again. Steeped in truth.

We were silent as I pulled up to the curb in front of Maya's house and cut the engine. She turned to me, waiting until I met her eyes to continue.

"Since we're doing this, I think we need to go all in. We'll go out to her place tomorrow and ask around. We need to find out who last saw her outside work, and when. Meanwhile, you go through everything you remember about Friday, until we figure out what happened."

"That was the plan this afternoon." I filled her in on the series of events that led to my learning about the cameras in the first place. "I was about to check the hard drive for the missing footage, but Ollie came in. All I could do was cover my own ass, and then I saw you, live on camera. I should have checked for it while we were in there tonight, but I forgot all about it after seeing the locker."

"That's pretty understandable, though. That was—yeah." She gathered her stuff from the floorboard and opened the door, leaving no room for argument. "It's fine. We'll regroup tomorrow and figure out a way to make it happen."

"Okay," I said, because there wasn't another answer. If she insisted on staying part of this, all I could do was whatever she needed.

I walked her to her door because it was late. Because I was paranoid. Because I simply didn't want to leave her side. It had nothing to do with my feelings, which had long ago snapped the leash and dashed into the wilderness without me, and everything to do with the bone-deep need to protect her. To see her safely inside, and to work, and to everywhere, as long as I was the reason she needed protecting.

"I'm so sorry about all this," I blurted once we reached her door. "I shouldn't have dragged you into it. I should never have said a word to you."

"Hey. No regrets." She bit her lip, grabbed me around the waist in a rough, surprise squeeze, then shoved me toward the sidewalk, like I wasn't already reeling. Her hair stuck to her cheeks; her face was a wild muddle of worry and frustration. "I'll text you in the morning. We need to get as much done before work as we can, but we need to split up after and clock in separately. Unless Mickey talks, as far anyone else knows, you and I are strangers."

chapter 18

I poked at the dome of butter on my pancakes, wondered if ordering them was as good an idea as it seemed at the time, then decided I didn't care enough to worry. I was halfway down the stack before Maya finished the first bite of her breakfast sandwich. Her place setting was messy with spilled salt and about eight empty sugar packets, the contents of which she'd stirred directly into her hot chocolate.

The surreal haze in my brain had begun to clear, leaving a single, all-important priority at the forefront: Maya's safety. I'd been up half the night pacing around the dark house and staring through the windows, ears alert for disturbances at every point of entry. I'd finally fallen into a restless doze, woken about sixteen times, and only really calmed down when I'd given up on sleep and gone for a sunrise swim. Maya's text had been waiting when I left the pool; apparently, she'd been restless too. Now she sat across from me in the vinyl booth, hair gathered back from her face. She wore a flowered wrap skirt, a blue halter top, and shimmer powder on her cheeks and shoulders. I couldn't stop looking at her.

I steeled myself for what I knew I had to say next. My personal feelings were of garbage-level importance right now. I couldn't keep her close without risking her life. Which meant I couldn't keep her close at all.

"Maya," I said with literally no lead-up, "I think you should quit Frightmares."

"I'm not quitting Frightmares, Dave."

"Okay, but I *need* you to quit Frightmares. You saw the chaos. You got bad vibes off Seth. You saw Bethany's things. This is real. You need to get out while you can."

"Too late. I am officially one with the chaos." She took a huge gulp of her sugared hot chocolate, set the mug back on the table, and leaned toward me, eyes shifting around the dining room to make sure the other six Denny's customers weren't listening in. "Dave, do you really think I'd ditch you now, *especially* after last night? When you were literally ready to sweep me into your arms and carry me to safety?"

"Forget that. I can't let anything happen to you. I won't."

The beat of silence following those words went on just long enough for me to start thoroughly hating myself. Even the Daves were quiet. Maya dropped her eyes to her plate for a split second, then refocused on me, a tiny smile creeping across her face.

"Anyway," she continued, "I think we need a plan. One of us should ask around work about Bethany. I figure I'll do that, since I don't actually know her."

"Right," I croaked, covering my shame with a gulp of orange juice. "Plus, I'm pretty unattached to most of the cast—I'm the high school kid, they all have adult lives. Aside from Josie, Ollie, and Mickey, we don't really hang out. If I start asking questions out of nowhere, and I approach the wrong person—"

"Exactly. But I'm neutral, and I'm new, and I'm literally filling her shoes. It makes sense that I'd have questions about her role, how she played it, why she left, et cetera. And meanwhile, you and I need to figure out a way to interact without looking suspicious. As long as Mickey keeps quiet about our little . . . *incident*, no one has a reason to think we know each other at all. Right?"

"Right. Except for Josie. She saw us talking at Blacklist last week when I stepped on your foot. And on my car that time."

"I don't remember her from either night."

"Oh, she was there. If Josie doesn't want to be seen, you won't even know she's in the zip code."

I realized too late how weird that sounded—like Josie had been incognito on purpose, hiding from a girl she'd never met. And yeah, technically that had been exactly the case, but holy shit, the last thing I needed was to have to explain to Maya how her involvement in this fucking travesty of a situation had begun with Josie's attempt to hook us up. And now the situation itself had led to Mickey *thinking* we were hooking up, when really we were *pretending* to hook up, so as not to get caught trespassing and clue-hunting. Could it be any more convoluted, was the real question.

The reminder of Maya's fangs on my mouth sent a thrill over my skin—one that ramped up to a full-body shiver at the unreal sight of her across the table, insistent on sticking by my side. A spark of hope worked its way up from my gut, even as the Daves stirred into action, ready to talk me down.

Don't count on it, buddy, came the expected mutter from the left. *She's in this mess too deep to quit, and that's all it is.*

Maya, unaware of my sad-boy internal narrative, set down

her food and rummaged through her bag, coming up with a blue glitter pen and a dog-eared green leather journal the size of a Stephen King paperback. A Post-it, two dried flowers, and a bronze coin fell from between the pages before she'd even unwound the wraparound strap.

"Wow. You seriously carry that thing around with you, like, every day?"

"I'm a poet, Dave. This is my travel notebook. Now." She uncapped her pen and opened the journal to a blank page. "About that plan."

The address on Bethany's driver's license led us to a weary-looking two-story complex off Orange Blossom Trail with a drained-dry pool and a parking lot with more potholes than spaces. There was no one around but a guy in a Sobik's Subs shirt and board shorts, dozing in a frayed lawn chair beneath the single scraggly palm tree planted in the median.

"Do you see her car?" Maya asked, scanning the lot as we climbed the stairs to Bethany's apartment.

"I don't know what her car looks like. Plus"—I gestured to our surroundings—"as you can see, Frightmares pays shit. For all I know, she didn't *have* a car."

"Are you sure you actually met her, or is she just a voice in your head?"

"It's not like we saw each other outside work. Seth always drove her around in his truck, and she bummed rides off Josie and Ollie a couple times, but no. I *didn't* know her very well, actually."

Harsh, but true, Bethany snickered as we stopped at an apartment door. Its peephole was scratched; its teal paint flaked off when I knocked, revealing the original bright coral color beneath. *And yet, here you are.*

I mulled that over, wondering what I'd do if Bethany actually did answer. Would I scream? Would I have an aneurysm? Would I collapse right there in the hallway if I came face to face with a girl I'd convinced myself was dead?

"Hey," Maya said, softly, "I didn't mean it like that. I know I sound like an asshole, well, a lot of the time, so maybe you should do the talking here. You're definitely better at *likable*."

I didn't have time to retort. The door opened, but it wasn't Bethany. A Black girl in a calf-length sundress and deep plum lipstick leaned against the doorframe, eyeing me across the threshold. She was as tall as me, and catwalk-thin.

"Hi," I began, "I'm looking for Bethany? Bethany Blake?"

"And you are?"

"Oh. I'm Dave, and this is Maya. We work with Bethany over at Frightmares—the haunted house? Do you know where I can find her? It's kind of important."

There's an understatement.

"Nah, she's not here. She's off with her boyfriend."

It took a minute for that one to land. When it did, I glanced at Maya, whose face was a master class in *WTF*. It was a pretty good mimic of how mine felt.

"Oh," I said, trying to recover without going full dumbass. "So, she's off with . . . Seth? Seth Tinetti?"

"God no, she's been done with him. He showed up here a few weeks ago, high on something. She threw him out, and that was the last I saw of him. She's with some other guy now. Levi, or something like that."

"Who the hell is Levi, Dave?" Maya hissed, earning a raised eyebrow from the girl.

"Levi, huh?" I racked my brain for anyone I knew with a name even marginally close. "Do you know where I could find *him*? I mean—I'm sorry to bother you like this, but it's important. Are you her roommate?"

"I'm Callie." Her expression shifted from suspicious to vaguely worried. "And as for Levi, I expect you'll find him when you find her. Why? Is she okay?"

You don't know the half of it.

"I need to see her, is all. She hasn't come in all weekend." Technically, it was not a lie. Beyond that surface lay too many things I couldn't commit to voicing, so I leaned hard on the Dave smile, knowing I had maybe another ninety seconds before this girl got sick of us and shut the door in my face. I couldn't even blame her. "If it's not too much trouble, could you tell me when you last heard from her? Please?"

"I don't know. Sunday? Let me check." She left the door cracked open and returned a moment later scrolling through a phone in a yellow rhinestone case. "No, it was Friday. Right around noon on Friday. Here."

She held out the screen so I could read it.

> Hey girl, just a heads up. I won't be home when you get back. Going down to that

casting call with L, then checking out the scene in South Beach. Leaving tonight after work and calling out tomorrow, which means I'm probably fired, but IDGAF. Bigger and better things ahead!

Callie had replied, and there was a whole back-and-forth exchange after that, mostly about Miami nightlife and how much Frightmares sucked. None of it told me anything more important than what the time stamp confirmed: Bethany had sent the text on Friday, hours before our shift began. I had no reason to think it was anything but legit.

But if Bethany *was* in Miami, with or without some random guy, what was her stuff doing in her work locker? If she wasn't dead, what—*who*—had I found in the sarcophagus?

"Thank you for this," I said anyway, because Callie deserved all the thanks for entertaining my bullshit in the first place. "Do you happen to know anything about her boyfriend? Where he lives, what he does—"

"Sorry, I never met him—she didn't bring him around here." She paused, considering. "I mean, maybe she has, but I've been on location up in Atlanta for the past two weeks. Just got back last night."

"And you really don't know who she's with, or where she is? She hasn't checked in with you or anything?"

"Hon, I'm not her mama. She's a big girl, she's off with her boyfriend, and that's the end of my involvement. Thanks for stopping by."

She stepped back into the apartment, door already closing

141

on her parting words, leaving us with the buzz of tree frogs, and traffic, and a blaring TV, audible through someone's window. Maya and I stared at each other in the hallway, buried beneath a landslide of new questions. I had no idea how to go about answering any of them—and no clue what we'd find if we tried to dig our way out.

chapter 19

I showed up to work that afternoon, brand-new lock in my pocket, hoping I was early enough to beat Ollie and Maya to the breakroom but not so early I'd be standing around like a tool waiting for everyone else to arrive. The parking lot, however, was full. My usual spot was occupied by a black-and-white police cruiser.

This was it—Bethany had been found. I could finally tell my story.

I parallel-parked against the building and ran for the front doors, some primal, fear-burst instinct screaming at me to find whatever cops had shown up and tell them everything before a sledgehammer crushed my skull, or a machete swung out neck-height across a doorway to sever my head from my shoulders. I yanked open the lobby door, ready to do a full home-run slide through to the hallway if need be. Instead of the faceless murderer I'd braced for, however, I found—well, everyone else.

Most of the Frightmares cast was in the lobby. Brennan, Ronnie, Lena, and Cori huddled in their little Swampland Cannibals clique near the ticket booth, conversing with each other in hushed voices. Our Demented Doctor, Hank, hovered off to the side alone, as usual, drinking a Fanta and playing a game on his phone. Suzanne appeared in the doorway of the lobby restroom, adjusting the bib collar of her doll costume and waving to Jillian, Hank's "experiment," who'd just stepped in from the employee entrance to the backstage hallway. Dara and Maggie, already in their stilts and Murder Circus costumes, loomed head and shoulders over everyone. And in the middle of the lobby, studying the framed cast headshots displayed on the wall, was Maya.

She was also in costume, eyes smoky, lips red, hair twisted into sleek spiral curls. She looked wildly gorgeous and perfectly at ease. She turned as I approached; a small smile flitted across her face as our eyes met, nearly blasting me off my feet.

Focus, asshat, Bethany snarled. *You're not here for that right now.*

"Hey," Maya called, giving me a fake shy wave. "Dave, right?"

"Hey, new girl." I strolled over, grin in place, letting everyone witness my smooth, smooth charm, and our very new and unfamiliar level of acquaintance. "Back for more?"

"Couldn't stay away." She gestured to the headshots. "Lots of pretty people here."

"Aspiring actors. Yours should fit right in."

YES! Chill Dave yelled as Bethany groaned, Anxiety Dave gasped, and Maya's cheeks went pink. *THAT is how you do it, son.*

I gestured for her to follow, and we walked away, pretending to casually chat until we reached the tour's exit—the vestibule between the lobby and the Demented Doctor set. The second we were out of sight, she grabbed my hand and broke into a run, pulling me along the dark hallway and into the mock operating room.

"What's happening?" I hissed as she ducked under the barrier, motioning for me to join her behind the white privacy curtain set up around the gurney. I made my way back there, wincing as my hip jostled the metal tray of surgical instruments neatly laid out for tonight's shift. "Are there really cops here? Is it about—"

"No." She shushed me, cocked her head toward the sound of footsteps passing outside the room's employee entrance, then continued in a loud whisper, "They're inquiring about a missing person. Some guy named Chet."

"Chet?" The bottom dropped out of my gut. "Are you serious?"

"That's what I heard Josie tell Ollie. Everyone's out in the lobby because the cops are set up in the office, pulling us all in one by one for questioning, and Loretta's freaking out about the timetable, and— What the hell is going on here, Dave? Who's Chet?"

"You don't know him," I muttered, frantically sorting through my memories of the night he'd quit. When *had* he left, exactly? What had he said? "He was our Undead Graveyard guy before— well, Friday. He got hurt on set and walked out in postshow."

"You have got to be goddamn joking. Tell me you're joking, Dave."

"I am definitely not. He's *missing*? Is that all you heard?"

"I don't know what I heard—none of this means anything to me." She bit her lip, eyes wide and scared and ringed in shadows. "For all we know, Chet is that Levi person, and he's 'missing' be- cause he's off in South Beach with Bethany. Are you sure you don't know *anything* about a Levi working at Frightmares? Maybe before you started here?"

We'd covered all this during the drive back from Bethany's place. Still, I racked my brain. Again, I came up empty.

"I'm positive. Everyone knows Bethany and Seth were a thing, but if she had a new guy—well, you heard about that the same time I did. It could explain why she was so upset that night, though. I saw her and Seth arguing in the hall. I thought she was dumping him right then, but maybe it happened earlier. Maybe she told him there was someone else."

"God." She swallowed hard and lowered her voice to a whisper. "Was he angry? Like, angry enough to—"

She didn't finish the sentence. She didn't have to.

"He seemed more sad than angry. And when I found her—" I winced at the blur of that memory. "You didn't see that set. It was a disaster when I ran out, but completely organized when I came back. Even the mummy was fixed. None of that fits with what I know of Seth."

"But is he really that consistently incompetent? Or are you underestimating him because he wants you to?"

I considered that, wondering why I'd been so quick to dismiss Seth from the start. He *was* creepy, Maya wasn't wrong about that. He was also resentful, and moody, and definitely mixed up in some sketchy dealings outside of Frightmares. Still, "consistently incompetent" was a painfully accurate descriptor—he could barely get his costume on straight most nights. I'd watched him fail so often, writing him off was practically a reflex.

But what if I *was* underestimating him? What if the loser persona was a facade, designed to hide a more sinister truth?

"I don't know," I finally muttered. "It's possible, I guess, but I've worked here for months—if it's an act, he's playing a serious long game. And if that's the case, how does it tie into the Chet thing? Is that linked to Bethany, or is it a separate thing? How much should we tell the cops?"

"Dave, that's really your call. I'll back you up with what I know, but I literally *didn't* know either of them, and—holy shit, we are *so* far in this now. We'll have to explain everything we've done, and we'll have to *justify* it. 'Dave saw something scary but now it's gone' won't do it."

She had a point. What Maya and I had done was shady as hell even *with* an explanation—and we'd gotten busted before we'd even begun. If Ollie or Loretta had caught us last night, instead of Mickey, we'd have been completely screwed. My hopes were riding on the locker: when Ollie cut the lock off for Maya, he'd find Bethany's clothes, and her bag with her ID. That would raise suspicions at the very least, without me having to say a word. Hell, the cops were already here, poised to take the whole situation out of my hands.

"Her stuff," I said, glancing over my shoulder, weirdly paranoid, as if a third person were in the room with us, standing silently on the other side of the curtain. I shuddered and shook off the thought, trying like hell to calm the chills on the back of my neck. "That's our only proof she's gone. Once the cops see it, they'll follow up with their own investigation."

"What if they don't? Dave, someone is missing—*for real* missing. And the last time you saw him was the same time you last saw Bethany alive. If I were a cop and knew how deep this went, I'd be looking pretty hard at *you.*"

"Then we'll stay late again tonight and find the missing footage from last weekend. We know the trick with the door, we know the password, we know to disable the cameras. We need to finish it."

"Sounds like a plan," she grumbled, pressing her hands to her face. "I'm sure it'll go as well as every other thing here."

"It'll be okay. Maya." She didn't remove her hands, just moved her fingers so one eye glared through. "It'll be okay," I repeated.

"You're right—we're too far into this to walk away now. But I *will* get you out of it, all right? I promise."

"I trust you." She dropped her hands and offered me a weak smile, then pulled out her phone, eyes bugging when she checked the screen. She stepped back too quickly, nearly falling over the IV stand, its looping tubes, and attached blood bag. "Shit. Come on. We're going to be late."

We crept across the set and to the employee door, Maya a few paces ahead of me. She ducked around the curtain, opened the door, and stopped short with a little gasp. I froze in place, instincts telling me to hang back. If things were about to take a bad turn, at least I'd have the element of surprise.

"Oh, hey." Maya's voice was pitched high, louder than usual, so I heard it clearly through the curtain. "Hey there—is it Seth?"

"Hey. Hey . . . Maya."

There was a long silence. I shifted my weight silently, inched around until I could see them through a crack in the curtain. Seth looked like a pile of garbage—his hair was matted on one side, and his face was puffy beneath his zombie makeup, like he'd spent too much time sleeping facedown. His eyes were bloodshot but huge, his pupils deep-space voids. He stood way too close to Maya.

What was he doing? Had he been passing by? Had he been lurking there the whole time on purpose like a stalker? Or had he just spaced out in the hallway and drifted to a stop? I hadn't seen him in the lobby, but had he seen us? Had he followed us—or, more accurately, had he followed Maya?

I bit the inside of my cheek in frustration, wanting nothing more than to bust through the curtain and put myself between them.

I can't blame you. This is a little too close to déjà vu.

She was right. The last time I'd run into Seth in the hallway was Friday night, when he'd cornered Bethany by the restrooms. The lead-up to my last real-life conversation with her.

"What are you doing in my set?"

Hank's voice nearly sent me out of my skin. I bit back a scream and whirled around, expecting to find his tall, lanky form looming in the vestibule doorway.

The room behind me was empty.

I peeked back through the curtain; Hank was in the hallway, standing directly behind Seth. He was already in costume, his usually messy dyed-black hair slicked back beneath his head mirror. His black rubber gloves reached his elbows, and his white lab coat was artfully spattered in F/X blood. His eyes would have been creepy enough even without the help of his vintage surgical magnifying glasses. That guy pretty much never blinked.

"I hope you didn't disturb the instruments," he continued. "Jillian likes to keep things *just so.*"

"Sorry about that," Maya said, in the bright, fake tone she used for all her Frightmares interactions with people who weren't me. "I didn't touch the set—I was looking for the breakroom, but I think I got turned around? Do you think . . . could you maybe walk me over there? I'm supposed to find Ollie and get my locker opened."

There was a weird silence. Hank stared at Maya, waiting for her to move aside, clearly not planning to walk her to the breakroom or any other place. Seth glanced back and forth between them, apparently unsure if he was still part of the conversation.

"Yeah, okay," Seth finally answered when Hank didn't speak. "Come on."

I didn't hesitate. Before Hank could squeeze past Maya and catch me creeping around his precious set, I pivoted right and booked it through the vestibule to Dolls Alive!, then through there and into Captive Countess. Josie's bag was on the dresser, but the room was, thankfully, otherwise empty. I skidded to a stop, practically ripped down the curtain, and slammed through the employee door, nearly plowing into Seth and Maya, who were just rounding the corner. They both jumped a mile. Maya actually shrieked.

"Jesus Christ, Dave," Seth howled. "You can't just bust out a door like that, man. You want me to stroke out right here in the hallway?"

"Sorry, Seth," I said brightly, like I wasn't seconds from a breakdown myself. "Hey, new girl. Have you guys seen Josie?"

"Oh. Sorry, I don't think I know her." Maya bugged her eyes at me, half annoyed, half impressed. "We were just heading to the breakroom."

"Cool. Me too."

I strode ahead of them and sailed through the breakroom door, carefree Dave Gardiner, not at all on the brink of nervous diarrhea. Once out of Seth's sight, I rushed to my locker and fumbled the new lock out of my pocket, twirling the dial with shaking fingers. The lock popped open on the second try, just as I heard Ollie's voice greet Maya from the hallway. I casually opened my locker, hooked the new lock through the handle, felt the sweat pop out under my arms in relief.

"I ran into a slight problem, though," Ollie was saying as he and Maya entered the breakroom. Seth hovered behind them in the doorway, looking vaguely confused, like he'd decided to leave but stalled out midstep. "I can't find the bolt cutters—or the tool-box, for that matter. I can have Loretta lock your things in her office tonight, or—"

"You looking for this, Oll?"

I turned at the sound of Mickey's voice. He squeezed past Seth and set the toolbox on the table, giving me a nod in greeting. He was already in costume, painted gold except for his hands and face. I returned his nod, darted a sideways glance at Maya, who was very deliberately looking everywhere but at me.

"Always," Ollie said. "You're the best, man."

"I didn't do anything but damn near break my foot on it," Mickey said. "It was shoved behind the backdrop in my room, sticking out at an angle—just far enough to catch my toe when I went past it."

"Wonder who left it there," Ollie muttered. He and Mickey both glared at Seth, not that he noticed. His eyes were swollen and bloodshot, and still locked on Maya. "You okay, Mick? Do you need an ice pack, or—"

"Nah, I'm fine. As long as that mummy's working, I don't need a thing."

"Right on. Let's get this open for you, Maya."

Maya returned Ollie's smile, super casual, as if she wasn't about to fly out of her skin. Sweat broke out beneath my collar as Ollie cut the lock. He swung the locker door open and chucked the broken lock into the trash, pausing to touch his headset ear-piece as a broadcast came through.

"Yes? Okay, Loretta. Thanks." He passed Mickey the bolt cut-ters and gestured to the locker with his chin. "Maya, you're all set there. Dave? Everything good with you?"

"Me? Sure." I smiled so hard my face hurt. "As always."

"Great. They want you in the office for questioning. Everyone else, preshow in ten. Seth, you ready? SETH."

"What?" Seth tore his eyes away from Maya, blinked Ollie into focus. Rubbed a hand across his face, leaving a smear through his makeup "Oh. It's fine. I mean, I guess so? I mean—"

"Oh, Christ, man, really? Look, are you good to go tonight, or do I need to put you on tours?"

"Oh. Yeah, I'm good. Sorry. I'll be—I—"

"Oh, *hell* no, you won't put him on tours, Ollie," Mickey broke in, slamming the lid of the repacked toolbox. "Seth, we got two cops in the boss's office, and you're in here smelling like Burger King and bong resin. If you don't get it together, they'll search *your* fucking locker, then they'll see what you've got stashed inside it and this whole place'll get shut down."

"It's okay," Ollie said. "He'll be fine. Won't you, Seth? Everything's cool. Come on, let's get you set up for showtime."

Seth nodded, but his eyes were back on Maya. A tremor passed over his face; his mouth pursed suddenly, then flattened to a sorrowful line, like it hurt to look at her. Like he was almost looking *through* her, at some devastating thing that only he could see.

"Seth?" I hedged, wondering. "Are you—"

"I'm fine," he broke in, voice rasping over the words. "I'm just about as good as I'll ever be."

He made no move to leave until Ollie took him by the shoulder and steered him gently out of the room. Mickey followed them, threw a wink at me around the doorjamb as he turned the corner. I stood there like a dumbass, staring at the space where he'd been, then let my gaze drift to Maya, who hadn't moved, hadn't spoken, hadn't made a sound. Whose eyes were wide and horrified, fixed uncomprehendingly on Bethany's empty locker.

⁓

Josie squinted into the Captive Countess prop mirror, leaning into the dim circle of lamplight as she blended the edges of the "bruise" on her jawline. I craned my neck to peer around her, fumbling with the stupid cravat. This goddamn costume. If the hunt for Bethany's killer didn't unravel my sanity, the job itself would eventually do the trick, thread by excruciating thread.

After her initial shock in the breakroom, Maya had pulled it together almost instantly. She'd stored her stuff in the locker and secured it with her own lock; by the time she'd turned around, her face was a tranquil mask. I'd held her eyes for a brief, terrifying moment, seeking reassurance, offering solidarity. Then I'd headed to the greenroom first, continuing through to Loretta's office, where the cops waited for me.

The police questioning had been quick, but surreal. They'd asked how I knew Chet, how long I'd known him, if we hung out outside work, and when I'd last seen him. All those were easy to answer truthfully even with the Daves yelling their opinions on exactly how much talking I should do about which coworker. But the plan to turn the locker into a big reveal had vanished, and Maya was right: if I started spilling my guts, with Chet *actually* missing, I'd either get blown off or become a person of interest. I wasn't about to drop the Bethany grenade now, especially while my parents were unreachable. My only option was to pull off a better organized repeat of last night: pretend to leave, prop open the exit, hide until everyone else was gone, then dig through Loretta's computer until I found the missing footage.

Maya had been in her place with the rest of the cast when I returned, sitting primly in a chair, as if eagerly awaiting Loretta's notes. If I hadn't known how aware she was of every single person in the room, I'd never guess she was anything but the oblivious new hire. Josie had spent the entire meeting whispering with Mickey, both of them shooting not-so-covert glances at me. Maya, to her credit, had played her role perfectly—she hadn't even twitched their way. I'd been less successful at the whole casual facade thing. Unsurprisingly. By the time Loretta wrapped things up, I'd slid so low in my seat I was almost horizontal.

As it turned out, though, getting caught by Mickey in the mummy room was a lucky break. Loretta praised Maya during preshow for her last-minute improvised work the night before, then volunteered Mickey to give her the official Frightmares backstage tour. Mickey had begged off, claiming he needed to fix some goddamn thing in the mummy room (which was likely a legit excuse), then suggested I take over in his place. With every eye in the room on me, I'd flashed the Dave smile, followed it up with a lazy wave, and pretended not to notice Josie and Mickey's subtle fist bump and Maya's barely contained blush.

My friends, in their heroic quest to hook me up with Maya, had unknowingly hooked me up with what I'd needed most—an excuse to be seen with her. It gave us a free pass to talk and wander around Frightmares together without attracting attention. Most importantly, it made it that much easier for me to keep her safe.

Of course, now I had to deal with Josie. And I had to act normal.

"That's wild about Chet, huh?" Josie said, adjusting her corset. She grimaced at her reflection and turned to face me, leaning against the dresser. "The cops are acting like he's off on a bender or something. I'm sure he's fine, though."

"I hope you're right. What do you think happened?"

"How should I know? Maybe he took off to the 'Glades or Daytona or something. Maybe he dusted off his headshot—I heard there was a casting call in Dade County this past weekend for some movie franchise. I was thinking about going myself, but." She shrugged, gestured to our surroundings. "Self-doubt and apathy. Never a good combo. Plus, Ollie didn't want to take off work. Anyway, the last I saw of Chet was his back as he walked out. Then I went with you to Blacklist and set you on the path to bliss."

"To—what?" My heart sank as her crimson pout spread into a wicked grin. "Oh."

"I was *going* to kick your ass for ditching me again last night," she continued, climbing into the mattress hole, "but Mickey showed up. And do you know what he told me?"

"I'm sure I can guess." I groaned, adjusting the wig. Wishing I could go ahead and wear it backward until my face cooled to normal.

"Dude, you didn't waste a *second*. Not even a week ago you were, like, stalking this girl at the coffeehouse—"

"I was *not* stalking her."

"—and now you're sneaking around at work, doing your thing *in costume*. Putting us all to *shame*. DAVE FREAKING GARDINER. Making Mama *proud*."

"God. What would it take for you to stop?"

"More than you've got in your arsenal, baby son. But seriously."

She settled into the bed, smiling up at me as I slipped the ropes around her extended wrists. This job was so weird. "I'm proud of you. You got back out there. You took the chance. You became the wild card. *And* I kept my promise. I haven't told *anyone* you knew her before she started here. Which is literally killing me, in case you wondered."

"Not even Mickey?"

"Not even Mickey. Not even Ollie."

"Oh Jesus, Ollie knows? Am I getting, like, written up for workplace fraternization, or—"

"What for? He's fraternized with me in every room of this workplace for two years. He doesn't care if you date a coworker. He didn't even seem surprised."

"Okay, then. That's okay. We're not dating, though. Me and Maya. I mean—"

"Hush, child. All in good time."

"Whatever you say, Countess."

"That's what I like to hear." Her voice shifted, a note of concern slipping into her tone. "But other than that, *you're* okay, right?"

My fingers stilled on the rope, a split second too long. I had to force myself to look her in the eye.

"What do you mean? I'm fine, I guess. Everything's normal."

"Dave, please. You left during our shift on Saturday, you're skipping the meetings, you're ghosting everyone—you're a mess. Ollie would've written you up, like, six times already if this wasn't so completely *not* normal."

"I'm sorry, Jo." I sat on the bed next to her fake legs, horrified at how badly my hands shook as I pressed them to my face. Every moment since I'd found Bethany had been a performance; that it had taken this long for the facade to crack was actually impressive. "I'm okay. If you could maybe make sure Ollie doesn't stay mad, I'd be even better."

"He's not mad at all—he's worried about you. We all are."

Screams and laughter drifted through the door, mercifully cutting the conversation short. I stood and got in position for the scene, wondering how long it would take before word of me and Maya got all the way around the place. A day? A couple hours? Seeing as Ollie hadn't reamed my entire ass, Mickey must have skipped over the *where* and *when* details of the situation. It wouldn't make sense if he'd told, I guess—why would he go to the trouble of setting me and Maya up with the doorstop and covering our tracks, only to sell himself out by association the second he saw Jo and Ollie? I had to trust him.

I readied my ax, braced for my cue, and hoped I could manage to keep it together before everything came crashing down.

chapter 20

There was nothing to do but wait.

Once the overhead lights came on in our room, signaling the end of the shift, I helped Josie out of the bed and we reset the scene, buoyed by the surprisingly successful evening. Despite my nerves, everything had gone smoothly. The tours were timed perfectly, the props held together, the actors—and the lights—had stayed on all night. Even Seth had pulled through, which had literally never happened in my time at Frightmares. Ollie's earlier pep talk must have been intense.

Postshow was a blur of Loretta's smiling face and ecstatic hand gestures. Since we didn't have to sit through an hourlong litany of our failures, all Maya and I had to do was be patient. On any other night, our best bet would have been to blend into the chaos and sneak away. There *was* no chaos tonight, though—no smokescreen of anger to conceal our actions; no broken sets; no disasters to push Ollie into overtime. Not that he got paid overtime, no matter how late he stayed.

So, instead of hiding behind a curtain or some ridiculous thing until everyone was gone, Maya left first. Instead of hanging around to chat, she grabbed her things from her locker and disappeared. To anyone else, it looked like the shy new girl was slipping away before she could land on anyone's radar. What she actually did, though, was wait until Mickey was in the breakroom, distracted by my super hyped-up chatter, then sneak down to the mummy room and leave through the emergency exit, propping the door open just enough so the alarm wouldn't engage. When Josie, Ollie, Mickey, and I finally made it to the parking lot ten minutes later, I found Maya perched on the hood of my car, exactly where she'd told me she'd be, watching the rest of the vehicles leave one by one.

"Guess you won't be joining us after all, Davey," Mickey said, nearly knocking me over with a slap on the back. "It appears you've got other plans."

Ollie winked at me over Josie's head and tightened his arm around her shoulders.

"Be nice, Mick," he said. "Unlike you, Dave's got better things to do than be my third wheel."

"You're lucky to have me," Mickey replied. "You need *all* the help you can get with Madame Jojo."

"Damn right he does," Josie drawled, slipping her other arm around Mickey's waist as he and Ollie fist-bumped over her head. She grinned at me, threw Maya a goodbye nod past my shoulder. "You guys should come meet us when you're done . . . chatting. Interacting. What have you."

Play along, dumbass, Bethany murmured. *They're handing you a cover story. Go with it.*

"Shut up," I hissed, over Mickey's graphic reply. "You guys are about to get me ditched."

"Oh, she's not ditching *you*, son," he chuckled. "Mark my words."

I walked away to the sound of their cackles, cheeks burning. Maya smiled as I approached, like everything was normal-level chill. She'd removed her fangs but not her makeup, changed back into her skirt and halter top. Her flip-flops sat on the hood next to her bag. The thought of her witnessing that conversation made my stomach churn, but we had bigger problems.

And we also had an audience.

"Still in costume?" Maya asked as I approached, motioning to me. Her welcoming expression was edged with a tension I hadn't seen from a distance. "I feel so underdressed."

"I was distracting them," I muttered, tossing my street clothes, keys, and wallet beside her bag and sliding onto the hood. "I couldn't keep an eye on everyone *and* change my clothes."

"I'm messing with you, Dave. Wear it all night if you want. Or you can change when we're done with 'what have you.'"

"You heard them, huh?" Awesome.

"Oh, I heard them, all right. They are fully on board with the us 'ship—which, while awkward, is exactly what we want. It makes it that much easier to . . . you know. Sneak off together. Are they still looking?" She let her hand drift toward mine, traced her fingertip lightly over my knuckles as I nodded. "Okay. Let's give them a show."

CHRIST, screamed Anxiety Dave as my heart froze in my chest. *What is she saying? A show of what? Does she mean the "what have you"? Are we okay with this?*

Dude, YES, Chill Dave crowed. *We are okay with ALL of this.*

"Play within a play?" It was all I could manage. She held my eyes, shrugged one shoulder, and laid waste to my senses with a slow, curving smirk.

"If you say so."

Well. This was a moment that could go all *sorts* of ways.

I stared at her, let my smile stretch out to match hers. Turned my hand over and dragged my fingers across her palm. Tested the waters and gave her the reins.

She took it there, not me. She ran her nails up my arm and trailed her fingers back down to mine, coaxed them into aligning with hers, fingertip to fingertip, palm to palm. Raised them between us like a reflection. Like the inmate and visitor in a prison movie, connecting from opposite sides of the glass.

"Your hands are so much bigger than mine," she teased, batting her eyes. "You must be so strong, and powerful, and . . . dexterous."

I almost lost it. It would have ruined the performance to laugh my ass off, so instead I played along. I may be lacking in many ways, but when it came to this brand of roleplay? I'd *always* been unmatched.

"Absolutely," I answered. "My fine-motor skills are ten out of ten."

"Oh, no doubt. You must be exceptionally good at things like . . . heart surgery. And Jenga."

"I'm good at all the games." I gave her a wicked grin.

"I bet you are."

"You know I am. And *you* are absolutely crushing this scene, Maya."

Her name sliced through the facade. She kept the smile on her face as Mickey rode by on his motorcycle, followed by Josie and Ollie in the Jeep. When mine was the last car left in the lot, Maya dropped the act.

"Sorry," she whispered, pulling her eyes from mine, letting her hand fall and her lungs empty.

"I'm not."

That one came out on its own, like someone braver than me had commandeered my voice. A smile flickered across her lips, tiny and intriguing. Like maybe she *wasn't* really sorry. I was about to double down when she spoke.

"So, *that* took forever. I almost texted you to call it off—that one tall guy was, like, creeping around by the fence for ages. I thought he'd never leave."

"Who, Hank? The doctor?"

"Not him. The cannibal one."

"Ronnie." I'd never gotten a creepy vibe off him, but at this point, what the hell did I know. "He's not still here, is he?"

"No. He drove off just before you guys got here. It looked like he was waiting for someone—or hanging back on purpose, waiting for the lot to empty out. I don't know. Maybe it was nothing. But it made me nervous anyway." She glanced over her shoulder at the door, then scanned the parking lot again, eyes darting between the patches of streetlight and shadow. "We need to get back inside before someone sees us. And we should search for anything weird, or out of place. Maybe Bethany left something else behind. I checked around Vamp between tours, but nothing caught my eye."

"Looking for an 'out of place' thing is pointless," I said, heart sinking back to reality and the moment before she'd taken us off the map. "This place has fake weapons, and props, and mannequin parts all over, and nothing is organized—like, we could have a poltergeist that got off on moving stuff around and literally no one would notice."

"Wonderful. I guess this all hangs on whatever footage we can scrape off that computer. We'll just have to do our—"

"WHAT DO YOU WANT FROM ME, MA?!"

Maya and I both jumped at the shout, which came from the lobby entrance, around the corner. I heard the door slam shut, then two pairs of footsteps, heavy and angry on the sidewalk. Seth stormed into view and yanked open the back doors of the company van, which was parallel-parked in front of the building. Loretta swept past him to load a box of file folders into the van, head held high. Her shrill voice rang through the night, reaching us easily.

"I SUPPOSE FORWARD TRAJECTORY IS TOO MUCH TO ASK, IS THAT RIGHT? A TWENTY-THREE-YEAR-OLD MAN PUTTING A TOE OUT INTO THE WORLD, MAKING A PLAN, TRYING TO BETTER HIMSELF—FAR TOO MUCH FOR A MOTHER TO EXPECT. I CAN SEE I'VE CLEARLY CROSSED A LINE HERE, SETHY."

"YOU CAN'T JUST EVER LET UP, CAN YOU?" Seth screamed back. "WHY SHOULD I TRY HARDER WHEN EVEN MY BEST ISN'T GOOD ENOUGH FOR ANY OF YOU?"

"YOUR BEST? YOU STILL HAVEN'T CLEANED OUT THIS VAN FROM THE WEEKEND, WHEN I ASK YOU A HUNDRED TIMES. YOU LEAVE YOUR ARBY'S IN HERE TO ROT AND STINK UP THE WHOLE THING AND WON'T EVEN TAKE IT THROUGH A CAR WASH. SO, IF THAT'S YOUR 'BEST,' THEN—ARE YOU LOOKING AT YOUR *PHONE*? I AM SPEAKING TO YOU, YOUNG MAN.

NO RESPECT. NONE. AND THEN TO HAVE THE GALL
TO—"

The tap of Maya's finger on my arm distracted me from the
rest of the fight. She gestured to the emergency exit with her
head and slid off the car. I followed, knowing we wouldn't get
a better chance. We needed to slip back inside before Seth or
Loretta saw us seeing them.

The mummy room was dark and silent, already swept and
reset for tomorrow's shift. We propped open the door and pulled
back the set curtain, crossed to the employee door together, and
peered out into the backstage hallway. It was quiet and empty, lit
only by the emergency safety lights at either end.

"You stay here," I muttered, like there was anyone around to
hear me. "Loretta probably won't come back in, but if she does,
only one of us needs to get caught."

"Dave."

Her hand closed around mine, stopping me halfway out the
door. Dragging my eyes to hers. She started to speak three different times, before finally whispering, "Be careful."

I let my fingers tighten around hers, briefly. I had to force
myself to let her go.

It was a quick trip down the dark hallway to the far door of
the greenroom—the one beyond the camera's reach. The desk
lamp was on, and the chair was still warm. Adrenaline screamed
through my veins as I woke the screen saver, pulled up the camera, and checked the live feed, my guts a mess of nerves and ice.
I was cutting this too close. I fully expected to see Loretta on the
sidewalk, or in the lobby, possibly even outside the greenroom
door, but the building, as far as I could tell, was empty; the company van was no longer parked on the curb. She and Seth had

finished their spat and driven off—or, more likely, had driven off while still screaming at each other.

I'd managed to dodge the cameras getting back into the building, but to be safe I disabled them anyway, took a deep breath, and made myself concentrate. The first thing I did was locate the employee records, which were as much of a mess as anything in the place. The main folder opened easily enough, but Loretta was either more tech-savvy than I'd realized, or even she knew better than to leave everyone's confidential information unguarded. The individual folders were password-protected—and she'd actually swapped out *Sethy* for a less obvious and more secure option, one I didn't have time to guess. Instead, I maximized the window, took a picture of the screen, and moved on to the real challenge: the missing footage.

My years spent in the pool had done little to prepare me for a hacker side gig. Growing up with my sister, however, whose keyboard skills were both musical and technological, had taught me a few things. I'd come to her last year in a panic, after I'd snuck Cate in while my parents were on a date. Trent Roznor's nanny cam had picked up more than my mother needed to see, a fact I only realized once it was too late.

"You can't 'just delete it,' douchewagon," Roz had huffed. "Hitting Delete doesn't remove a goddamn thing from a machine. It marks the file as available to write over, which means it tells the computer that the file counts as freed-up space and can be replaced by new footage. Then it stays where it is until the computer needs that space."

She might as well have been speaking in tongues for all I knew at the time, but here and now her words were finally making sense. Considering how many times that fucking camera had stopped working over the past few days, there was a good chance Friday's files had yet to be overwritten and were still somewhere on the hard drive.

Or not, Bethany said. *As far as we're concerned, anyway. They might be in there, but you're not Roz. You don't know how to find that crap. Even Loretta doesn't know, and it's her machine.*

"Because it all 'goes into the online,'" I whispered. "'Into the online, and *poof.*' That's what she said. Which means—"

It's in the cloud. Holy shit.

I was so close. I started going through Loretta's mess of icons one by one, sifting through a ridiculous number of documents and folders, looking for any access point. I was on the edge of desperate, ready to do a full rage-sweep of her desk, when a notification bubble appeared in the lower right corner of the screen: an automatic OneDrive backup, just completed.

I smashed the cursor on that before it could disappear, typed *Sethy* into the password prompt, and nearly cried with relief when a window popped open on the screen—Loretta's cloud drive security backup. Row after row of folders, labeled by date.

It was all here.

Except it wasn't. Whole days were missing from the past weekend—Saturday and Sunday both. The cameras must have been offline the entire time. I clicked through to last night's folder, which had similar gaps in operability, though it did still have the footage of my dumb ass sneaking around with Maya. I didn't know what to do but leave that there and hope Loretta never had the knowledge or the need to go back and check it. I'd have figured out a way to trash it, but for one crucial detail: it was hard proof that Bethany's locker *had* been full when we checked it. I'd turned the cameras off afterward—whatever happened to her things between then and now hadn't been recorded. Still, the proof existed. It had been real.

There was no helping it, so I went back to the beginning—Friday night. I pulled up all four feeds from the postshow time slot and played them simultaneously. Watched Chet walk out and Bethany push past him as she fled the greenroom. Saw Chet trash his locker in the breakroom, then leave through the lobby doors. Watched myself intervene in Bethany's argument with Seth. Saw Seth kick the wall and slam into the men's room. Blinked back real tears at the footage of Bethany and me, walking back to the greenroom side by side. Seth came out of the men's room a few moments later and went the opposite way, disappeared down the hall to the other end of the building, where the cameras didn't reach. I saw myself leave with Josie through the lobby, watched Ollie head down the hall to Vamp, carrying a bucket of cleaning supplies. Watched Mickey wander into the breakroom, then out again, and then—nothing. A solid half hour of empty hallway, and the video cut off completely. There were no files recorded or stored after that until Monday afternoon, presumably when Loretta noticed the scratched lock and discovered the system failure.

Either the cameras had crapped out on their own, or someone had turned them off.

I scrolled absently through the Friday footage again, enlarging and collapsing each window, looking for anything out of place. I was about to give up when my eye caught a movement in the corner of the ticket-booth feed, right near the end of the recording. I backed up and zoomed in, tracked the legs of a grainy figure limping along the sidewalk from the parking lot to the auto-locked lobby doors. The legs stopped in front of the doors, which rattled, as if the person attached was trying and failing to pull them open. I clicked over to the lobby feed, head whirling, bottom dropping out of my soul, as Chet appeared on camera, slammed his hand against the glass, and retreated, limping back around the corner to the parking lot.

Chet, who was last seen leaving through the front doors, had returned to the building, and very possibly gone in through the back. Chet, who was now missing, hadn't left first, after all.

Hands shaking, I pulled out my phone and took several pictures of Loretta's screen, focusing on Chet's date- and time-stamped presence. I closed out of the OneDrive and pushed away from the desk, ready to get Maya and get the fuck out of Frightmares so I could process what I'd seen and what it meant.

I'd barely gotten my footing when the lights went out.

chapter 21

I sat perfectly still, mouth like sand, pulse building to a sprint. The darkness was utter and complete—the lamp, the computer—everything was off, leaving me in seething, suffocating blackness. Someone had shut off the lights. Someone had slipped into the office behind me, eased the door closed, and flipped the switch. Someone who might now be standing behind my chair, raising a knife inch by inch, moving it to rest on my exposed throat.

If I didn't turn around, it would be okay. If I didn't move, or breathe, or acknowledge the person behind me, they'd go away. They'd move silently back to the door and the only thing I'd hear would be the click of the knob, and the slow shuffle of their retreat. It would turn out to be nothing, just like the Taco Bell wrapper in my car—benign and safe. A misunderstanding, not a murderer.

All I had to do was wait it out, and I would stay alive.

It's a fuse, dude, Chill Dave said. *Remember the shitshow on Memorial Day? Go flip the breaker and quit being such a goddamn baby.*

I closed my eyes, willing my heart to slow to normal as I thought back to the holiday weekend. Seth had plugged too many cords into a breakroom outlet and blown half the building's lights out right as the first tour began. Josie and I had thought it was a normal chandelier malfunction until Loretta had burst into the room through the employee entrance, whisper-screaming at me to troubleshoot the breaker panel in the Dolls Alive! room. I'd raced next door and slammed every single breaker switch off and then on again, plunging the entire building into total momentary darkness, but ultimately fixing the issue in time to return to my place. My messing around with the cameras had probably tripped a fuse. That was all it was.

I slid out of Loretta's chair and thumbed open my phone flashlight, braced for the sudden illumination of a face, or a blade, or a silent figure standing inches from my chair. The office was empty. I was alone; the solid black void of the greenroom lay beyond the open office door.

I made myself move forward, one step at a time, followed the circle of light across the deserted greenroom. The hallway was pitch-dark—even the emergency lights were out. My phone light reached down the hallway, illuminating the storage room door on the left and the employee door of Captive Countess on the right. Beyond that was a wall of shadow. The air conditioner had shut down too—*was* this actually a fuse issue, or had there been a citywide power outage? Had the whole of Orlando plunged into darkness?

The building thrummed with a heavy silence, broken only by my footsteps and the in-out *whoosh* of my increasingly panicked breath. The air was already going stale. The artificial AC chill had ebbed, revealing the underlying scent of Frightmares: The sharp pine of floor cleaner. The acrid whiff of popcorn someone had burned in the breakroom microwave. The stomach-turning reek of something dark and rotten and animalistic beneath the April Fresh Febreze Loretta used on the greenroom furniture. Mickey was right—we probably had rats. Again.

Dave, if you do not get your shit together, I swear to god. Get to the breaker panel and turn on the lights. Then go back to Maya and GET THE HELL OUT OF HERE.

"Sorry," I answered Bethany aloud. "I'll be okay. I can fix this."

I crossed the hall and slipped into the Demented Doctor employee entrance. I picked my way backward through the tour path, followed the vestibule through to Dolls Alive!, and shuffled behind the draperies until I reached the breaker panel.

I had no idea which switches went to which outlets, or even if every fuse in the building had blown—Loretta and Seth had manually turned off all the lights during closing. Only the lamp in the office had been on when I reentered the place. For all I knew, that was the only one with an issue. I wasn't about to test every bulb in the place, so I did what I'd done the last time I'd had to deal with this panel—I turned every breaker off and then on again, then flipped the wall switch next to the employee door. It worked. The lights came on in Dolls Alive!, and the air conditioner whooshed back to life. Everything was fine.

There was nothing left for me to do in Loretta's office and it was getting way too late to mess around. I needed to get back to Maya, get us both to Blacklist, and spend the rest of the night flirting in front of Josie, Ollie, and Mickey until our cover story sold itself. Who knows what the hell the three of them would say if we took much longer to show up? That thought alone was enough to get my ass in gear. It was time to go.

I closed the breaker box, flipped the light off, stepped out from behind the curtain and into the set. Captive Countess was right through the vestibule. It made sense to follow the tour path back to the mummy room instead of venturing back into the stinking hallway and risk getting caught on camera again. I'd disabled them, but the whole deal with the fuse and the breaker panels could have undone that—for all I knew, they'd rebooted and were fully operational, waiting to catch my dumb ass in action once again.

Don't take chances, Bethany hissed. *Go through the vestibule. Turn the lights back on if you have to, but GO.*

I was three steps from the curtain when everything went wrong.

I don't know if it was the pressing darkness, or a barely audible breath, or an out-of-place movement at the edge of my flashlight beam. It could have been an instinct; the same skin-crawling prickle I'd felt in the pool. The unmistakable weight of an unseen gaze, the subtle waft of someone else's sweat, the presence of another human, far too close and trying to be still.

The Dolls Alive! room was exactly what it sounded like: a child's playtime gone wrong in a nursery of nightmares. The small table was laid for a tea party, three chairs occupied by animatronic dolls controlled by floor panels. The fourth chair, where Suzanne sat during performances, was empty. Floor-to-ceiling shelves of tattered stuffed animals and collectible porcelain dolls bracketed the scene; detached doll heads with plucked-out eyes and carved-up cheeks lay scattered over the table and floor. Wind-up toys were clustered with demented-looking rubber babies and toddler-height figures in pigtails and ripped dresses, grinning at nothing through too many teeth. A few were even life-sized—a ghoulish, carved-wax Peter Pan, taller than me. Freddy Fazbear himself, Loretta's big splurge of 2018. An Annabelle replica, perched on a stool. A marble statue of an angel in long, white robes, watching over the room with its smooth, blank face.

As the two biggest cast members, Mickey and I were constantly tapped to carry in new props, move set pieces, rearrange existing scenes, and perform general grunt work no one else felt like doing. I'd never worked the doll room, but I'd been in there dozens of times for many reasons, not the least of which was troubleshooting the goddamn breaker panel.

I'd never seen that angel before in my life.

I stared at it, dread seeping into my bones. I had maybe four seconds to act—to turn and run through the vestibule, or through the employee door. Or I could quit being a scared little shit and run toward it—stride into the scene and shove it over, watch it topple in a pile of cloth and wings and plaster limbs. One of many mannequins added and removed at Loretta's whim, draped in robes, wigless head cloaked in a full-coverage morphsuit mask, tiny mesh patches over its sightless eyes. Nothing more than another effective prop in Frightmares's creepiest room.

Yeah, another "mannequin." That assumption didn't serve you too well last time, Dave—wouldn't you agree?

The realization was a slosh of ice water over my skin. My blood turned to sleet. Sweat broke out along my back as my vision went hazy, mind whirling, trying to remember who I'd seen leave, or return, or if I'd ever truly seen anything in this place for what it was. What if someone else had died today—during the shift, or even after, while I'd been busy charming Maya in the parking lot? What if another one of my friends was propped up in here, rotting in that costume, blending into the horror-show scenery until the smell grew too strong to ignore?

What if you already *smelled it, dude? What if that wasn't rats at all?*

There was another body beneath those robes. I'd never been surer of anything in my life.

The thought made my insides churn, but I couldn't run—not this time. I'd call the cops. I'd call them right now, without taking my eyes off this angel. I'd get in serious trouble, maybe even get arrested. I'd absolutely be fired—not that I cared—and who the hell knew what this would do to my scholarship status or my future.

None of that mattered. I couldn't let another body vanish on my watch.

I had to see who was under that mask.

My phone buzzed in my hand—an incoming text from Maya. I ignored it, took a step closer to the angel, then another, bracing myself for sickly-sweet rot and maggot-filled eyes. Then the smooth, blank face turned toward me, slowly, until its gaze met mine.

There was a split second of absolute silence—stillness—a suspension of reality and belief, during which my brain disengaged from my body and convinced itself this was all a dream. Then the angel bolted forward all at once, hitting the barrier and swiping for me with white-gloved hands.

I didn't stop to think. I ran.

The vestibule was pitch-dark apart from my phone light. I burst through the curtain and into Captive Countess, skirted the barrier, and ran for the emergency exit that led to the back end of the parking lot, and Maya, and the howl of a triggered alarm system. I had to set it off before a well-aimed blow could crush my skull and my corpse could get stuffed into a clown suit, or laid out in the Vamp casket for someone else to find. The alarm would attract attention, maybe bring witnesses, or at least give Maya time to get away. Whatever happened, I had to open that door.

My hand was seconds from making contact when I got body-checked from the side. The angel and I flew sideways together in a swirl of my black cape and its white robes, slamming into the dresser hard enough to knock the wind out of us both. A sharp pain shot through my hip. My phone flew out of my hand and disappeared beneath the bed. I threw an elbow into the blank face and hiked a knee into the flurry of cloth, felt it connect with a hard, muscled mass—a thigh, or maybe an abdomen. It was enough to bend them double, giving me an opening to slip free—and fight.

I spun around and laid hands on the first thing I saw: the mechanical leg, resting innocently on the bed next to the Josie hole. I brought it down hard on the angel's back, driving them to their knees, then swung the leg like a baseball bat, connecting with the side of their head. I grabbed the whip off the wall, lashed out with it once, and jumped onto the bed, leaping from the mattress over the barrier in an adrenaline burst of strength, cape billowing out behind me like I was goddamn Batman.

Unfortunately for me, I was definitely not Batman.

The cape caught on the barrier as I landed, yanking me backward by the throat. The world rocked; instead of breaking, the strings knotted, garroting me as my back slammed against the railing. I felt a layer of skin shred off beneath my costume as my ribs scraped the edge of the wood, but then I *wasn't* falling—I was being dragged upward. The angel had me by the cape from the other side of the barrier. They were reeling me in like a fish, as I gasped for a breath that wouldn't come.

They were choking me out.

My head was jerked sideways, my feet scrabbled for purchase against the carpet. My vision swam with tiny pricks of light. My limbs tingled between pain and numbness. The world went gray at the edges as the strings tightened around my throat. The angel hauled me closer until we were face to face, eye to mesh-covered eye. They tightened their grip, determined to drain the life from my body.

What they didn't count on was that body being fully accustomed to reaching past its limits. They didn't count on these lungs, honed over years of discipline and training, being primed to go without air.

Instead of fighting, I focused. Instead of tugging feebly at the cape or flailing my arms in useless pinwheels, I got my feet beneath me, made a loop of the whip, and swiftly brought it up between us. I hooked it over the angel's neck and yanked each end as hard as I could.

The effect was immediate. They released their hold on my cape, hands flying up to claw at the whip. I gave it another good yank, let go, hauled off, and punched them square in the face. Something crunched beneath my knuckles; blood bloomed red across the white mask as they stumbled, falling back into the Josie hole with a muffled yell.

Throwing my cape over my shoulder, I fell to my knees and crawled under the barrier, grabbed my phone from where it lay half under the bed, and rolled back to the main path just as the angel got their footing. I saw them vault the railing as I sprinted through the vestibule, heard their footfalls right on my heels.

I swept through the curtain to Vamp and immediately went blind.

chapter 22

The air was a solid, pale gray swirl in the circle of light from my phone. My antics with the breaker panel must have tripped an already malfunctioning fog machine. I could hear it hissing steadily as it puffed out clouds of chemical mist, but I couldn't see a single thing—not the open casket, or the graffitied brick-wall backdrop, or the floor beneath my feet. I couldn't even see the exit.

I heard the swish of fabric behind me, then a gasp as the angel caught up, stumbling through the curtain into the fog. I had a split second to run, sight or no sight; instead, I reacted instinctively— and my instincts took me down, not forward.

Pressing my phone to my chest to smother the light, I dropped to a crouch and scuttled away, heading for the far vestibule. The air was clearer close to the ground; I could just make out the edge of the curtain in front of me. Assuming the angel was still fumbling around in the fog, I had maybe twenty seconds to make a break for it, get through two vestibules and another room before I reached Attack of the Mummy. The thought of Maya waiting in there for me, unaware of the danger I was literally leading straight to her, turned my limbs to rubber. A twenty-second head start was nowhere near enough. I had to move faster than this.

I launched myself into the vestibule curtain and found my footing, scrambled to my feet, and ran swiftly through the dark. I was reaching for the gap in the far curtain when something hit me from behind, pitching me into Murder Circus.

My phone flew from my hand as we hit the floor. The angel was not, as I'd assumed, feeling around sightlessly in Vamp. While I'd been inching through the fog, they'd charged ahead, making up the distance in mere seconds that I'd managed to put between us. Now they were beneath me on the ground, one arm locked around my throat. My shoulder howled. My heels thumped helplessly against the carpet. My already aching lungs were empty.

I snapped my head back, felt the arm loosen as my skull connected with their face. Their gloved hand still gripped my billowy shirt, so instead of fighting, I grabbed the hand and yanked it across my body, used the momentum to roll us both under the barrier and into the set, through the scattered straw and into the striped big-top tent. The central support pole was mostly for show; it didn't stand a chance against my well-aimed kick. The angel yanked their arm free of my grip as the whole tent came crashing down on us in a whoosh of staticky nylon and flimsy wooden dowels.

I clawed my way through a gap in the fabric and rolled out of reach, slammed into the legs of the giant animatronic clown that hovered over the scene, accidentally knocking over the single pair of stilts resting against the wall behind it. The stilts clattered to the floor; the clown teetered on its pedestal, threatening to topple. I scuttled out of the way and gave it a good, hard shove, sent it straight down onto the angel, who was fighting to free their wings from the tangle of the tent fabric. The clown wasn't heavy enough to stop them, but it would slow them down long enough to let me get away.

I crawled back under the barrier, grabbed my phone, and hauled ass toward the final vestibule between me and escape. I could see the light from the mummy room around the edges of the far curtain. I was so close.

"MAYA!" I screamed, stumbling through the darkness and throwing aside the final obstacle between me and the room. I vaulted over the barrier, cape flying, heart racing. "MAYA! RUN!"

"Dave?"

She stood in the middle of the set, waiting. Her face twisted from bewilderment into shock, then horror. I turned in time to see the angel burst through the vestibule curtain, skirt the barrier, then stop in their tracks at the sight of her. Their robes were covered in floor grit and streaked in blood; their breath hissed through the mask, quickening as they took a slow, deliberate step toward us.

I didn't bolt, I didn't yell. I did the only thing I could think of to get her out of there.

I grabbed the edge of the sarcophagus with both hands and yanked it sideways as hard as I could—pulled it straight down off the pedestal and onto the angel. I heard them shout as they hit the floor, but I was already moving, barreling straight at the propped-open door. Maya's shriek blasted through my ears as I lifted her off her feet and carried her, quite literally, into the parking lot.

"Dave," she gasped, stumbling as I set her down. "What's happening?"

"GET IN!" I howled. "GET IN THE CAR!"

I kicked the doorstop out of the way and shoved the door

closed, braced my shoulder against it just in time to take the brunt of the angel's weight as it collided with the other side. I dug my feet into the gravel and gritted my teeth, every hit rattling my bones as Maya ran for the car, which was still parallel-parked next to the building. The angel hammered on the door, unconcerned by the alarm, undeterred by the sarcophagus, the projectiles, my fists, and every other thing I'd used to fight back.

I couldn't hold this door shut forever. I was the only thing standing between Maya and the angel. If they killed me, they'd have to kill her too. They'd arrange us in grisly poses somewhere in a fucking Frightmares set, or disappear us into a lake, or the groves, and continue to play their bloody game over and over until all my friends were dead.

I had to stop this. I had to get us out of here.

Maya grabbed my keys and the rest of our stuff off the hood, unlocked the doors, and climbed in through the driver's-side door. The reverse lights came on as the engine roared to life, and then she was driving backward, pulling straight up next to me, and throwing the car into park just as the angel gave a final thump on the door. Maya climbed into the passenger seat as I sprinted around to the driver's side and practically dove in after her, slamming and locking the door behind me.

I stared at the employee exit, expecting to hear the alarm wail and see the angel bursting from the mummy room, but everything was quiet. My vision blurred; the adrenaline seeped away in a whirl of exhaustion, pain, and razor-sharp terror that made my head spin. I couldn't drive like this. I could barely see straight. I rubbed my hands over my face, pressed my palms to my eyes. Damn near jumped a mile when I heard what sounded like the click of the employee door. I raised my head, looked wildly around, but the door was closed; the alarm was silent. The parking lot, apart from us, was empty.

"Dave," Maya hissed. "What the *fuck* was that?"

"I don't know. I don't know," I gibbered. "I was on the computer, and the fuse—and I thought it was another body. And then I went to get a closer look, and it looked back at me—chased me through the rooms—and I almost—"

"A closer *look*? Why didn't you come straight back here? I texted you when the lights went out, but you didn't answer. Then I heard a crash, so I propped the door open and was about to come after you, when—"

"No." The vehemence surprised even me. I turned to face her, heart nearly stopping at the shock on her face, the wide, dark eyes, the frightened tremble of her mouth. I held her gaze and spoke clearly, making sure she didn't miss a thing I said. "Don't you *ever* run into the dark after me."

"But—"

"There's a chance one of us might die before this is over," I continued over her protest. "If it comes to that, you need to save yourself. *Promise* me, Maya. *Please*."

I squeezed my eyes shut in relief as she finally nodded, opened them just in time to see the blank, white, blood-stained face rise up into view through the window at her back.

The yell burst from my throat a split second before the rock made contact.

The window cracked but didn't shatter—a fractured starburst webbed out from the point of impact and the rock arced down once more, but I was already throwing the car into reverse. I was already stomping on the gas. The Honda leaped backward in a spray of gravel, Maya's scream slicing through the thud of a second impact, as the rock hit the hood instead of the glass. The angel fell forward on their own momentum, landing in the space where the car had been. My headlights caught them on hands and knees, one wing gone, face mask almost entirely red, and then my tires were spinning. I was jerking the wheel to the right, practically riding on the rims as the car swung out of the lot backward into the thankfully deserted street. If I'd missed the exit and hit the fence, we'd have wrecked.

Maya clutched my sleeve as I shifted into drive; the streetlights caught the tears on her cheeks as the pedal met the floor. I peeled out in a screech of tires, leaving a trail of rubber and a bloody angel in my wake.

chapter 23

Frightmares disappeared from the rearview in seconds, but I didn't slow down until it was miles behind us. I kept my eyes on the road and my foot on the gas, waiting for the inevitable breaking point—for the snap of my nerves, or the literal collapse of the cracked window. For Maya's quiet tears to turn to sobs and shatter my heart. Instead, she wiped her face and sat up straight, broke the silence with a shaky sigh.

"Can we go to your place?" she finally whispered. "My mom thinks I'm out with you guys. If I show up now, like this, she'll—"

"Of course," I said. "Maya, I—"

"Who *was* that?" she burst out, cutting me off. "How did they get inside? Were they just, like, *waiting* for you, or did they break in, or—"

"I never saw their face. But I think—" I swallowed hard, voice catching at the idea of speaking a name, of painting a familiar face on the person who'd killed Bethany, and who, just now, had tried his hardest to kill me too. "I think it was Chet."

I felt her eyes on my profile, felt the shock wave of her stunned silence. Whatever name she'd expected me to say, it wasn't that one.

"*Chet?* You think that was Chet back there—and Chet killed Bethany? Oh my God. Oh my God, Dave, did you see it on camera? Did you see what happened to her?"

"No. But I saw him come back." I filled her in on the contents of Friday night's security file. "He must have gotten inside somehow and killed her," I concluded, "and now he's gone on the run. It's the only thing that makes sense."

Maya was quiet for a minute, processing what I'd said. I turned in to my subdivision, checking the road behind me for the thousandth time to make sure we weren't being followed. The neighborhood was still and dark, the sidewalks ringed in streetlights and broken by shadows. There were no other cars on the road—not behind me or ahead of me. We were okay.

"How does *that* make sense?" she finally asked as I pulled into my driveway and cut the engine. "You found her on Saturday, right? Then she disappeared—but Chet wasn't at work that day, was he?"

"No. Not that I saw."

"Okay, so you're suggesting he snuck back in on Friday, killed her, and set all that up for . . . someone to find on Saturday? And he hid in the building overnight and all that day so he could disappear the body afterward—but now he's missing, but also he just appeared and chased you in a weird costume, and tried to kill us both? Dave, that makes *no* sense. At all."

I stared at her, silenced by her undeniable logic. She was right. What had been so clear a moment before didn't actually make sense *at all*. What was wrong with me? How had I arrived at that conclusion? From five seconds of video footage?

I was so desperate for answers, I'd looked at an image on a screen and twisted it past every possible rationale. If this was the apex of my detective skills, how the hell was I supposed to solve anything?

Goddamn it, Dave, Bethany snarled as I climbed out of the car. *Get it together and* think.

That was the problem, though—I *couldn't* think. I couldn't wrap my head around what had happened in that doll room. I couldn't even trust my memory anymore—had the person chasing me been tall or short? Did they smell of flowers or sweat? Cologne? Smoke? Were they broad or narrow or thin or heavy? I didn't know. I could barely remember what *Chet* looked like at this point, and I'd just seen him on camera. Every recall was a rush of white, a splatter of red. A blur of fear and curtains and headlights and darkness. And forget the exact details surrounding the day I found Bethany—my brain had stashed those into a deep, dark corner ages ago out of pure self-defense. I just didn't *know,* and it was going to get me killed.

Her too, Dave. It'll get Maya killed too, and what then? Some hero you are—no wonder it's all an act with you and her. Get your play-within-a-play ass inside and set the alarm. The only way out is through.

I climbed out of the car, eyes landing on the broken window as Maya carefully shut the passenger door. I'd have to come up with a cover story for that shit too, of course, not to mention the dented hood—my parents would want to know *all* the whys behind those repair bills.

It was too much. I braced my hands on the roof of the Honda and bowed my head, gasping in the muggy night air. I was so close to coming undone.

You're losing it. LOSING. IT. Bethany's voice grew louder, as if a tiny her actually *was* perched on my shoulder, shouting into my ear. *How are you keeping this girl alive when you can't even hold yourself together? How are you keeping* you *alive? DAVE. CALM DOWN.*

Too late, muttered Anxiety Dave. *Panic attack in ten, nine, eight—*

"I'm sorry."

I said it out loud, without thinking. Maya was at my side in an instant, sliding in between me and the car, slipping her arms around my waist. Keeping me steady on my feet.

"It's okay," she breathed into my shirt. "We'll be okay, Dave. It's not your fault."

I let my arms wrap around her and held on until I caught my breath. She was so much smaller than me. Her arms were strong, but tiny; her ear was exactly level with my heart. All I wanted was to lock us both in the house and keep her safe. I wanted to erase the fear and sorrow in those eyes and fill them up again with peace.

The last thing I wanted was to let her out of my sight.

Eventually, my grip on her loosened. I led her inside, engaged the dead bolt, set the alarm, then turned off the porch light and turned up the track lighting. The living room appeared at the end of the hall, empty and comforting and familiar.

"Is it okay if I wash up?" Maya asked, gesturing to the downstairs bathroom. "I need to get this stuff off my face."

"Sure. My mom has some makeup wipes in the top drawer. I'll go—yeah."

I waited until she'd closed the bathroom door before heading upstairs to clean up and catalog my injuries. The cape strings had left a thin, red mark on my neck, like the stage-makeup version of a slashed throat. My knuckles were tender and swollen. The right side of my torso was scraped and raw, splotched with purpling bruises from armpit to waist. My body ached, and I'd need to keep an eye on my iffy shoulder, but my face had been spared. From the neck mark up, you couldn't even tell I'd been in a fight. The same could probably not be said for the angel.

I changed into basketball shorts and a T-shirt, chucked my costume in the laundry room, and washed my face, grateful for clean skin and soft, fresh clothes. Staying in that costume a second longer than I had to was pure torture; every moment at Frightmares the past few days had been another facet in the lie. One more layer to the public face I could never scrub away. Maybe that's what was wrong with my head.

Among other things, Chill Dave muttered. *You're definitely solid on the pathetic asshat front, though, so there's that.*

Seriously, Anxiety Dave chimed in. *Maya Green is downstairs waiting for you, and you're up here feeling sorry for yourself in a mirror. Think you can be near her without going fully ballistic, or do you need to cut your losses and take her home now before she's scared of you, too?*

"I get it," I answered them out loud, turning away from my own reflection. Turning out the light as I left the room, the night weighing heavy in my bones.

I found her in the living room, cross-legged on the floor, back against the couch. Her face was downcast and exhausted, eyes ringed in shadows. Still, she smiled as I walked in, inviting me to sit. I sank down beside her, wishing I could erase the horrors of the night and talk to her like a normal person, about something that wasn't murder. Wishing I could shrink the world to a circle of lamplight, until there was no space for anything that wasn't real.

I'd barely gotten settled when I heard the swish of the doggie-door flap and the scrabble of tiny toenails on the kitchen floor. Trent Roznor skidded to a stop in the doorway, stared at us, then beelined straight for Maya. He pounced onto her lap, quivering all over, tongue out and tail going wild. I cringed, seventeen apologies at the ready, but Maya didn't need them. She scooped him up like a baby, laughed as he nuzzled into her shoulder.

"Oh my goodness. Aren't you the most precious little gentleman? Yes you are, you are the best good boy of all the good boys. What's your name?"

"Oh. That's Trent Roznor." I shook my head at her raised eyebrow. "My sister named him after herself."

"I didn't know you have a sister. And she named the dog Trent—wait. Is your sister Rosaline Gardiner? From the Blacklist open-mic nights? She's awesome."

"Some would say," I muttered. "And she would agree."

"I guess it runs in the family," Maya mused. "Overachieving. Her with the piano, you with the pool."

"Yeah, but we literally couldn't be more different. She's a total diva and, like, a baby goth, and she hates everyone. She's basically the human version of this dog."

"Really? She seems so friendly."

"She is. Friendly is an excellent cover for introversion. I guess that's one thing we do have in common."

"You? You're an *introvert*?" She smiled softly at my grimace, absently fiddling with Trent Roznor's ear. "I'd say I'm shocked, but I guess I'm past being shocked by anything tonight. God, that was so fucked up—that thing really tried to kill us. And it was so surreal, it feels like it didn't even *happen*."

"Maya, I'm so sorry." I wanted to reach over and take her hand. I didn't dare. "I never meant to get you into—"

"Stop. I got myself into this. Though—yeah, my summer vacation plans did *not* include living a horror movie with Dave Gardiner. Especially after . . ."

"After what?"

"After *life*. You basically lived in this perfect bubble, all through high school. You and Cate, and your million friends, floating through the world. Stuff like this doesn't happen in bubbles like that—right?"

"Yeah, well, you know how bubbles work. Brush up against something solid, and it's game over." I dug a knuckle into my eye, pressing back against a sudden sting that felt way too close to tears. I was a *mess*. "That bubble in particular was especially fragile."

"It was especially shiny. And you were the brightest thing about it." Her gaze dropped to the dog. "You were Dave Gardiner, king of the school. Smiling at everyone, sailing through life. You were—well, *everything*."

"Dave Everything." I shook my head, managing the smallest of smirks. "Leader of the Varsity Douche Squad."

The reminder of her own words blew away whatever she'd planned to say next. Her soft smile turned to a grimace, like she wished she could forget that's how she'd seen me. But how could I even be mad? I'd spent years perfecting my gleaming image. It wasn't her fault she'd bought into it alongside everyone else.

I watched her carefully, wondering if I'd ruined everything. Or if, more likely, there had been nothing left to ruin for—yeah. Several days, now.

"That was an asshole thing for me to say," she finally muttered. "I know you're—look, you should know that even before all this, you weren't the worst, by far. Mostly douche by association. Douche-adjacent."

"You're not wrong, though," I said, sighing, not bothering to hide a chuckle. Douche adjacency. I'd practically lettered in it.

"But making those assumptions," she continued, "that's on me. I never looked past the others, so I never really saw *you*. Now I feel like I finally *do* see you. In a way . . . I didn't expect."

Her voice faltered, like she'd said too much when she hadn't meant to say anything at all. But that couldn't be right, could it? That *too much* existed, and it made her smile soften, and her cheeks go pink—that *couldn't* be right. This couldn't be happening.

Dude, one of the Daves muttered. *Tell her.*

My breath caught around the words. The other Dave was losing it, screaming at me to shut up before I steered this moment straight into the sun. Before I wrecked myself on this girl, and her words, and her razor-wire eyes.

Shutting up was no longer an option. Whatever I said could bring the world crashing down—or it could open up the skies. Either way, the wreck was happening. It was always going to happen.

"Maya. You're *all* I see."

Might as well put the pedal to the floor.

"Oh," she finally said after an excruciating, too-long silence. "Wow. This is—oh, this is bad. This is destined to end in misery."

Welp, you had to try, said Chill Dave as my heart collapsed. *Salvage those shreds of dignity and back the hell off.*

"Yeah, I get it. Sorry." I looked away, hating every Dave I'd ever been. Forcing my face into neutral like it wasn't about to melt off my bones. "Anyway, it's fine. Before a thing can end in misery, it would have to actually begin."

"I know," she whispered. "I think it already has."

Her voice hooked into me, lifted my gaze to hers. I stared at her, waiting for a punch line that never came. She looked nervous, hesitant, like she was braced for—what? *Rejection?* Like I might laugh, or blow her off, or drop-kick her into the friend zone and pretend she hadn't ripped a hole in my universe?

This wasn't some play within a play. This wasn't a panicked, fake kiss in the mummy room, or a staged flirtation on the hood of my car. This had roots in spilled coffee and spoken poetry, and a girl who'd changed me with her words. I'd been lost to her from the start. If our hearts overlapped even the slightest bit, that was enough for me.

I shifted closer, then leaned in, gave her plenty of time to dodge, or shove me away, or yell *psych*. She didn't.

It was the moment I'd wanted since the first night I'd seen her at open mic. My hands cupping her face, her lips meeting mine halfway. Her fingers threading through my hair, pulling me close, then closer. It was perfection, a full-body rush like nothing I'd known—cut through with a god-awful racket, a familiar, skin-crawling, metal-saw whine.

It was Trent Roznor, my sister's very own fur-covered blasphemy, who would *definitely* take a dump right on the area rug if I didn't slam the brakes on the single best moment of my life and put him in the yard.

I broke away with a groan, wishing it were possible to temporarily banish the dog to another dimension. Maya blinked at me, flushed and breathless, furnace-eyed, and I had about half a second to realize she looked like that because of *me*, when her eyebrows drew together, and she frowned, nodding past me at Trent Roznor.

"Is he okay?"

"Yeah. I'm sorry. I just need to . . ."

The words trailed off as I looked at him—*really* looked at him. He stood facing the front door, muscles tense, ears laid flat, lip curled up over bared teeth. His tail stood straight up, and all his hair was on end. I'd heard him bark at nothing a million times. I'd seen him stalk garter snakes, and chase lizards, and hide from the neighbor's cat. I'd seen him trot after dragonflies, snapping his little jaws. I'd never seen him act like this.

"Hey. Trent, what's up, boy? Are you—"

"Dave." Maya's sudden grip on my arm cut me off. "Someone's there."

I followed her finger, which pointed not to the dog, but to the door, and the flash of movement behind the frosted-glass window. The long shadow that fell through that window and across the entryway. Trent Roznor took off after it, threw himself against the door, growling and scratching and barking.

For a split second I was a useless block of ice. My lungs seized and my vision went hazy, rocked by the same fear that had left me a gold-painted, sweat-soaked mess, flailing around in a RaceTrac parking lot. What would I see if I approached the glass, cupped my hands, and pressed my eyes to the pane? Would it be a friend checking up on me? A stranger, searching for someone at the wrong house? Or the bloodied white face of the angel mask, staring back at me?

I turned to Maya, ready to stammer out half a plan—tell her to run upstairs, or out the back door. To follow me through the yard, jump the fence, and run through to the next block over, before whoever was outside got in. All of that vanished when I saw her eyes. They were huge and terrified, and looking to me for help.

The fear drained away, leaving nothing but fury.

One second I was on the floor, the next I was on my feet, racing through the hallway, slamming the alarm keypad until it disengaged. I flung open the door and burst out into the driveway behind the dog, who bounded into the grass and ran in a circle, yipping and snarling, like he didn't know which nothing to latch on to first.

That's all there was out there—absolutely nothing.

I heard other dogs barking, probably in response to Trent Roznor. I heard a squeal of brakes, soft music drifting from an open window. A car's subwoofer and a motorcycle and the long, loud blare of a horn. No suspicious rustling in the bushes or hurried, retreating footfalls. Nothing in either direction but an empty street.

Maya appeared at my elbow as I stared into the shadows, cursing the curved road and wishing I had someone to follow—to punch, to chase down, and tackle, and beat into the ground. I'd run my ass off earlier that night, flight mode taking hold and sending me through the maze of looming clowns and toppling props. Now fleeing was the furthest thing from my mind. Now I was more than ready to kick some ass.

Someone had come onto my property, stalked around my front porch, scared the dog, and scared Maya. If they'd broken in, she'd have been a target too. If they'd attacked us, she could have been hurt—or worse. Because of me.

Screw running away.

Whatever had happened at Frightmares had officially fol-

194

lowed me home. I could no longer shut my eyes or talk myself out of it. I definitely couldn't assume that whoever killed Bethany wouldn't pursue me into the world beyond the sets. It was time to quit messing around and find out what was going on.

It was time to solve this, before it all blew up in my face.

chapter 24

We sat on opposite ends of the couch, Trent Roznor curled up between us like a snoring throw pillow. I'd missed about eighteen texts from Ollie, all of which turned out to be Josie, badgering me to either show up at Blacklist or officially cancel so she could go home. I'd sent a quick apology, which she answered immediately with a middle finger emoji and four black hearts. It was fine. She was fine.

I'd offered to take Maya home, but she'd shaken her head, insisting on going through what I'd found on the computer. After being attacked and possibly followed home, we couldn't afford to leave it until morning. She'd insisted I tell her everything, too—from the moment the lights went out to the moment I'd returned to her. I relived it dutifully, showed her the marks on my torso and neck. Watched the color in her cheeks drain right back down to nothing.

"So," she finally said, "we're dealing with a true psychopath, is what you're saying. Someone who killed Bethany, dragged you into their sick little game, and literally lay in wait for you tonight."

"Looks that way," I said, sighing, far too calm considering the weight behind that statement. "So, what have we got? Because I am all for getting out of this game sooner, not later."

As it turned out, Loretta wasn't about to make the quest for

Levi easy on us. Her employee files, in addition to being disorganized, were labeled with first initials and last names only. No first names at all. Maya sat cross-legged, her notebook on one knee, my phone balanced on the other as she wrote down every name in the photo of Loretta's employee files.

"I made a separate list of *L* names," she finally said. "First and last initials both. No stone unturned and all that."

I shifted Trent Roznor to my other side and moved closer to Maya so I could read over her shoulder.

K. L. Coombs
L. Hanks
L. Mattison
L. Ramirez
L. Towers
L.J. Tyson
L. Yang
A. Langford
I. Lazaro
R. Leclerc
C. Lee
M. Levinson
H. Long
S. Lydell

"Lotta *L*s in this place," I observed.

"We definitely do have some *L*s. Do any of them mean anything to you, or did we almost get murdered for nothing?"

"I know a couple—that one's Cori, and that's Lena. And these other three are former cast members. None of their names are even remotely close to Levi."

"Former cast members. So *that's* awesome." Maya sighed, crossing through the names I indicated. "I guess Loretta having an organized list of current employees was too much to ask."

"Oh, absolutely," I said, remembering the disaster of the computer's desktop. "But the people who quit this place aren't really trying to spend a lot of time on the premises. None of them would come back even to hang out, much less stage a murder. For all we know, this Levi guy doesn't work there, and never did."

"And for all we know, we see him every day." She set her notebook aside and shifted to face me. "Dave, we can't dismiss it. Do you know how many women die at the hands of their romantic partners? Too many to ignore. And if Levi *didn't* kill her and is just some random guy, wouldn't he have shown up looking for her by now? Especially if they were supposed to go away together?"

"Maybe, maybe not. They couldn't have been that serious— he hadn't even met her roommate. Maybe he thought she ghosted him and moved on."

Ghosted by a ghost, Bethany quipped. *Cute.*

"Or maybe," Maya said, "he's out there wondering what happened to her. I really think we need to find him." She studied the picture again, brow furrowed. "I see my own file in this, and yours, too, but I don't know how many of these are stage names. Can we assume Loretta used legal names in official records, for taxes and stuff?"

"I think she did. That's Josie's real name: J. Morello. It follows that all the names on the files are legit. But I don't even *know* everyone's last names, much less whether they're real or not."

"Who else uses a stage name? It'll take forever to go through all these, but if we can eliminate everyone we know who *isn't* Levi, that should at least narrow down our suspects."

"I'm not sure—Ronnie? Suzanne? I *think* Brennan does. I know Mickey does. Seth doesn't."

"Yeah, I think we can safely say Seth isn't Levi. But Mickey..." She paused, studying the list. "Did you hear a motorcycle when we were outside, or was that just me?"

"I . . ." I trailed off, head aching. I *had* heard a motorcycle, threaded through the other background noises. I'd heard one the other day when I was in the pool too, when I'd thought someone was breaking in at the gate. As for Mickey's whereabouts on Friday night, I didn't remember seeing him at all after postshow. The video footage I'd found showed him leaving the breakroom before the cameras cut off, but when he'd left the building and where he'd gone was a question mark.

But it didn't fit. Mickey had to clock out early when Loretta put out rat traps. He was basically made of muscle, and the last guy you'd want to pick a fight with, but he was a good person. He wasn't a killer.

"No," I said. "It can't be Mickey."

"Dave," Maya said gently, "I hate the idea too. He seems so nice, and I know he's your friend, but—"

"It doesn't make sense, Maya. Why would he leave her in his own set?"

"Maybe he put her there in a hurry, thinking he'd get rid of her later. Then he was called on to work Vamp and didn't have time to move her."

"But he didn't fight back on switching sets at all—in fact, Ollie wanted to put Josie in Vamp, but Mickey said he'd do it because he used to work that room. If he knew Bethany was in there, he'd have at least stalled long enough to move her, right? Because he had to know she'd be found."

"So would anyone. No one in their right mind would have left her out like that—unless they were trying to set *Mickey* up to take the fall, but it ended up being you, instead. Or"—she pressed her hands to her eyes—"maybe we're trying too hard to justify this, and 'Mickey Styx' is"—she checked her notes—"M. Levinson, aka Levi. It sounds too obvious, but sometimes *obvious* also means *true*."

"If Mickey were seeing Bethany, there's no way he'd keep it secret," I insisted. "He'd have made out with her in the greenroom during postshow just to piss off Seth. Anyway, we saw Mickey leave with Josie and Ollie tonight—and unless he shrunk himself down to fit into those angel robes, it wasn't him. That guy wasn't short, but he was shorter than me."

"So is everyone at Frightmares, except—well, *except* Mickey."

"Exactly. If I'd had that fight with him, I'd be fucking dead." I shook my head at Maya's pitying expression and doubled down. "I think we need to look harder at Chet. Find out where he is, what he knows, and why he tried to get back in that night."

"Okay," she conceded. "I trust you. If you say it's not Mickey, I'm on board. And unless you think it was a woman in those robes—"

"It wasn't. Jillian or Maggie could have fought me like that, but neither of them are tall. None of the women in our cast are."

"Know what would *really* help narrow this down? If there was literally anyone at Frightmares who wasn't openly sketchy or weird." Maya rubbed her hands over her shadowed, weary eyes. "So. You think of a way to track down Chet. I'll focus on the Levi angle. Between the two of us, we'll come up with something. We have to."

"Okay, but can we do all that tomorrow? I can't talk about this anymore. I can barely think."

"I know the feeling. Not talking about this sounds pretty good to me."

She closed her notebook and set it aside, then leaned against my shoulder, wrapped her arms carefully around my battered torso. I felt her relax into me as I pulled her closer. We sat there together as the minutes bled away, staring through the front door's window at the dark and empty night.

chapter 25

We walked into Frightmares hand in hand on Wednesday, which was Maya's idea. "Us" as a concept, she'd rationalized, was practically workplace canon by now; avoiding each other would seem more suspicious than leaning into it. Not that I was arguing. The way she'd kissed me when I'd dropped her off that morning, right around four a.m., would have been enough to convince any witness we were a thing.

We split up after preshow, during which our close proximity had inspired plenty of raised eyebrows and *you go, Dave* grins. Maya headed down to Vamp, while I made a last-minute detour to deposit my sadly deceased phone in my locker. The beating it had taken the night before had left it on life support; it had succumbed to its injuries right before Loretta called places. Between the phone and the car window, my parents were going to lose their shit.

I was about to swing around the corner into the breakroom when I heard a wet cough, followed by a moan, then a frustrated mutter that slowed me to a stop. I waited just out of sight, instinct telling me this was not a talk I wanted to bust in on.

"Seth," I heard Ollie say, "what you do off the clock is your own business. But man, I can't have you coming into work like *this*. You can barely keep your head up."

"You don't get it," Seth answered, voice fluctuating between harsh and barely audible. "It's—on and off for days now. Holes—flickers—every second I'm awake—it's like I'm dying, and there's no way out. It keeps getting worse, no matter what I do."

"The only way out is to get help. You need to see a doctor, someone who specializes in—"

"*Specializes.*" I could hear the venom dripping from his slurred words. "Quit acting like you know what it's been like for me, Ollie. You don't know shit."

Silence. I held my breath, wondering if it was too late to sneak away before the yelling started. Ollie was known for his patience—it was the main reason Loretta had promoted him to begin with—but everyone had a limit. If Seth *only* got written up for this, he'd be getting off easy.

"What I know," Ollie finally said, tone even, but only barely, "is that whatever's happening with you needs to *stop*. Get your head on straight. If you can't perform, it'll throw off the whole night. People will want refunds, we'll get slaughtered online, and we'll lose new *and* repeat customers. I've seen the numbers this past month. It's not good, man. Summer tourists will give us a boost, but the next few weeks could make or break the whole place. If you hurt the business, you hurt your mom. I know you don't want that."

"Nah, man." Seth's voice broke on the words. "I don't."

"It's okay. It'll be okay. We're all here to help you if you need it. I promise, everything will work itself out."

I heard footsteps in the hall behind me and started moving again before I got caught eavesdropping. I strode into the breakroom like it was any ordinary day, pretending surprise at the sight of Ollie hovering over a personified layer of hell. Seth was a glassy-eyed mess of streaked makeup and uneven latex; the way his hands were shaking, it was a miracle he'd been able to apply it at all.

"Hey, guys," I said, easy-breezy, casually concerned. "Seth—dude, are you okay?"

"He'll be fine," Ollie answered, when Seth didn't manage to do more than blink at my dumb grin. "Hangovers: do not recommend."

"Sucks, man. Let me know if you need anything."

Seth's issue clearly went beyond a hangover, but that was their business. I opened my locker and went through the motions of storing my phone, trying like hell to hear the whispered conversation behind me, which seemed to mostly consist of Ollie soothing and Seth apologizing. I dithered in the breakroom as long as I could before heading across the hall and letting myself into Attack of the Mummy.

The room was quiet and empty. The ritual props were artfully arranged, and the sarcophagus was back in place, as if I'd never pulled it down onto my would-be killer. As far as appearances went, it was like last night had never happened.

You already hear *things,* Bethany snickered. *How do you know you're not* seeing *things, too?*

That wasn't my concern, though—the evidence lay in the ache of my ribs and the marks on my body and throat.

I walked past the set and through the vestibule, heading down the tour path to Captive Countess. Murder Circus was similarly undisturbed, and Vamp was clear of fog. Maya looked up in surprise as I entered, a compact mirror in one hand and a bottle of

F/X blood in the other. She set both in the casket and walked to meet me face to face, the barrier between us. Her hands covered mine on the railing, concern etching lines in her powdered-white forehead.

"Hey. Is everything okay?"

"I don't know," I said. "Everything looks back to normal—which, honestly, is pretty much the opposite of okay. Being back in here—"

"Yeah, I am also not a fan. If we hadn't been there last night to see it—"

"—it would seem like we'd made the whole thing up."

"Exactly. I don't like any of this. Everyone here is either all smiles or, like, full uncanny valley. Except Seth, who spent all of preshow staring through the side of my face. I didn't know the human eye could go so long without blinking."

"Yeah, about Seth." I filled her in on what I'd overheard in the breakroom. "He was really messed up—worse than I've ever seen him. I don't know what his deal is, but if he shows up in here tonight and tries to corner you, my room is right on the other side of that curtain."

"My hero."

"I didn't mean it like that," I began, face heating. "Just—if you need anything—"

"I know how you meant it, Aquaman. I was teasing." Her fingers tightened around my knuckles. "I'll be okay. And if I'm not, I'll come find you."

The overhead lights flickered, signaling the start of the first wave of tours. I returned Maya's small smile and hurried next door, where Josie was already settling into the mattress hole. I helped her into the ropes and positioned the leg beneath the sheet, head whirling and stomach heaving. Last time I'd seen this leg, I'd been swinging it at someone's head. Yet here it was, exactly where it should have been.

Sounds like a pattern, Bethany whispered. *Things in this place . . . they do seem to self-correct, do they not? Undisturbed limbs. Reconstructed tents. Dead bodies that seemingly walk away all on their own. Almost like you invented the whole damn thing, huh?*

I'm not inventing it, I told her. *Maya saw those things too. Not all of it, but enough.*

True. Unless you're inventing her too.

"Dave? You okay?"

I blinked back to the outside world, gave Josie a bright grin that scraped the borders of insanity.

"Sure am. Ready for the show?"

"When am I not?" She nodded to Ollie's phone, which lay on the dresser. "Could you put that in the dresser drawer? Ollie was supposed to come get it before showtime, but he has yet to materialize."

"Yeah, he probably won't. He's in the breakroom, talking Seth through his hangover."

"Irony is not yet dead, my friend," she drawled, rolling her eyes as I set the phone in the drawer next to a pack of chandelier bulbs, a plastic bag of zip ties, a tube of F/X blood, and a rubber eyeball. "Irony is, in fact, literally Ollie judging someone's hangover, when he spent last night getting wasted while we were waiting on *people*"—she shot me a death glare—"who never showed."

"Oh, that. We . . . lost track of time." I felt like such a knob, tacking a smirk onto the end of that sentence. Still, Josie's answering grin was worth the lie. If even a fraction of the truth came out, things could only get more complicated. "Sorry you got stuck babysitting those assholes."

"Just the one asshole. Mickey took off early, so I got to hoist my one true love into the Jeep by myself. Again." She sighed. "He's, like, consumed by managerial stress. I get that the promotion was a big deal for him, but frankly, if *I* had a flying fuck to give, I wouldn't waste it on Frightmares."

"Is he okay?"

"He'll be fine. Last week was rough, but he's been much better since—"

The approaching screams and laughter from Maya's room cut the conversation short. For the next half hour Josie and I did our thing, fell into our usual performance rhythm, and everything spooled out as planned. I was resetting the scene for the third time when the overhead lights came on—the end-of-shift fluorescents, not the chandelier.

"What the hell?" Josie squinted in the sudden glare. "Did we get sucked into a wormhole? What time is it?"

"Not closing time, that's for sure. I'll go see what happened."

I left through the employee door, resisting the urge to check on Maya. There was protective concern and then there was annoying condescension. The last thing I needed was to blur that line.

The hallway was brightly lit and empty, but I heard voices— agitated half-whispers, choked moans, and shushing sounds. I crept toward them, half expecting one of the employee doors to burst open in a swirl of bats, or the angel to come sprinting around the corner with bloody robes and outstretched hands.

From the looks of things, that theory might not have been farfetched.

My vision doubled, then snapped back into focus. I blinked at the mess on the floor ahead of me, wondering if *this* was the hallucination—if, of all the unreal stuff I'd seen in the past few days, this was the thing my mind had tricked into reality.

A high-pitched ringing began in my ears, swelling to a steady keen as I quickened my pace, every cell in my body screaming at me to quicken it in the opposite direction instead of toward the streaky, spattered trail of dark red blood connecting the employee entrance of Undead Graveyard to the breakroom door. I was only half certain it even existed, but if it did—if someone was hurt, or worse—I had to help. I couldn't keep running away.

I nearly collided with Ollie in the breakroom doorway. He was leaving as I was entering, speaking over his shoulder to someone in the room.

"Ollie, what's going—" The words died in my mouth at the sight of Seth hunched over in a chair, Loretta holding a red-soaked towel to his face. "Jesus. What happened?"

"He blacked out," Ollie muttered, looking past me into the hallway, checking for a larger audience. "Fell face-first into the barrier in the middle of his show. A customer had to find me in the booth and send me in after him."

"Is he okay?" I whispered back. "I mean, do you think he'll be—"

"I don't know, Dave. Honestly, he hasn't been 'okay' for a while now."

"No," Loretta chimed in, overhearing us. "He hasn't. I called an ambulance. This is too much. You hear me, Sethy? It's too much. I can't fix this with the first-aid kit. I—"

Her voice crumbled. I shifted uncomfortably, feeling like I

should be a few more feet away from this conversation, or maybe a few more feet outside the whole damn building.

"I'll move Ronnie or Brennan into Undead," Ollie said, turning away from me. "They can wing it for tonight. But we need to discuss the . . . long-term options, Loretta. Sooner rather than later."

Loretta pressed the towel into Seth's limp hand and followed Ollie into the hallway. Their hushed voices drifted back to me, too low to decipher. I moved carefully into the room, hesitant to leave Seth alone in case he blacked out again. His makeup was smeared; his zombie latex was peeling off in chunks. Aside from the fresh blood, it was hard to separate the injuries from the disguise.

"Hey, Seth," I said, feeling all kinds of useless. "You need anything?"

"Man, where do I start. Maybe a Reset button. Or a time machine." He squinted at me over the towel. "Oh. Hey, there. Dave?"

"Um, yeah? Are you—"

"Thought you were Ollie for a second. Can't even fucking see straight anymore. You're real, though, right? You look real. Hey, how's Maya? How's your girl?"

"She's not my—" I swallowed the rest of my automatic protest, reminding myself that, as far as the Frightmares cast was concerned, Maya and Dave were Officially a Thing. Not that Seth would remember this conversation, but still. "She's fine. It's all pretty new, so. You know how it is."

"Yeah, I do. I miss that. I just really miss—hang on to it, okay? Do right by her, while you still can." His eyes watered; he gestured to himself with his free hand. "Try to at least do better than *this*."

209

A wave of pity rolled through my gut. Seth had been a mess for a good, long while—everyone knew that—but I hadn't seen how truly broken he was before now. I hadn't realized that the shift between delusion and reality was his new normal, or that the line between the two was growing thinner by the day.

It was terrifying, how thoroughly I could relate.

"We're all doing our best, you know?" I finally said. "It'll get better."

"Sure it will, kid. Sure it will."

My reply was lost in the clamor of Ollie, Loretta, and two EMTs hurrying in from the hallway. All of them beelined for Seth, and no one needed me to stand uselessly off to the side, so I crept back to Captive Countess. Josie was leaning against the dresser, scrolling through Ollie's phone. She smiled through fresh lipstick as I approached the barrier.

"There's my baby son. Everything okay?"

"No. It's bad. It's Seth."

"Of course it's Seth—that boy is a series of poor life choices. What happened?"

"He passed out during the show and busted his face on the barrier railing. Loretta had to call an ambulance."

"Are you serious? God. I'll go see if they need help."

She set the phone on the dresser and ran out of the room, hiking up her corset as she went. I stared at the phone for a split second, a terrible, risky idea forming in my mind. I *should* wait for the phone to go dark, then put it back in the drawer. Maybe even carry it down to Ollie like the good boy I was. I definitely shouldn't pounce on it before the screen could lock, open Ollie's phone contacts, and scroll until I found Chet's name.

Seth wasn't the only one fueled by poor life choices.

210

Ollie had the contacts sorted by first names. I found Chet's info easily enough, then scrolled farther down to the *L*s, scanning the screen for any sign of a Levi, or maybe the missing first names from Loretta's files. Ollie was far more efficient than Loretta, though—his list was current employees only, all stage names as applicable. It made sense. His job was to wrangle the cast, not keep track of a zillion different legal names, memorize them, then match them with their alias every time he had to make a call. He even had *Josie Manning* in there instead of *Joanna Morello*, and she was his girlfriend.

I scrolled back to Chet's contact info and stared at it, wishing I had my phone camera. I was never going to remember this.

Maybe, Chill Dave whispered, *you don't have to.*

Impulsively, I pulled up their text history and started typing.

> You there?

I hit Send before I could talk myself out of it, eyeing the screen like it might explode into dust. When the text went to read, my heart stopped; when Chet's reply appeared, I nearly collapsed.

> Hey man. Didn't expect to hear from you.

I almost dropped the phone in my haste to reply. I had to play this off—sound enough like Ollie so as not to raise suspicion, yet somehow extract the information I needed. It would help if I'd known Chet apart from a few work-related exchanges, but he'd never been big on after-hours gatherings.

Man, where have you been? I finally typed. The cops came by—no one knows where you went. You okay? Need any help?

> To answer your questions: 1. out in Ybor—
> didn't tell anyone why/when because it
> was nobody's business. 2. Cop thing was
> a misunderstanding. 3. No problems on
> this end. It's all good.

> Glad to hear it. Any chance of you coming
> back? We could really use you on set.
> Buy me a beer once you're back in town
> and we'll call it even. Maybe I can talk you
> back into the Graveyard.

I held my breath as I hit Send. By the time the reply appeared, I was on the verge of my own blackout. Maybe the ambulance had room for one more.

> Deal. Tell you what, I'm headed back in
> tomorrow morning. I need to drop off a
> couple props that ended up in my car.
> What say we meet at Frightmares around

noon, go grab that beer, and come to an understanding?

Right on. See you then.

I waited for the Read notification, then deleted the conversation, palms sweating, heart racing. I'd done the thing. I'd set our search in motion, located a missing person, and possibly located Bethany's killer. Even if I was wrong about that last part, I could still get some answers. I'd at least find out what he knew and what he'd seen. If I was right—well. Either way, this nightmare would finally end.

By this time tomorrow, everything would be okay.

chapter 26

Maya and I outright declined the postshift Blacklist invitation, opting to park in front of her house and make out in my car until her dad texted her to cut it out and say goodnight. After making me promise to pick her up at eleven so we could work out a plan to deal with Chet, she'd kissed me one last time and gone inside. I'd driven home on an endorphin high, skin melting, heart on fire.

I was too jacked up for sleep. Instead, I swam laps until two a.m., brain shifting between replaying a highlight reel of the past few hours and worrying over the impending meetup. The rest of my night was spent playing *Assassin's Creed*, roaming around the house in the dark, compulsively checking the windows and doors, and talking myself into breaking my earlier promise to Maya. Plan or no plan, I was definitely *not* bringing her along to confront Chet, even though it meant she might never speak to me again.

Fatigue caught up to me before sunrise; the morning passed in a series of restless naps. I left my house at 11:23, cringing with guilt as I bypassed the turnoff to Maya's street. Orlando was a blur of shimmering pavement and midweek tourism, the sun's glare rimmed by distant banks of fat, black thunderclouds. The forecast promised scattered storms, which meant I'd be meeting Chet either beneath sheets of rainwater and forks of lightning or in a seething fog of heat, humidity, and mosquitoes. Meanwhile, all I really wanted was to blow the whole thing off, turn around, and drive straight to Maya's. We could send Loretta a joint resignation, curl up together in front of a movie, and leave Frightmares in the past. Instead, I was driving there alone, braced for the final act of everything my dumb ass had set in motion.

If someone had told me a week ago I'd be ghosting Maya Green the exact second it looked like I might have a real chance with her, I'd have blocked that person on every platform—yet here I was doing exactly that, when she'd done nothing but show up for me time and time again. My phone was broken, so I couldn't text her, and telling her face to face would end with her buckled stubbornly into my passenger seat, waiting for me to cave—which made ditching her my only real option. We'd barely escaped our last attempt at a Frightmares mission. I couldn't lead her into another that was almost guaranteed to end just as badly.

The lobby was dark and empty when I arrived. The trash bin next to the ticket booth was overflowing and buzzing with flies, the deserted sidewalk littered with the usual candy wrappers and cigarette butts. Despite Ollie's daily routine of cleaning the glass, sweeping the concrete, and chiseling the splattered lovebugs and old gum off the building's various surfaces, Frightmares always looked like it was minutes from being condemned. At night, that aesthetic worked to our advantage; during daylight hours, it just looked sad.

I wasn't about to park in the fenced-in employee lot and risk getting trapped. Instead, I parallel-parked at the curb and ducked beneath the front awning, waited in the shade next to the trash bin. Sweat gathered on my skin, pooled at my temples and collarbone and lower back. I'd gotten here early, according to the clock in my car; it had to be past noon by now, but there was still no sign of Chet. There was no sign of anyone.

"Dave?"

I spun around at the sound of my name, pulse rocketing through the top of my skull. Seth ambled down the sidewalk toward me, a can of Four Loko in one hand, the end of a pizza crust in the other. His face was a mess of cuts and bruises, nose swollen, lips scabbed. His mirrored wraparound sunglasses weren't enough to hide what looked like a matching set of black eyes.

"Hey, man." I had to force that one out in neutral, stomach dropping at the sight of his truck parked four storefronts down, in front of the pizza parlor. I hadn't even seen it.

Try paying attention for a hot second, Dave, Bethany hissed. *Trust me when I say this guy is a wild card you absolutely do* not *need.*

I couldn't agree more. Judging by Seth's expression, he felt the same about me. I wondered if he remembered what he'd said to me back in the breakroom—or if he remembered anything at all about last night. At least he recognized me this time.

"What're you—I mean, you're here early," he said, stuffing the last bite of crust into his mouth. "Is there, like, an employee thing, or—"

"Not that I know of," I hedged. "I'm meeting up with—well. Chet Perez. We were texting, and—"

Seth's demeanor changed instantly the second I mentioned Chet. He clapped me on the shoulder, grinning, like we had a tight, secret bro bond no one had bothered telling me about.

"Hey, me too—that kid owes me damn near a grand, and he

went on vacation. If he's got money to disappear, he's got money to settle up, am I right? Said we'd meet here and make good. You didn't pay him already, did you? Or is this a two-birds thing?"

"What? I don't—"

"Don't bother waiting on his ass, D-boy, I can hook you up. Whatever he's holding came from me anyway, and, hey—at least I showed up, huh?"

Ignoring my weak reply that D-boy was not, in fact, looking to be hooked up, Seth dug out his phone and voice-texted Chet.

"Yo, you on your way, or what?"

The reply buzzed through seconds later. Seth pushed the sunglasses up on his head and squinted at the screen. His eyes were swollen nearly shut; the bruises were bad enough to make me wince. He must have caught that railing *right* in the face.

"Huh. Says he's already inside." Seth held the phone so I could see the text thread. "Putting stuff back in the storage room, whatever that's about."

"He has a key?"

"The number of keys we've had go missing—they might as well be Halloween candy, the way Ma hands 'em out. No one tells me that stuff." He downed the last of his Four Loko and tossed the can in the direction of the trash bin, shrugging when it bounced off the rim and onto the sidewalk. "Time to go get paid."

He fumbled with his key ring, his hands shaking too much to function. The key skittered over the metal faceplate, landing everywhere except in the goddamn keyhole—the painfully obvious answer to Loretta's mystery of the scratched-up lock. I was weighing the pros and cons of offering to help versus shoving in front of him and doing it myself, when he managed to get it together and unlock the door. I followed him inside, head swimming with the heat and the stress and too many pieces that didn't quite fit.

If Chet has a key, that means he can come and go any time, dude, Anxiety Dave squeaked. *He could have snuck back in on Saturday to clean up the mummy, no problem. He could have been the guy in the angel robes who almost ended you NOT FORTY-EIGHT HOURS AGO.*

But if he has *a key, why didn't he use it Friday night, when he tried to get back in?* Bethany whispered. *And if he* doesn't *have one, how is he already inside?*

Who cares? Chill Dave said. *What you need to focus on* right this second *is what Chet'll do if he's expecting Ollie, and you walk up with Seth. You don't even have a phone on you. If things escalate, do you at least have a plan that doesn't involve standing there like a dumbass?*

I did not, in fact, have such a plan—because how do you plan for anything when absolutely nothing adds up? Chet was missing, but now he wasn't. He couldn't get in the building before, but he was apparently in there right now. He'd been reliable enough to have a Frightmares key, but had no qualms walking out with zero notice. He was savvy enough to deal for Seth, but reckless enough to party on the profits. None of those details fit with *anything* Maya and I had found. None of it made any sense in context with Bethany's death.

"Hey," I began as Seth relocked the door behind us and headed for the backstage hallway. "You feeling okay? Your face and all?"

"Yeah, I'll be fine. They gave me Percs at the hospital, so I am feeling *no* pain."

"So, you'll be cool, right? With Chet? I'm not looking to fight. Or get in your business. I'm just here to talk to him."

"But is he here to talk to *you?*" He slapped me on the back again. My hands ached to shove him across the room; I had to force them into my pockets. "Lesson one, D-boy: never show up empty-handed, even if it's just pepper spray. Shit won't go down nine times out of ten, but that tenth time . . ." He eyed me, a tiny smirk playing over his busted lips. "What's the matter, kid? You scared of something?"

Oh, hell *no,* Chill Dave drawled. *We did not get this far just to back down from Seth Tinetti.*

"Not at all," I said, flashing that Dave smile. "Why? You think I should be?"

We stared at each other, unblinking. He looked away first.

"As long as Chet has my cash, there won't be a problem in the world."

The lights were on, but the hallway outside the greenroom and restrooms was empty. We rounded the corner together, expecting to find Chet leaning against the wall, or texting, maybe still messing around with the props. The storage room door, however, was closed. The hall, apart from what was fast becoming the Frightmares trademark stench, was deserted.

"What the hell?" Seth muttered. "Where is he?"

"He probably ghosted us."

"Dude, he better damn well not have. If this is how he handles business, that kid'll go missing for real someday." He pulled out his phone again and spoke into the voice-text app. "Chet, man, this ain't funny. If you don't—"

"WHO'S THERE?"

An electric jolt slammed through my veins. Seth's phone clattered to the ground. We stared down the still-empty hall, sensing the unseen presence just around the bend. The shout had come from somewhere close by but out of sight, down near the entrance of Dolls Alive!. Was there someone in the building other than us and Chet—or was it actually Chet himself, playing some sort of messed-up game?

"THE HELL YOU MEAN, 'WHO'S THERE?'" Seth yelled back. "THIS IS MY MA'S PLACE—YOU TELL *ME* 'WHO'S THERE.'"

"Seth?" Josie peeked around the corner, eyes wide, bewilderment written all over her face. "You scared the hell out of me. How did—"

She stopped short at the sight of me. Her eyeballs practically dropped from their sockets.

"Hey, Jo," I said, sheepishly. "What's up?"

"*Dave?* What are you *doing* here?"

She walked toward us, Ollie's phone in one hand, a Starbucks iced coffee sweating in the other. Her eyes were wide and confused, rimmed in dark green shadow that matched her halter dress. The soles of her steel-toed Docs squeaked on the linoleum, echoing weirdly in the quiet hall.

"We're supposed to meet someone." Seth eyed her warily. "What are *you* doing here?"

"Ollie had to turn on Loretta's computer. He can access her desktop from his devices, but she must have turned it off last night, because he couldn't log on." She rolled her eyes. "He's being a butt—he didn't want me to tag along, but I needed something from my locker, and then he had to break down some boxes in the greenroom, and—"

A hollow ringing swelled in my ears, blotting out the rest of Josie's explanation. Loretta had shared her desktop with Ollie.

This was a problem.

He could see what happened on her screen in real time. And if he could access the desktop, he probably knew Loretta's passwords—which meant he could get to the camera footage. He could pull up the live feed. He might even be able to see what I'd done in OneDrive. My guts turned to ice at the idea of Ollie, lounging in the comfort of his own home, watching me and Maya follow through on the string of bad decisions that defined the past several days of my life. And now he was in the greenroom and would definitely want to know why I was sneaking around in here with Seth hours before shift. This was *bad*.

Calm down, Bethany said. *If he'd seen any of that stuff, you'd both have been fired days ago. The Chet thing is obviously blown, so be cool, and focus on getting out of here.*

"Okay, well, we should probably go." The words came out of my mouth, but they felt far away, as if shaped by someone else's voice. I grinned wildly, taking what was definitely not a casual step backward. Seth and Josie stared at me, like I was the one high on Percs. "Since our guy's not here and all. I'll see you tonight, right, Josie? Or—"

"Jo, baby, you ready? Just need to drop these in the break-room, and—hey."

My heart sank. Ollie appeared around the corner and stopped at the sight of our little gathering, confusion clashing with surprise on his face. He had a stack of file folders in one hand and a retracted box cutter in the other. Two sleeves of paper coffee cups were tucked beneath his arm.

"Hey, man." Seth was the first to break the silence. "Everything good?"

"Fine," Ollie answered, eyes moving back and forth between us. "Taking care of business."

"Us too. We were supposed to meet—"

"WHAT THE HELL?"

Josie's yell blew apart the rest of Seth's explanation. She gripped Ollie's phone like it was frozen to her hand, gaping at the screen.

"Oh my god. Ollie. Ollie, *Chet* just texted you."

Oh, shit, Chill Dave muttered as I froze, hoping my face was set in neutral. *Probably should've blocked that number on his phone while we had the chance, huh?*

"Chet?" Ollie pocketed the box cutter and peered over Josie's shoulder at the text, read it aloud with an eyebrow raised. "*'I'm here, man, just like we arranged. Check the storage room for what you've been missing.'* Arranged? I never—what the hell *is* this?"

"Missing?" Seth scoffed. "He wants to come in here and talk about what's missing—when he takes half my supply and disappears? I didn't drive all the way out here to play hide-and-seek in the goddamn storage room."

"You were meeting *Chet*?" Josie yelped. "Dude, did they find him? Is he okay?"

"He won't be if he doesn't pay what he owes me. Get that door open, Dave. If there's no cash in there, I'll track his ass down and *show* him what's missing. I'll—"

The sentence turned to a gurgle. The pizza, the Four Loko, and whatever else Seth had eaten that day shot from his mouth and nose in foul chunks and splattered at his feet. Ollie's files and cups clattered to the floor as he spun away, gagging. Josie's shriek ricocheted off the walls. Her coffee cup hit the ground, its contents splattering her boots. I recoiled instantly, choking on a breath I wish I hadn't taken. If I'd had anything in my stomach, I'd have tripled the size of Seth's vomit puddle without breaking a sweat.

I'd done exactly what he'd asked: I'd reached past Josie and opened the storage room door, revealing piles of props, stacks of mannequin parts, and—yes—the thing we'd been missing. The source of the stench we'd explained away over and over, blaming the building foundation, spoiled food, our rat problem. Now it hit us all full in the face.

Chet was in the storage room, all right. From the looks of it, he'd *been* in the storage room, for way more than a couple days. His face was a bloated, rotten monstrosity, skin sagging on the frame of his bones. His eyes were half gone; so were his lips— they'd been chewed away in several places, exposing his teeth. Like something had crept in for a taste, scampered away, then returned for more.

Looks like we'd been right about the rats after all.

"Oh God!" Josie wailed, turning away from the sight. "No. Oh my God."

"Ah, Christ. Jesus *Christ*. What did you do, man? What did you *do*?" Seth's skin was ghost-white beneath his bruises as he turned to Ollie, shirt splattered with puke, face twisted with horror, confusion, betrayal. "This was *never* part of the plan."

chapter 27

I couldn't move. I couldn't breathe. The hallway doubled in length, tilted sideways, stretched out beyond comprehension. Reality shattered, re-formed, and broke apart again as I vaguely registered a growl of thunder, a whiff of petrichor, the muted thud of raindrops on the roof. Seth stood there seething, an angry red flush spreading from his neck up to his battered face. The sight of Chet's body had snapped him right out of the Percocet-induced calm.

"The *what?*" Josie finally choked out. "The *plan?* Seth, what are you—"

"You said you'd handle it." He ignored her and advanced on Ollie like a dog, bowing up his shoulders, clenching his hands into bruise-speckled fists. "You promised."

Ollie's eyes, though, were two question marks. He didn't look caught, or guilty, at Seth's sudden burst of rage—he looked as baffled as I felt. What was happening?

"Hey—handle what?" Ollie stepped carefully sideways, holding Seth's gaze. Moving the focus away from where Josie stood and keeping it on himself. "What *plan?* Dude, what are you talking about?"

"He was distribution, man!" Seth yelled. His hands clawed at his own cheeks, pressed too hard against his swollen eyes. "I told you I needed that money. You said you'd get it off him and fix everything. But this—this isn't fixing it, man."

"Jesus *Christ*, Seth!" Ollie shouted back. "Get your head on straight. I never said I'd fix a damn thing for you outside this workplace—I told you to find a side hustle if you needed extra cash, not get into some messed-up drug ring. I definitely never told you to drag Chet into any of it."

"But you went after him. You said his foot was lucky—I mean, luck—and you went while I drove, remember? And you said it was okay, but—"

"I said—*what*? You're high out of your goddamn mind. Listen to yourself—*nothing* you're saying makes sense. I didn't do *this*. Why would I kill anyone?"

"Because you're Levi."

I nearly blacked out at the sound of her voice. My legs went numb; my skin burned, then froze, then prickled with icy terror. I turned around slowly, wishing with every beat of my heart it would be anyone else on earth, even though I knew exactly who I'd see at the end of the hallway.

Every eye went to Maya as she strode toward us. Her sandals slapped against the floor. Rain dotted her T-shirt and cutoffs and glittered in her hair, which was pushed back from her flushed, determined face. This was suddenly so much worse.

You happy now, bro? Anxiety Dave screamed. *You could've done the smart thing for once and quit this place last week, but no—you had to be all up in here like it's an episode of goddamn* Riverdale. *Are you the big hero yet? Or will you only let this end when the girl you love is dead at your feet?*

225

"Maya," I croaked. "What are you—"

"Doing here?" she retorted, quickening her pace. Panic welled in my gut, spilled out into the quickly shrinking space between us—twenty feet, then ten. "What are *you* doing here without *me*, Dave? I had a bad feeling all shift last night, so I put the doorstop in the Egypt room exit. When you didn't show up this morning, it was pretty easy to figure out where—"

Her words ended in a gag as the Chet stink hit her. She stopped short, eyes bugging out as they landed on the storage room and its rotten, hideous contents.

"Oh my *God*." She bent double, dry heaving into her cupped hand. "What the hell is *happening*?"

"Maya, go." I slammed the storage room door and started toward her, every instinct screaming at me to get her out—get her into open air and far away from Frightmares, no matter what it took. "Go back out the Egypt door and get help. Go *now*, before—"

"I'm not leaving you here!" she shouted through her hand. "He's Levi Towers." She looked past me to Ollie, whose face was absolutely blank. "I'm right, aren't I?"

"Wait. Why is that relevant?" Josie's head swiveled back and forth between Maya and Ollie, confusion poking holes through her terror. She scrubbed the tears from her cheeks with a trembling fist. "What's his name got to do with this?"

"Oh my God, Josie!" I yelled. "His name is *Levi*? And you *knew* that?"

"What the hell are you talking about? I've been with him for two years, Dave, of course I knew it. Oliver's his stage name— I thought *you* knew that, and—" Her voice rose, in volume and octave both. "Could someone *please* start making *sense*? Ollie—

Seth—someone had better *tell me* what's happening, or I *swear* I will burn this place to the ground."

"She doesn't know any of it," Maya whispered. Her eyes widened as they met mine, fear seeping in around the edges of her tough-girl stare. "Dave—"

"Know *what?*" Ollie interjected, eyes on Maya. "You have some weird theory about me, go ahead. I'd love to hear what you think you know."

"It's on your headshot in the lobby." She stared him down without flinching, even as she took another step backward. "Oliver West. Levi Towers. The only anagram that fit."

It was so simple I could hardly look at her. While my dumb ass had been texting a dead guy's phone, Maya's poet's brain had unraveled the answer. She must have been up all night working on it—trying every possible combination of letters on the headshots, matching them up with the names on the employee files until it clicked. The Levi thing had sunk its hooks in her the second we'd heard about it. She'd been right all along.

"Okaaaay," Ollie said. "I guess you . . . cracked that code? Seth's over here accusing me of *this*"—he gestured to the storage room—"actual *dead body* he found, and you're talking about *anagrams?* Jesus. Jo, give me the phone. We need to call the cops—who already *know* my name, by the way. Not like it's even a secret."

"It might not be a secret," Maya said, "but literally no one here calls you that. Except maybe Bethany."

Any modicum of chill Ollie had maintained blew apart. His outstretched hand dropped to his side, phone forgotten. His face went gray; his blue eyes bugged in their sockets. His mouth listed open like the door of a broken sarcophagus. Nothing came out. Not a single sound.

"Bethany?"

Seth's shaky voice cut through the silence. He swallowed and blinked, visibly wincing. Like the name itself hurt more than his face.

"Ollie," he began, "how does she know—"

"She *doesn't* know Bethany," Ollie snapped. "She doesn't know *anything*."

"I know enough to make a pretty good guess," Maya shot back, standing straight again. "I know Chet came back here Friday night and tried to get into the lobby. I know he walked around to the parking lot, where you can get in through the mummy room door. I know he probably did that at the very worst possible time, Seth." She turned to him as she spoke, her tone taking on a gentle edge. "That's what happened, isn't it? He *did* come back that night. You can tell me."

Seth stared at Maya, unblinking; then something in his expression shattered. His focus shifted past her to the wall, like he couldn't stand the sight of her—or, more accurately, like he couldn't bear to meet her gaze.

"I don't remember," he finally muttered. "Chet texted my burner after he walked out—said he'd be back with my money after closing. I had to stay late and fix the mummy—but then— there's this hole in my head, you know? This big, gaping blank space, where some really important shit should be, and I thought I put her in the van—but when I drove out to the groves, she was gone. I forgot Chet even showed up, until—Ollie, I don't know how it happened."

Maya's eyes met mine as Seth's words settled over the puke-spattered, rot-scented hallway, seeped into my head, and locked themselves into place. He'd skipped over the finer points, but it was easy enough to piece together the aftermath: he'd meant to *move* Bethany—stuff her in the van, dump her in the groves. Instead, Chet had shown up in the parking lot, likely while Seth was hauling the body from the room to the van. The rest had spun out from there. In the chaos, Seth had left the plan, the details, and the rest of reality in one of his many blackouts, hidden Bethany instead of moving her, and everything that happened next had been incidental. Chet was collateral damage. The sarcophagus was a choice of circumstance, unrelated to Mickey, or me, or anyone. If they'd been in Vamp, she'd probably have ended up in the coffin.

No one in their right mind would have left her out like that. Maya's words from the other night had touched, unknowingly, on the simple truth: Seth *hadn't* been in his right mind. Not that night, or any night since. He'd been a wreck for a long, long time. It was one of the many reasons he'd gotten dumped in the first place.

Either way, he'd done it. He'd killed Bethany.

"It wasn't even for me," Seth continued. "The money, I mean. I was gonna use whatever he brought in after his cut to help out my ma. That's all I wanted. But I can't do this anymore, man. I don't even know what's real."

"Seth," Ollie broke in, gently. "It's okay. You don't have to—"

"I *can't*," Seth repeated. His voice cracked, his face collapsed around the grotesque twist of his mouth. "I tried, Ollie—I did everything just like you told me. But I can't."

"Oh my God," Maya whispered. Her eyes widened in horror, darted between Ollie and Seth. "Seth, what did he tell you? What did he—"

"Ollie, what are they talking about?" Josie stepped in front of Seth, into the path of Ollie's furious gaze. "What *did* you tell him? What did you *do?*"

"I didn't do *anything!*" Ollie yelled. "I don't know what he's talking about. *He* doesn't even know. He needs to get help—*that's* what I've been telling him. Look at him—he's barely lucid. Seth, man, you need to calm down. Think about what you're saying. You need to sleep this off and get your head straight."

I blinked through the déjà vu as Ollie's pleas spooled out, an echo of every interaction I'd heard them have over the past week: Seth rambling, Ollie talking him down. Seth suffering, Ollie soothing. One relentlessly silencing the other every time he tried to speak.

For once, though, Seth wasn't in the mood to be silenced.

"The thing is," he broke in, "I've *been* thinking. I've been thinking hard, man. And I know that means shit to you. And you, and you." He pointed at Josie, then at me. "But you—" His finger drifted to Maya, then curled into a shaky fist. He tapped himself on the chest, eyes achingly desperate. "*You* see me, right? You don't know me, so you might actually listen—believe— and I know she's dead. I remember her on the floor, next to that mummy, and I remember having no idea how she got there. But the last thing I *do* remember before that, was walking through the graveyard vestibule and into that room and seeing the curtain swing closed on the far side. And not a minute later, *he* came walking through it."

Every eye followed his pointing finger to where Ollie stood.

"Seth," Ollie began, voice low. "You don't know what you're saying. You need to—"

"He freaked out on me," Seth continued, "going off about

how could I do this, what happened, why did I kill her. Saying I'd had a blackout—and at the time, I thought he must be right."

"I *was* right," Ollie hissed. "You were high as shit—you still had whatever you'd just snorted all over your face, for Christ's sake."

"I know!" Seth shouted, turning on him. "But something wasn't right—'cause you *whispered* at me. Any normal person would've yelled their head off and called the cops, but you were already talking about how you knew I didn't mean to do it, and this would get the place shut down for sure, so we had to hide her to protect my ma. You sent me to get the van, and when I opened the door, someone was there—Chet, I think, I can't picture it for sure, and the rest of it is gone—but I couldn't have killed Bethany. I *couldn't* have. I don't know shit anymore—half the time I can't tell you what day it is, or where I left my goddamn truck—but I know I loved her. And I never *once* touched a hair on her head. So, you tell *me* what happened that night, *Levi*."

They were squared off now, chest to chest, flame and hydrogen, ready to blow. I saw Josie move from the corner of my eye, shifting slowly into the space behind me. Maya stood frozen not six feet away. The length of my body, from head to toe. Way too close to their standoff. Her huge, frightened eyes found mine, sending a jolt through my heart. I needed to get her out.

"Maya, run," I hissed, holding her gaze. I took a careful step forward, ready to launch myself between her and them before everything exploded. "Go. Now."

"No," Ollie said. His voice was low, but steady. Not argumentative—he didn't bother daring us to disobey. That, for him, had never been an option. "No one's going anywhere."

"Bitch, try to stop me." Seth spread his arms wide, dangerously close to chest-bumping Ollie. "You're done giving me orders, you little—"

His words skittered into screams. Ollie's face never changed. His hand, however, had moved lightning-fast—slipped the box cutter from his pocket, thumbed the blade upward, and slashed in an arc through the air between them. Seth staggered backward and fell into me, howling, both hands pressed over his spurting cheek. We went to the ground together, taking Josie down with us. Ollie's phone shot out of her hand and spun down the hallway; my head smacked the cinder-block wall as I fell, snapping the world into a funhouse blur of colors and screams. I shoved Seth off me and staggered to my feet, shook my head until Frightmares settled into focus.

What I saw nearly stopped my heart.

Ollie had easily closed that final six feet between him and Maya. He stood behind her, calm-eyed and tranquil, forever patient. One hand was fisted in her hair. The other hand lay almost casually against her collarbone, fingers wrapped around the box cutter. The blade caught the glare of the overhead lights as he pressed it firmly to the fragile skin of her throat.

chapter 28

My stomach hollowed out. The floor rocked as I took a step forward; I ignored it and took another one. Ollie shifted his grip on the box cutter, stopping me in my tracks.

"Maya." The words felt thick on my tongue. "Are you okay?"

"She's fine," Ollie answered for her. He leaned forward until his cheek lined up with Maya's and put his lips right against her ear. Held my gaze without blinking as he spoke. "One more word out of you, sweetie, and I take your tongue. Understood?"

Maya's eyes slid closed, the blade shifting dangerously against her flesh as she nodded.

"Good. But if I even *think* you or your boy over there are trying to run, this goes straight through your neck."

"Ollie!" Josie shrieked from the floor. "What are you *doing*?"

"When'll it be enough, man?" Seth climbed to his feet and made his unsteady way to my side. His words were slurred; his severed cheek split as he spoke, gaping like a second mouth. It must have hurt like hell, but he didn't pause. "Let her go—she was never part of this. She's just a kid."

"She was sneaking through the place like a rat from day one," Ollie snarled, backing down the hallway. Taking Maya with him, farther from me with every step. "Saw her myself, live on camera—and unless you want to watch this 'kid' bleed out right here, all three of you will do exactly as I say. Now."

There was no other choice. He gestured for us to follow, and we did. He stopped at the door to Captive Countess, waited as we filed inside. Maya's face was blank; her eyes were fixed on the floor. I wanted nothing more than to rip the box cutter away and body-slam Ollie into another dimension. He must have seen it on my face because he shuffled backward as I passed, avoiding my gaze.

"In the set, all of you," he barked. "Touch that exit door, and she's dead. Seth, open the top drawer and get me the plastic bag."

My veins went icy as I recalled the contents of the top dresser drawer: Light bulbs. A prop eyeball. F/X blood. Zip ties. It didn't take a genius to guess which one Ollie was after. Seth's face, when he saw them, blanched beneath its mess of bruises.

"Ollie. Man, can we talk about this?"

"Seth, we were in this together. We still can be. Put a set of those on her and do what I say, and I'll let you walk out of here." Ollie hauled Maya past the barrier and over to the dresser, box cutter firmly at her throat as Seth fumbled with the zip ties. "Jo, get Dave tied up. Put him in the bed."

I backed away, but only made it a few steps before the bed frame hit my calves. The only thing keeping me from beating Ollie's entire ass was the box cutter; the way his eyes darted between me and the ropes indicated he knew better than to drop his guard before I was securely restrained. If I didn't stay on my feet, we were all dead.

"You don't have to do this, Josie," I hissed, heart breaking at the defeated lines of her face as she moved toward me. Shock, sorrow, and horror blended seamlessly beneath an utter lack of surprise. She wouldn't look at me. "Run—get out of here. I've got your—"

"Keep that up and see what happens," Ollie cut in. "Josie. Now. Unless Dave wants to watch me carve you up next."

I lowered myself to the mattress, seething with rage, ass wedged uncomfortably in the Josie hole. Her lips trembled as she leaned over to fit the restraints around my wrists. Her breath was low and erratic; her skin smelled of sunscreen, and fear sweat, and the sharp, cedarwood bite of her perfume. Her hands, however, were steady on the ropes. The tip of her finger slipped into my palm, quickly tapping out our code: one, two, three.

Ready or not.

My eyes stung, my blood raced, sweat broke out across my neck and shoulders as her message came through, loud and clear. She was my partner. She had my back.

It was showtime.

I didn't dare meet her eyes. I didn't try to jerk free, or fight, or kick her off me and leap from the bed. Instead, I let my own eyes fall shut, summoned every shred of hopelessness and despair until my face felt like a match for Josie's. Focused every bit of self-control I had on keeping my body still and my hands limp until the right moment. I would get one chance, and only one, to make this work.

When our shitty leather straps had snapped, Ollie had bought the rope to replace them, but left us to rig up the restraints. He had no idea I'd tied those nooses with an emphasis on safety rather than function. If he'd done the job himself like he was supposed to, we'd be screwed; now, we had the tiniest of upper hands. I had to take his focus off Maya and let him think I'd given up.

"What was your big plan, dude?" I said, voice tight with a fear that may not have been completely faked. "Jump me and Seth both with your box cutter? Leave us in the storage room and hope Loretta never went looking for the smell?"

"Not quite. I set it up last night—gasoline and rags in a couple key rooms. An electrical fire in a building like this? Even Loretta wouldn't be surprised."

It was too simple to be a lie. Whether he'd planned to bar the exits, or overpower us, or lock us in the storage closet with Chet was incidental—Ollie's Act Three ended with Frightmares in flames, and me and Seth trapped inside. He'd leave us here, burn the place down, and show up later in a state of shock and manufactured grief as the firemen sifted through the ash for our corpses. He'd have cooked up a new cover story by then, likely one centered on the drug money dispute. It wouldn't be hard at all to throw Seth under the bus for all of it, especially on the heels of his public blackout and ongoing downward spiral. No one on earth would take his word over Ollie's—hell, up until the box cutter appeared, I'd had zero problems believing this was all on Seth. Even *Seth* had believed it.

Ollie really thinks he'll walk away from this clean, Chill Dave snarled. *Oh, hell no.*

I couldn't just yank my wrists free and dive across the room, though. Unless Ollie dropped the box cutter, following through with my base impulse to leap over Josie and tear his fucking head off would trigger a guaranteed bloodbath. I couldn't call his bluff and risk Jo or Maya on the off chance he really was all talk. I had to stay calm. As soon as he was gone, I'd slip free of the nooses and find a way to get us out. For now, I had to play victim. I had to let him think he'd won.

"You don't have to do this, man," I pleaded over Josie's shoulder, desperate to keep him talking and distracted. "I get why I'm here. I do. I saw too much—I wouldn't leave it alone. But let Maya go, okay? She's not part of this. She only wanted to—"

"She made herself part of it. Didn't you get Chet's text?"

"What? No. My phone broke the other—" I stopped, every fiber of my soul cringing at the realization. He'd kept Chet's phone. Of course he had. He'd kept the phone and texted himself only moments ago, while we were in the hallway, probably hitting Send right before he came around the corner. Then he'd stood there and watched our faces change as he read that text out loud, knowing exactly what would happen next.

Way to solve the case and save the day, Chill Dave groaned. *I guess you* could *be more of a dumbass, but I'm just not sure* how.

I thought I'd been so slick, posing as Ollie. Getting the tone just right, setting up a friendly meeting, when I'd literally been texting him, *as* him, from his own number.

I deserved to die like this. I really did.

Ollie watched me as it sank in, a tiny smirk playing across his lips.

"Figures. But just so you know, 'Chet' texted you right before he told 'me' to check the storage closet, confirming he had the oxy you'd told him to bring. If your girl had stayed home, this could've all gotten pinned on him as a deal gone bad. Or, you know, if this waste of space over here hadn't messed up his one job Tuesday night. But what else is new, right?"

"*Seth?*" My eyes leaped from Ollie to Seth, whose shoulders slumped at the sound of his name. His hands stilled on the zip tie circling Maya's wrists as he turned to meet my furious gaze. I gaped at his bruised face and swollen eyes, stomach flipping. *I'd* done some of that damage—the railing had messed him up good, I'd seen the aftermath of that myself. But he'd looked like hell *before* he'd blacked out. I'd written it off as a hangover and bad makeup. I'd written *him* off, like everyone else, assuming him incapable of more than his usual failings.

He'd been more than capable, though, of putting up a fight. He'd choked me. He'd tackled me. He'd chased me through Frightmares, violent and relentless, in wings and robes and a blank, bloodstained mask.

He'd been the angel all along.

"What the hell did I ever do to you, man?" I shouted, nothing fake about the rage surging in my chest.

"Ollie said you knew," Seth muttered. "He said you found Bethany, and if you talked, the business would get shut down for sure. I don't care about myself anymore—I know I'm done. But this place is everything to my ma. Ollie texted me as I was leaving that night, said he saw you sneaking in on the cameras. 'Go full Ghostface if you have to,' he said. So, I did." He shook his head, eyes full of pity, and sorrow, and genuine shame. "You should've quit while you could, Dave. I wish you'd left when you found Bethany and just stayed gone."

It made sense—perfect, horrible sense. Seth had argued with Loretta while Maya and I were on the hood of my car. While I'd gone in through the side door and snuck to the office, Loretta must have driven off alone, none the wiser. Meanwhile, Seth had let himself in through the lobby, disarmed the alarm, donned the angel robes, and shut off the breakers. After that, all he'd had to do was wait for me to wander straight into his white-gloved hands.

If I'd run any slower that night, I'd be dead. If I'd been weaker, or injured, or off my game even in the slightest, he'd have killed me.

I should've known it was him. The way the sight of Maya had stopped him in his tracks—he'd reacted like that since day one. Like if he stared hard enough at Bethany's replacement, she'd turn to him and smile with the face he'd loved. Like he couldn't bear to see a stranger where his girl had been. If I'd put those details together sooner, it would have been obvious.

We might not be trapped here, waiting to burn.

We're dealing with a true psychopath, Maya had said. And I didn't doubt we were—but almost none of this had been Seth's idea.

"So yeah, Seth messed it up for me, himself, and everyone else," Ollie said. "I'm sure you're all thoroughly shocked. But, like I said, it's too late now."

"It doesn't have to be," I said. "You can stop this any time you want."

"I honestly wish I could." Ollie gave me a small smile, sadness creeping into his voice. "For what it's worth, Dave, I'm sorry. You're a good kid, even though you're dumb as hell." He gestured to Maya's wrists with his chin, impatience hardening his voice and straining the seams of his calm demeanor. "Quit screwing around, Seth. Get those on tighter, hook it to the drawer handle, and get her ankles, so she can't run. Do it now, and you walk out of here—or you can stay with them and die. Your call."

Something gave way in my chest as the box cutter fell away from Maya's throat. I caught her eyes over Seth's shoulder, not daring to broadcast even a drop of reassurance. Hers were frightened but calm, not a tear in sight. Tough to the end.

Ollie waited until Seth was looping a zip tie to the drawer handle before crossing to Josie, taking the bag with him. She backed away from him, leading him to the foot of the bed. I braced myself, expecting him to hit her, or shove her down. Instead, he took her by the shoulders and guided her to the floor, kneeling beside her as he spoke.

"I didn't want *you* here either," he told her softly. "I told you to stay home for a reason, but you never listen, do you? You always have to push back, every time I tell you no."

She didn't answer. She didn't flinch. He reached out to smooth her hair, trailing his fingers gently across her tearstained cheek.

"I never wanted to hurt you, Jo. And I'm—" His voice broke as he looped a zip cord around her wrists and pulled it tight. "I'm sorry. Seth's not wrong—this was never part of the plan."

"Okay," she whispered. "It's okay, Ollie. I love you."

His hands stilled. He stared at her, lips parted, searching for words.

"You—what?"

"What do you mean, *what?*" Her voice went hard at that; her lips curled up in an insulted snarl, even as her eyes overflowed. "We said forever, remember? Thick and thin. I've never said that to anyone else, you *know* that. I swore I'd love you till the end of my life. If *this*—right now—is the end? *I* kept that vow. Even if you didn't."

"*Josie!*" I screamed, hoping like hell I could pull off an improv

240

when I was closer to wetting my pants than winning an Oscar. "What are you *doing?*"

She didn't so much as glance my way. She hovered on her knees, meek and submissive, cheeks wet, lips parted. Gazing at Ollie with eyes that leaked perfect, fat, black mascara tears. She was the Countess, braced for the downswing.

She was the wild card, about to blow up his game.

"You wouldn't have kept it," Ollie muttered. "I cheated on you, Jo—I didn't plan it, but I did. Bethany was going to tell you. She was going to ruin everything."

"*You* tell me, then. There's no limit to 'thick and thin,' not with us. Tell me your side—everything—and I can forgive you. I swear."

Ollie studied her, taking in her loving smile and unwavering gaze. I snuck a look at Seth, who'd gone completely still. His shoulders tensed, his breath had quickened at the sound of Bethany's name. His head turned slowly toward Ollie. I caught sight of his expression as the pieces came together—his jaw was clenched, his mouth was a line. His eyes were incandescent.

He's never heard this story either, Bethany whispered. *He had no idea.*

"You already know about the first time," Ollie began. "She'd been fighting with Seth—he was high as shit, he'd blown her off again, stranded her without a ride so he could go close a deal. Same old story. She stayed late with me that night, and—she was really upset, and I know that's no excuse—I never meant for it to go further. But whenever I stayed late after that, she—"

"She stayed too?"

"Yes," he whispered, shamefaced. "Every time. She came up

to me Friday before shift, said she'd made plans to go down to that goddamn casting call together, make it into a getaway weekend. She wanted to be with me out in the open, where we wouldn't run into anyone we knew. I said no, and she freaked out—she was a mess that night, remember? Spent half the shift melting down. After you and Dave left, she caught up to me and said I had to make a choice or she'd go straight to you and ruin everything we had. I told her I was done with ultimatums, and with her, and she slapped me—" He faltered, shuddering, squeezed his eyes shut, as if he couldn't stand reliving it. As if he'd relived it already, a million times since. "It escalated. She started screaming, and I grabbed her by—I didn't mean to *kill* her. I wanted her to *stop*. Now everything is ruined anyway. *We're* ruined, Josie. I'm so sorry."

"No, baby," Josie breathed. "We're not ruined—I've always been here for you, Oll. I'm *still* here."

I shifted quietly, darting my eyes to Maya. Her eyes were locked on Seth. Blood still trickled from his face and down his neck, soaking the collar of his T-shirt. His hands, for once, were steady. The right one slid slowly into the front pocket of his cargo shorts, withdrew something small and flat. I heard a tiny *snick*; the silver gleam of a blade appeared inches from Maya's skin. He moved like a snake, slipping the blade between her wrists. The zip tie fell away like it was made of silk. Seth held her eyes for a moment, then turned his back on her, pivoting his focus to the scene spooling out near my feet.

I refocused on that travesty, afraid to breathe. The room was a hush of Josie's sniffles and the steady *whoosh* of rain on the roof— typical Florida thunderstorm, water riding on wind, drops thick enough to drown. Maya inched sideways, carefully making her way to the emergency exit. Had Seth reset the alarm? Had Ollie? Either way, once she reached the set curtain, stealth would no longer be a thing. She'd have to haul it aside on its squeaky runner. She'd have to open the door, which was loud as hell. Then she'd have to book it, as fast as she could, and hope her head start was enough to outrun Ollie. I began shifting my right wrist slowly, unlooping the rope from its false binding on the bedpost, trying not to catch his eye.

For the moment, though, I was the last thing on his mind. He gazed at Josie in wonderment, kissed the tears off her compliant cheeks. The rest of us might as well have already been ash.

"You really mean it, don't you?" he whispered. "We can still—? Oh, Jo. Here, don't move." He fumbled with the box cutter, sliding it carefully between the zip tie and her skin. "Are you okay? I never want to hurt you. I'd die first, I swear to God."

"I'm okay." She brought her forehead to his, cupping his face in her freed hands. "We're okay."

The box cutter thudded to the floor. Ollie's fingers moved gently over Josie's wrists, massaging the marks left by the zip ties. I glimpsed his face over her shoulder as her arms slid around his neck. His smile was soft and blissful. His eyes were half closed. His skin flushed pink with pleasure, then drained dead white all at once as the switchblade slashed through his back, unzipping the flesh across his deltoids.

"Oh, sorry, bro!" Seth yelled over Ollie's agonized wail. "I didn't *mean* to do it—it *escalated*."

He made another downward slash with the blade, slicing open Ollie's upraised arm. Ollie reared back to defend himself—to get

243

away—but he couldn't get his balance. He couldn't stand, or turn, or do anything at all. Not with Josie's elbow locked around his throat.

"JOSIE!" he screamed. "WHAT ARE YOU—"

"YOU DID THIS TO *YOURSELF*!" she shrieked. "I HOPE IT WAS WORTH IT, OLLIE."

Seth took another swipe but missed. He shook his head, dazed and off-balance. The cut on his face had reopened—he'd lost so much blood it was damn near a miracle he wasn't dead. Still, he managed to bring his foot down on the box cutter and kick it backward, seconds before Ollie's fingers could close over the handle.

Ollie's yell cut off abruptly. He clawed frantically at Josie's forearm, gasping for air, slammed his head backward into her mouth. She howled and tightened her grip, sank her teeth into the back of his flailing hand. Seth slashed wildly at him a final time, his bellow of rage ricocheting into a moan as Ollie's heel connected solidly with the side of his knee. Seth dropped like a sack of rocks; the switchblade flew from his hand and disappeared.

The bed frame jolted beneath me. Ollie reared backward once—twice—slamming Josie's head into the foot post. Her arms went slack for an instant, just long enough for him to throw her off. She collapsed, sliding out of sight. He crawled for the box cutter, which had spun away and lay by the dresser. Then Seth was back on him, rolling Ollie faceup and slamming his head into the ground, trying like hell to pin him down. Ollie's eyes were wide and furious—and locked on Maya, who'd made it halfway to the door. My heart stopped as she faltered, turned, and took a step back toward me. She didn't know about these ropes either.

Ollie wrenched a hand free and clawed it across Seth's wounded face. Seth fell to the side, yowling like an animal, and Ollie was pulling himself upright on the bed next to me, just as I freed the rope from its final loop. He was dazed, and trembling, pouring blood from his back and arm and the crescent on his hand where Josie's teeth had broken the skin. He was still going, like some unreal horror-movie monster. He was inches away.

Our gazes locked; something flared in his eyes, and for a brief, horrible instant, I saw my friend. He was sad and sorry, defiant and ashamed, thoroughly terrified, and desperate for an out. I gaped at him, seized by a deep, instinctive pity. I almost hesitated.

Then, Josie's fingers appeared at the footboard, curled over the railing as she pulled herself up. Her moans joined Seth's ragged gasps. He sprawled on the floor between us and the exit, barely conscious; his switchblade was God knows where. I was our only chance.

"GO! NOW!" I yelled, yanking both arms forward. The rope slid effortlessly through the headboard spindle, exactly as I'd rigged it to do. "MAYA. GO."

Her hair flew behind her as she sprinted to the set curtain, yanked it back, and slammed through the exit and into the storm. A gust of warm, thick air blew in, followed by a spray of rain. The door stayed open on its shitty hinge pin. I heard her footfalls splash through the parking lot as Ollie whipped around. I caught his shirt and hauled him backward; he dug his heels in, unrelenting. The fabric tore along the switchblade slash and came apart in my hands. He fell to his knees, scrabbling across the floor and out of reach. He was getting away.

YOU SCREW THIS UP, EVERYONE DIES, Anxiety Dave howled. *GET HIM ON HIS ASS ANY WAY YOU CAN, AND DON'T YOU DARE LET HIM GO.*

I yanked my hand out of the left noose and leaped from the bed, taking the rest of the rope with me. It flew back through the spindle and caught on the bedpost, yanking my arm back and damn near dislocating my shoulder. I couldn't stop—I had to reach him. It had to be enough.

It was. Ollie went to the floor, my knee in the center of his back, just as his hand closed over the box cutter. He twisted beneath me and lashed out with the blade, missing my leg by inches. I rolled away as he took another swipe, adrenaline-clumsy, gasping for breath. My head was a wasp nest; my shoulder wept.

Ollie pulled himself up on the dresser, box cutter clutched in one shaking hand. He radiated pain. Every move was stiff and stunted, like his body was one deep breath from cracking apart. I was on my knees and tethered to the bed; still, he was no match for me even on his best day—and this day was definitely not that. I got to my feet, eyes locked on his, braced for an attack that never came. Instead, he backed out of reach, turned toward the exit— then stopped, frozen to the spot.

Josie stood between him and the door, hair storm-blown, dress, arms, and shoulders soaked in red. Her fingers were steady and scratched bloody, and wrapped around the handle of Seth's switchblade.

"Is this the way you wanted it, baby?" Ollie whispered. "The thick and thin?"

He took a step toward her. Another. I was still clawing at the noose, which had somehow knotted up on itself. I hauled the rope

246

slack out of the way, frantically working the other end out from the headboard spindles as Josie raised the blade between them.

"Ollie. Stop this."

He slashed the box cutter halfheartedly through the space between them, less an attempt to connect than to make her back down. She flinched away but held her ground. He wasn't quick anymore. His confidence, his strength, the element of surprise, all of it was gone. Still, his arm made another clumsy, wide arc through the air. Josie feinted at him with the switchblade, face twisting in fury and frustration. Her reach was too short. Close enough to cut him would be *too* close.

"Do it." The words came out of him in pieces. "Only one of us walks out of here, Jo. I want it to be you."

"SHUT YOUR MOUTH!" she screamed. "You don't get to say who lives or dies. You don't make that call for *anyone* here."

Ollie was silent for a moment, then shook his head.

"Looks like you're making it for me."

He lunged at her, just as the rope pulled free of the bed frame. I turned in time to see Josie's body twist, her back shoulder drop, and her right boot snap forward, its steel-toed tip connecting solidly with Ollie's shin. He howled as he collapsed, catching her around the legs. The box cutter and the switchblade both went airborne. Then he was on her, knees straddling her waist, hands locked around her throat.

I sprinted across the room, pushing past fatigue, ignoring the throb in my shoulder and head. I had no plan. I had a rope, my rage, and a singular thought wailing through my head:

Take him down.

I never got the chance.

Before I could showcase my wide variety of ass-kicking skills, a figure appeared in the open doorway, enormous and windswept and covered in rain. Mickey stepped over Seth, crossed the room in three strides, and caught Ollie by the shirtfront, physically lifting him up and off of Josie. Ollie took a single, furious swing at Mickey; then he was flying through the air, right past my stunned face. He was crashing into the barricade and sliding to the floor, barely conscious.

Mickey was on him in a second anyway, pinning him down, motioning me over.

"Bring that rope over here. Get him tied up before—" He shook his head. "Man, I can't use that when it's wound up on your arm. Loretta needs to get some handcuffs, or some kind of useful shit in this place."

I grabbed the bag of zip ties from the floor near the footboard and tossed them over, then found the switchblade and went to work sawing the goddamn rope off my wrist. Mickey secured Ollie's hands and feet with about five hundred zip ties and left him there. He crossed the room to where Josie lay and crouched next to her gasping form.

"Jo, you okay? Jojo?" He brushed the hair out of her fluttering eyes. She blinked past him, dazed and unfocused. "Hey. Jo, come on. Come on back."

"Mickey?" she finally whispered. "How are you even—"

"I was online when you went live. I clicked on it in time to hear—well. I heard enough." He moved to check on Seth, who'd gone still. "Damn. Okay. That ambulance can make its entrance any time now."

"Maya," I blurted, shaking off the last of the rope and dropping it next to the box cutter. "Mickey, did you see—"

"She's fine. Girl almost dove in front of the motorcycle when

I pulled in, yelling about everyone tied up in here, and—" He cut himself off, chuckling at the grin splitting my face in two. "Go check up on her, Davey, before she passes out. I've got this."

If he hadn't already turned his attention back to Josie, I'd have full-on hugged him.

Instead, I ran for the door and into the storm, frantically searching until my eyes found what they were seeking—the most beautiful, unreal, awesomely mind-blowing sight I'd ever see.

Maya Green, alive and whole, splashing her way across the parking lot. Running straight for me, through a sideways gust of rain.

epilogue

The sky was a steely blue stretch of parasailers, aerial banner planes, and far-off storm clouds rimming the flat, gray ocean. The beach was crowded for a weekday, even though the waves were garbage. Umbrellas and towels were scattered across the sand, mostly occupied by sunbathing tourists and soggy, grit-crusted toddlers surrounded by bright plastic beach toys. Josie and I lounged on a blanket near the dunes, watching four seagulls fight over an abandoned bag of Doritos. A guy on a wakeboard skidded past Maya, veering dangerously close to the huge sandcastle she and Mickey were building down at the tide line. It was surreal, seeing them mess around like kids, when our last gathering had ended in us nearly being burned alive in our workplace.

Yeah. *Surreal* was definitely a word for it.

My parents didn't lose their shit *all* the way over my part in The Frightmares Nightmares, as the media called it, but they came close. It didn't help that they'd heard the news report while still at sea, the day before their ship returned to port. Luckily, they'd been too busy phasing between guilt and relief to do more than take my car keys for a couple days while the window got replaced. Since Maya's house was within walking distance, all it did was give me an excuse to see no one but her during my "punishment." Which, to be honest, was perfectly fine with me.

Now, three weeks after being almost murdered, I'd finally managed to sleep through the night for the first time since finding Bethany. I'd woken to a text on my new phone: Josie, asking me to hang out with her and Mickey. Our usual Blacklist/Denny's routine felt like a hard no on all sides, so when she'd suggested a beach day, I'd wasted no time collecting Maya and driving the hour east to Cape Canaveral. It was the closest thing we'd had to an actual date, which was something I needed to rectify ASAP. If we wanted our relationship to work in the real world, we'd have to venture into it at some point—an initiative neither of us had made much effort to take in the nineteen days since we'd made Us official.

It was borderline scary, the need to keep her in my line of sight—like if I so much as blinked, she'd vanish into nothing and it would be all my fault. I had to remind myself constantly that Ollie was locked up. That Maya was safe. That she was tough, and capable, and didn't need me checking around corners or lurking like a paranoid guard dog every time she left the house. The struggle, however, was very real—even now, in broad daylight on a well-populated beach, I couldn't take my eyes off her.

Josie was overflowing with news, everything from her new agency contract to the twenty thousand followers she'd gained since her video of Seth and Ollie's showdown went viral. As far as I was concerned, her actions had been key to us all surviving that day. She'd gone live on her promo account right before

Ollie had pulled the box cutter. Mickey had seen the notification, clicked on it to show support, and been treated to a livestream of Seth getting his face carved open in the Frightmares hallway. The phone had been knocked down the corridor moments later, but Mickey was already on his way. He'd found Maya in the parking lot and had her call 911 with his phone while he rushed to our rescue.

Once the ambulance arrived, followed shortly by the cops and Loretta, the place devolved into a mess of local media and yellow police tape, detectives and forensic experts and God knows who else combing over every inch of the building. They'd found Ollie's arson setup, Seth's stash in his locker, and, of course, Chet's body. Josie, Mickey, Maya, and I had been separated and questioned, which only led to more confusion and an official trip to the police station to give formal statements. Luckily, Loretta had declined to press charges against me and Maya for our multiple after-hours break-ins. And, to her credit, she'd also refused to capitalize on the real-life horror show that had played out in her establishment. Frightmares was closed until further notice.

My side of the story, it turned out, was the least of it. Between what we'd heard of Seth's side, and Ollie's confession in the aftermath, the rest had come together piece by piece.

When Chet had returned that night with the money, he'd caught Seth and Ollie preparing to load Bethany's body into the company van. Ollie told Seth to take care of Bethany and fix the mummy, while he went after Chet—who'd been caught easily, due to his injured foot. Seth, who was shocked, grief-stricken, and already high as hell, hid Bethany in the sarcophagus, dropped the mummy behind the set curtain, and left in the van. When he reached the groves and realized Bethany wasn't there, he panicked, went home, then blacked out again, waking with no clear memory of the night's events. He hadn't even known Chet was dead until I'd opened the storage room door.

While Seth was off driving around in the empty van, Ollie had lain low at Frightmares, waiting for him to return. When that didn't happen, he'd taken Chet's phone and put him in the storage room, knowing he'd have to wait until he had the van back to get rid of him. He'd already taken Bethany's phone off her, planning to send her resignation the next morning. When Josie had unexpectedly responded to the text, he'd replied back as "Bethany," thinking that was the end of it—until he looked up from his seat in the ticket booth during Saturday's shift to the sight of my gold-painted ass running down the sidewalk. Worried there'd been a glitch in the tour, he'd rushed to the mummy room and found Bethany on the floor. He'd grabbed Seth from next door while Loretta was giving the pre-tour speech to the next group; together they'd hidden Bethany behind the set curtain, reattached the mummy, and lifted the sarcophagus quickly back into place. Ollie had made it back to the booth before I returned and blamed his absence on a bathroom break.

That night, he'd snuck out before postshow and used his work-issued key to load Bethany into the company van. He then had Seth drive the van out and dump the body after closing, while he made sure to be seen leaving with Josie. He'd left Chet in the storage room because he simply never got the chance to move him—Seth was already deep in a grief spiral, and Josie had been on Ollie like a burr during their off-work hours, dragging him to the mall, and to Blacklist, and everywhere else she went. When Ollie saw Maya and me on the security feed, sneaking around after closing, he'd emptied Bethany's locker, sent Seth after me, and come up with a last-ditch idea to take care of all of us at once.

To say things hadn't gone according to plan was an understatement. At least he'd have plenty of time in his pretrial detention center to puzzle over what went wrong.

Seth, for his part, had gone straight from the hospital to in-patient rehab. From what I heard he was putting in the work to recover, physically and psychologically. And, though he'd racked up no small number of his own charges, he also threw Ollie to the wolves without hesitation, offering a full testimony in exchange for leniency. He'd spilled everything he knew—or, at least, everything he remembered.

He did know enough to lead the police to the groves, and the shallow, unmarked hole where Bethany was buried. Her body was recovered a week to the day after she'd died. Her voice hadn't been in my head since, a detail I only fully realized when, deep in a postnightmare conversation with the Daves, I'd caught myself waiting for her to chime in and got nothing but silence. I hadn't realized how much I missed her until she was gone for real, in every way.

I had to be okay with it. That voice had never been mine to keep.

A group of kids descended upon Mickey and Maya, who put them to work on the already ridiculously large sandcastle. Josie, who could always sense better than anyone my nervous energy and need for distraction, kept up a steady stream of commentary and conversation. Between that and the million questions she had regarding my parents' reaction and the physical therapy for my shoulder, I didn't get a chance to interrogate her until we'd been there half the day.

"So," I finally butted in when she paused for breath. "You and Mickey, huh? Is this a play-within-a-play thing, or the real deal?"

"Bite your tongue, child. I am absolutely done with men for the immediate future." She shook her head at my raised eyebrow. "Don't give me that Skeptical Dave look. He's the best friend I've got, and that's it."

"For now."

"For now," she conceded. "And yes, if I ever hate myself enough to start dating again, it'll probably be because of him. Someday. Maybe. He still feels bad about scaring you, by the way. If it helps, it was my idea."

As it turned out, I *hadn't* imagined the motorcycle in my neighborhood—it had been Mickey after all, doing drive-by stealth checkups at Josie's request. Me being a hot mess in the workplace had them more than a little concerned, but they didn't want to make a whole big thing out of it. Instead, Mickey had parked around the bend a block away from my house, approached on foot, and lingered just long enough to make sure I was safe at home. Apparently he'd done this a few more times than I'd noticed, which did little for my faith in my own level of awareness. Or Trent Roznor's future as a reliable watchdog.

"And speaking of 'more than friends,'" she continued, nodding to Maya, "I see you still owe me that Chipotle."

"You earned it after the way you saved us," I said, cringing at the memory of me stuck in those ridiculous ropes while she faced off against Ollie like the badass she was. "You were the perfect wild card."

"Everyone in that room was a goddamn wild card. Ollie most of all." She shook her head, staring bleakly at the horizon. "A love like ours doesn't happen every day, you know. Perhaps it's not too late to reconcile."

"Um," I hedged, stomach dropping at the thought. "That's— Wow. I get that you have lots of emotions tied up in this, Jo, but—"

"My *God*," she scoffed, cutting me off with a glare. "Do I really just scream 'desperation'? Like I'm still hot for a literal cheating murderer? Dave. If you don't start appreciating my sarcasm, I swear to God."

"Touché." I blocked her playful smack. "But, Jo—are you sure you're okay? I'm here if you need to—you know. Talk. Or if you maybe need counseling, I can ask—"

"You're sweet, baby son, but I'm covered. Right now, what I need is to move on. *All* the way on, from every aspect of that job and the life tied up in it."

"Can Disney casting handle Josie Manning, is the real question."

"They absolutely can't, but moving on includes being done with Greater Orlando. A girl I know from Blacklist is starting her own indie production company over in Tampa—like Kevin Smith but for horror, is her pitch. I went to high school with the boom guy, and he says they're looking for talent with SAG cards. Which I just so happen to be."

"The boom guy, huh?" I smirked at her eye roll, nudging her with my shoulder until she palmed my face.

"Yes, the boom guy. And yes, he is smoking hot—but he's also formed entirely of styling gel and bad decisions, so no thanks. Anyway, who needs a boom guy when I'll have *that* guy?"

Josie gestured to Mickey, who was now on his hands and knees at the water's edge, scooping out a moat around the sandcastle. Maya kneeled a few feet away, sorting through a pile of shells.

"So, you're not seeing Mickey, but you're bringing him to Tampa?" I raised an eyebrow at her faint blush. "What happened to moving on?"

"I can move on without leaving him behind. Some people are worth keeping close, wherever things end up."

We got to our feet as Mickey finished digging, seconds before the tide came in. He and Maya watched the moat fill with seawater, then rejoined us, abandoning their kingdom to the gleeful, shrieking kids.

"Ready to head out, Jojo?" Mickey said, gesturing to the darkening sky. "We should get back before those clouds roll in."

"Ready when you are."

He shook out the blanket as Josie said her goodbyes, pulling me into a long hug. They walked away side by side, hands almost touching, leaving us behind.

"Is she okay?" Maya asked, watching them go. "Mickey was all smiles, but I can tell he's worried."

"She's holding up. Not sure how she'll handle the trial coverage once it starts, but she'll be long gone by then. New job, new city, Mickey . . . I think she'll be okay. And if they don't work out, I hear there's a hot boom guy."

"Lucky her." Her laugh sent a thrill across my skin. "If only we all had a hot boom guy on the back burner."

"You can join them if you want." I grinned. "Swap your notebook for a SAG card. Tell your horror story to the silver screen."

"They're not ready for my horror story. Besides"—she nudged me gently with her shoulder—"I have my reasons to stay local."

"Yeah? Those must be some damn fine reasons."

Her smile set my pulse on fire. Her skin was spattered with seawater, not blood; her legs and feet were coated with sand, not zip-tied and bloated and rotting off in pieces. I smiled back, letting myself sink into those eyes. Refusing to picture them blank and lifeless, as they'd appeared in my nightmares ever since that day.

"So far, so good," she teased. "I'm hanging on to them as long as I can—if all parties involved agree."

"They do." I caught her hand, linking my fingers gently through hers.

She stood on tiptoe to kiss me, then slid an arm around my waist, rested her head on my shoulder, and stared out at the sea. I let myself breathe in the salt air, let the sun soak into my skin and the breeze brush my face. It was calm here—*I* was calm.

Maya and I would have the summer together, then see where things went from there. It could be good—it might even be great. And there didn't need to be a word for how I felt. Whatever Anxiety Dave might have labeled it in a haze of mortal terror, it was enough for now to bask in without giving it voice. I didn't need to say it to know it was real.

We had plenty of time to take things slow.

Sure, man. Can't wait to see how you and Maya Green mesh when you're not at the literal edge of death. I'm sure you two are super compatible.

I ignored Chill Dave and tightened my arm around Maya, scanned the beach for anything weird or out of place. Which was something I probably wouldn't stop doing for a long, long time.

Christ. I had to get it together. I couldn't keep looking over my shoulder for a glinting blade. I couldn't spend life sniffing the air for the reek of rotten flesh.

It's nothing, I thought, tensing as a shadow fell across the ground—the long shape of a figure, approaching from behind, drawing nearer with every step. Footfalls barely audible in the soft, dry sand. *It's no one. If I don't look back, I'll be okay.*

It was fine. Everything was going to be fine.

Acknowledgments

This book was inspired by, of all things, a typo. The fact that it now exists in tangible form is irrefutable proof that there is no One Correct Way to traverse the idea-to-book journey. This journey, however, would not have been half as enjoyable without the help of those who made it possible.

Huge thanks goes to my editor, Ali Romig, for taking a chance on an idea and letting me turn it into this book. I am so lucky to work with someone who let me bring the fun as well as the fear, and who shares my love of '90s pop horror. I've never had such a blast conjuring a story to life. Endless gratitude also to Wendy Loggia and the team at Delacorte/Underlined for everything you do. I am so excited and proud to publish under this imprint.

Christa Heschke, your constant support and encouragement never fails to astound me. Thank you for this and every opportunity you've brought my way, and for answering all my wild ideas with an immediate yes, no matter where they take us. I am so thankful for you, Daniele Hunter, and the rest of Team M&O for your amazing work and enduring confidence in me.

These pages would be glaringly incomplete without mention

of two of my favorite authors. Jill Corddry, without you (and my ridiculous phone) there would be no Dave. There would also be no one who so thoroughly embraces my visions or follows them so gladly down their weird and twisted paths. Thank you, always, for that—and especially for EVERYTHING. Ron Walters, thank you for so effectively talking me down off the many ledges on which I manage to strand myself, time and time again, and reminding me that I can in fact do this whole "author" thing. The EWC continues to shape my inane concepts into readable words—I am forever grateful, and so proud to know you both. May we three always inspire each other in the most ludicrous and perfect ways.

Jennifer Moffett, Alex Richards, Shannon Takaoka, and Shana Youngdahl, our chats and meetings have been an indispensable part of my creative process, and truly kept me going during these fraught times, when the easiest thing would have been to quit. Thank you for sharing your beautiful work with me, and for being your awesome selves.

Endless thanks and love always to my parents, family, and friends, and to the bloggers, booksellers, and readers who show up for me time and again. I can't tell you how much I appreciate every single one of you. Additional special thanks goes out to my drama club cohorts, summer series castmates and crew, and fellow Florida theater kids, for the many years of camaraderie, fun, memories, and inspiration. I wouldn't be me without you.

Cora (my unicorn baby) and Henry (who loves horror), you are my favorite and my best. You give life to all I do. I'm so happy to share my world and my stories with you, whether they be scary, funny, magical, or sus. I love you both, above all else.

Brandon, you deserve more thanks than I have space on this

page, for helping make my seemingly impossible goals so incredibly, wonderfully possible. I'm sorry I clogged the streaming algorithm with serial killer documentaries, pop horror movies, slasher flicks, and seedy crime dramas, but it was for a good cause. I couldn't do this work, or this life, without you.

Enjoy your stay.

TURN THE PAGE FOR MORE CHILLS FROM UNDERLINED.

CHRISSY

"'Die, you pig-faced bitch!'"

"Damn it, Kiki, we told you to never read the comments." Chase scolds Kiki without looking up from the video he's editing with intense focus.

"Do I have a pig face?" When Kiki looks up from her phone, she's near tears. She's the most sensitive soul on planet Earth. Also, somehow, the most lovable.

Emmaline sucks in a deep breath to suppress an eye roll, her fingers tightening on the EMF detector she's fiddling with. Emma is thick-skinned, with steel guts. She's smart as hell and will go to any school she wants next year. No doubt one of the Ivies.

This ghost detector is an Emma brainchild, just like a lot of our gear. Apparently, this one uses electromagnetic frequencies to spell out words. It mostly works.

"Oh my God, *no*," Emma groans.

"It's probably about me," I say. Kiki's pulsing with energy and I'm already on the verge of a headache. I throw her a reassuring smile and squeeze her hand. It does the trick. Her nerves settle and the throbbing in my head lightens.

Kiki's gained a few pounds recently, and despite the fact that the weight looks good on her, she's letting it get to her. It's not something she says to me; it's something that pops into my head. A thought that doesn't belong to my own brain.

Other people's thoughts often drop into my head like pebbles in a stream. Feelings out of place and unfamiliar, a voice that isn't my own, knowledge I shouldn't have and can't explain.

I run a hand through my hair and realize the reason Kiki's in my head is because I've taken my hat off to scratch my scalp. I throw the wool beanie back on and make a mental note to find a different, not-itchy hat for this weekend. Hats are my mind's protection from unwanted, intrusive thoughts and feelings, from both the living *and* the dead.

Cue that famous line whispered by the little kid in the movie *The Sixth Sense*:

I see dead people.

Wah-wah-waaah.

A blessing and a curse, right? Scares you shitless when you're three years old and you wake up to a shadowy man standing in your bedroom doorway. You're unable to move, too scared to make a sound. After countless nights of terror, you get fed up and tell him to go away. Surprise, surprise, he doesn't budge.

Shortly after he appears, your mom starts taking "special" trips to the hospital with your dad while you play at the neighbors' house. Eventually, she loses all her pretty hair and gets really skinny and sad, with hollows under her eyes. For two years, the shadow man appears in your doorway, faceless and silent. It's not until you're five years old that you finally ask him what he wants. This time he starts to move, to shiver, like you're looking at him through a glass of water. One second, he's in the doorway, the next he's right in front of you. No eyes, no mouth, no nose. A shadow where his head should be. You scream until you black out, and when you wake up in the morning, your mother is dead.

Everyone you try to tell pats you on the back with poor-little-girl-just-lost-her-mommy eyes. "What a horrible dream. That must have really scared you, huh?"

But what they don't know is that now the spirit world has got your number, so your childhood bedroom becomes a rest stop on the road to the great beyond. A holding cell for souls with unfinished business. Or those who die too soon. Sometimes violently.

Unfortunately—spoiler alert—there's no otherworldly psy-chiatrist to help you cope with all the dead people. You do even-tually tell your dad and he shrugs it off as silly kid's stuff. You realize you're all alone with this curse, so you're going to have to figure it out. You try lots of things to get the dead people to go away, to get them out of your head, but nothing works. No, they don't always want your help. Yes, sometimes they *just want to scare you.* The spirit realm is not the rainbows-and-butterflies place most psychic mediums (who are mostly frauds) will tell you it is. It's not black-and-white like that.

So you learn to deal because what other choice do you have?

You start sleeping with a pillow over your head because it drowns out the voices. Never completely, but just enough to let you sleep for a few hours at a time. You realize later that a hat works just as well as a pillow and is portable, so it becomes your number one fashion accessory.

Enter Chase Montgomery. He's cute and a nerd, so when he's assigned to be your partner for a film class project, you secretly jump for joy. Little do you know, your secret talent for communicating with the dead shows up on film. Streaks of light and orbs plague the camera in your presence. Chase not only notices, he also directly inquires as to why that could be. You try to make something up on the fly, but unfortunately for you, Chase and his mom are avid paranormal TV enthusiasts. Chase calls you out as exactly what you are, and it's the first time anyone has ever believed you.

He's also the first person who sees your curse as a blessing. He calls it a "gift." It's refreshing, though you wouldn't necessarily agree. He asks if he can interview you on his budding YouTube channel. The episode gains him one hundred new subscribers almost overnight, so he recruits his genius tech-geek bestie Emma to help him shoot a full episode of what starts out as *Ghost Girl*. You do readings for people and take your audience on what you call "ghost walks" of haunted Vegas locales.

In just a few short months, *Ghost Girl* gains a cute fan base of about ten thousand subscribers. It's impressive, but Chase is always hungry, never satisfied. He recruits Kiki Lawrence to do a reading with you. Kiki is TikTok famous for her feminist rants, dramatic makeup transformations, and viral dances in kaleidoscopic sixties-go-go-dancer-inspired outfits. Not to mention she's got the most beautiful color-changing hair on the planet.

Kiki's terrified yet charming reaction to your talk with her dead grandmother skyrockets the channel to fifty thousand fans. Turns out the people want a cast of characters, and when you're in show business, you learn to give them what they want. Just like that, the Ghost Gang is officially born.

Now you have friends and a purpose.

But what you don't have is anyone who understands. You're alone with the voices inside your head, and not even the scratchiest wool hat can keep them out.

Kiki gasps and it shakes me out of my reverie.

"Come on. Are you looking at comments again?" Chase asks, annoyed.

"No." Kiki tries to hide her phone behind her back as Chase makes a grab for it. He's quicker than she is. As he reads what's on the screen, his jaw tightens.

"What is it?" I ask.

Reluctantly, Chase turns the phone so we can all read the comment.

if i kill u will u stay with me forever?

"Yikes, stalker much?" Emma tugs nervously at the strings of her hoodie.

"It's hauntedbyher666," Chase says, frowning. He looks at me, his eyes worried. I know he thinks it's directed at me.

The problem is this isn't the first time we've heard from hauntedbyher666. The comments started about a year ago. We think it's a guy because, well, statistics point to online trolling being perpetrated mostly by men. His comments are usually about "killing u"—whoever "u" is—but he never goes into specifics. He just drops a murderous load in the comments and takes off. Other fans reply to him in our defense, but he never engages further. It's one and done, and then he disappears, sometimes for months.

We always report him, but somehow he keeps coming back. It's creepy as hell, but it never escalates past the comments, and there's not much the authorities can do about cyberstalkers until they basically come to your house waving a gun around.

"It's just some internet troll," I say, trying to reassure Chase. "Report it to YouTube."

Chase nods solemnly. He clicks the three little dots next to the username and flags the comment for harassment.

I do everything I can to stay out of Chase's head—always. He hates it when I hear his thoughts, but this time his feelings make his internal dialogue too loud to ignore.

Chrissy's in danger.

"I'm not," I say. I clap one hand over my mouth when I realize I've just responded to a private thought.

Chase groans out loud and slams his computer shut. He stands up and shoves his hands in his pockets before stalking to the pool house door.

Kiki and Emma exchange a knowing look from the plush white sofa across the room. Chase's family's pool house is all lush decor meant to impress guests, but we're pretty much the only ones ever in here to use the handmade marble coasters on the three-thousand-dollar Restoration Hardware coffee table. We keep the furry lavender throw pillows and crystal candleholders in pristine condition.

"Where are you going?" I ask him.

"Snack," he says, throwing the door open.

It slams shut behind him.

...

Chase blows off steam for a few minutes and comes back in a much better mood with an armful of snacks from his parents' overstuffed pantry. We gorge ourselves on Cheetos and Doritos and all variations of ee-tos, using paper towels to clean the dust from our fingers so we don't get it on the throw pillows, and wait impatiently for the final cut of our latest episode.

"Genius perfection," Chase finally exclaims, spinning around in his editing chair, eyes a little dilated from staring at the screen. Joy pulses from him like the score of a Disney movie. "Anyone want a final look before I upload?" He's not really asking.

The cursor hovers above the Publish button.

"We know that's rhetorical," Emma says, shooting up from her chair and over to the black bags she's lined up to load all our gear. She sets the EMF reader in its cushioned bag right next to the thermographic camera filter she assembled from materials she found on Amazon.

I watch the little gray bar on Chase's screen slowly edge forward. The video is a teaser for the Halloween special we're shooting this weekend. It's a sizzle reel of the last few months of episodes plus a reading at the Bellagio Ballroom on the Las Vegas Strip.

Most of our episodes are documentary-style, like *Ghost Hunters,* but without the Syfy budget. We're most funded by Chase's real estate mogul father when he decides to take a break from being disgusted by his son's Hollywood dreams. Also, Chase mows lawns on weekends to pay for our travel expenses, and Kiki worked out an influencer deal with an online store called Ghost Tech to get us discounted ghost-hunting gear.

Vegas is full of haunted locales, and we use the Montgomery name to shoot just about wherever we want (since most of the casino owners live in houses developed by Chase's dad).

Our first on-location shoot was at the Sandhill Tunnels, the site of a tragic car crash. We've filmed at the Luxor on the Strip, where too many depressed patrons have leapt to their deaths inside the pyramid. Then there's the Hoover Dam, which has a similar problem, and lest we forget, the corner of Flamingo and Koval, where Tupac was gunned down at a red light. Even in broad daylight, there's something eerie and sad about that intersection.

Chase pops up, stretching long. My eyes fix on the strip of tan skin showing between the hem of his T-shirt and his jeans. He's backlit by the three computer monitors set up on the wall-to-wall desk that he uses to edit in addition to his laptop. I don't realize I'm staring until he walks over to the snack pile and picks up a Kit Kat. He unwraps it, snaps it in two and shoves half into his mouth.

"All right, plan for tomorrow?" he asks, mouth full.

Kiki is already taking off her swimsuit cover-up like business time has ended, but with Chase, that's never the case. Her face twitches with disappointment and my heart clenches—she's right, we rarely *just chill.* Kiki rolls her eyes and flops down on the sofa, crossing her legs. Her newly pink-and-purple-streaked hair sits coiled on top of her head, beautifully contrasting with her dark brown skin.

Chase grabs a Mountain Dew from the mini fridge and hovers behind the sofa, holding the soda in one hand and opening the Waze app on his phone with the other.

"I've packed up most of the gear," Emma says. She yanks off

her glasses and uses the hem of her T-shirt to wipe them clean of any smudges.

"We should head out in the morning," Chase says. Kiki groans loudly. Chase messes with the Plan a Drive settings in the app. "It says the Hearst Hotel is only four hours away as long as we leave by eleven."

We're going to what is quite possibly the most haunted hotel in America in one of the most dangerous neighborhoods in Los Angeles in record-scorching SoCal heat on Halloween weekend, all without parental permission.

"I can't believe you're actually going to go through with this," Emma says, eyes on Chase. Chase is willing to make bold moves for the channel but has never risked the wrath of his parents in such a blatant way.

He shrugs, but he's sweating. "This trip is our ticket to one million subs. The benefits outweigh the risk."

"Taking your mom's Escalade to downtown LA without telling her?" Emma says. "You're a madman."

"We're there and back, just one night." Chase forces a grin. He simmers with nervous energy, ready to explode into a rolling boil any second. "What's the worst that could happen?"

"Why would you say that?" Kiki squeaks, covering her ears.

"We're doomed for sure now!" Emma slaps a hand over her forehead for added drama.

Chase frowns at both of them and crosses his arms over his chest, trying to hide the pit sweat seeping through his white T-shirt. I giggle, fully aware that they are (mostly) teasing him. Chase is serious about being serious, a trait he inherited from his dear old dad, who inherited it from *his* dear old dad— a fact that I know only because I catch occasional glimpses of

Chase's dead grandfather scowling at me from a second-story window.

We all told our parents different stories about where we're going on Saturday. Chase told his parents he's doing an SAT prep all-nighter at our school. Kiki told her mom we're going on a camping trip and Emma told her parents she's going to a robotics conference. As for me, my dad doesn't really notice when I'm not there, so I plan to leave him a stack of microwave meals in the freezer along with a note that I'll be back on Sunday.

Not that my dad would care that much anyway. He's got more of a fall-asleep-in-front-of-the-TV type of parenting style. Also, depression. My grandmother (whom I never met) shows up in my dreams sometimes begging me to get my dad on meds. I always remind her that I'm not a doctor and that he refuses to see one. She's not happy with how my dad is handling things in my mother's absence, but there's not much she can do about it from beyond the grave.

As for my mother, I've never seen her in spirit. Not one time. I tried to summon her myself once with a Ouija board in an attic and ended up with a back full of bloody scratches from malevolent ghosts. (Don't ever, ever touch—don't even look at—a Ouija board.)

Unfortunately, you can't pick and choose the ghosts you summon—they choose you.

"People," I say, drawing their attention to me before everyone's nerves get the best of them. Kiki told us recently to stop saying *guys* since it's not gender inclusive. "It's too late to back out now. The Halloween teaser is up. Our subscribers have been asking for this video for months."

What they've really been asking is for me to use my *gift* to make contact with Eileen Warren.

You see, the Hearst isn't just your average, everyday haunted hotel. It's also the site of one of the most internet-famous mysteries of the last decade.

Nearly ten years ago, after going missing for almost a week, the remains of twenty-five-year-old grad student Eileen Warren were found scattered in an elevator shaft. A month into the investigation, authorities released footage from hours before Eileen's untimely death. Her bizarre and erratic behavior led many Mom's-basement-dwelling internet sleuths to believe her death was not the accident the coroner had ruled it to be.

These Reddit detectives all have their own theories about how and why Eileen Warren ended up in that elevator shaft. But based on her posts and my own experiences with the paranormal, I have a sneaking suspicion that her visions were more psychic than psychotic.

"We're not backing out, we're just wigging out," Emma counters, chewing on her lip. Despite Emma's laissez-faire facade, lip chewing is her number one tell that she's nervous as hell.

"Can I swim now?" Kiki asks, arms folded and lips pouty. Her bikini is tie-dye and matches her hair.

"Go for it," Chase says. "I gotta go inside and finish AP calc."

"You're not done yet? I finished that at lunch." Emma yawns and stretches, rubbernecking Kiki as she leaves to splash into the pool.

"I finished that at lunch," Chase mocks Emma's not-so-humble brag. He chugs the rest of his Dew and then smashes

the can in one hand and Kobes it into the trash. "Eleven a.m. tomorrow. *Please* don't be late."

He shouts the last line for Kiki, who is always late to absolutely everything. She flips him off from her rainbow pool float, confirming that she one hundred percent plans to be late.

Chase groans and pauses to flip the light off inside the pool house. He looks back at me. "Coming, C?"

I stare past him at the faceless shadowy figure standing in the doorway. It's been many years, but there's no mistaking it. The deadly omen that haunted my preschool years, that vanished the day my mother died . . . is back.

"Chrissy?" Chase blinks at me with concern in his eyes. I'm frozen in place.

I shut my eyes tight and when I open them again, the shadow man is gone.

"Coming" is all I say.

 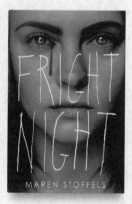 

1495